W9-CRN-797

Auntie Poldi and the Sicilian Lions

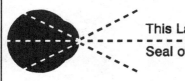

This Large Print Book carries the
Seal of Approval of N.A.V.H.

AUNTIE POLDI AND THE SICILIAN LIONS

MARIO GIORDANO

Translated by John Brownjohn

THORNDIKE PRESS
A part of Gale, a Cengage Company

Farmington Hills, Mich • San Francisco • New York • Waterville, Maine
Meriden, Conn • Mason, Ohio • Chicago

LIBRARY OF CONGRESS CIP DATA ON FILE.
CATALOGUING IN PUBLICATION FOR THIS BOOK
IS AVAILABLE FROM THE LIBRARY OF CONGRESS

ISBN-13: 978-1-4328-5068-5 (hardcover)

Published in 2018 by arrangement with Houghton Mifflin Harcourt Publishing Company

Printed in the United States of America
3 4 5 6 7 22 21 20 19 18

AUNTIE POLDI AND THE SICILIAN LIONS

1

Describes how and why Poldi moves to Sicily and what her sisters-in-law think of it. Unable to function without her wig and a bottle of brandy, Poldi invites everyone to a roast pork lunch, makes her nephew an offer he can't refuse, and gets to know her neighbours in the Via Baronessa. One of them goes missing shortly afterwards.

On her sixtieth birthday my Auntie Poldi moved to Sicily, intending to drink herself comfortably to death with a sea view. That, at least, was what we were all afraid of, but something always got in the way. Sicily is complicated — you can't simply die there; something always gets in the way. Then events speeded up, and someone was murdered, and nobody admitted to having seen or known a thing. It goes without saying that my Auntie Poldi, being the pig-headed Bavarian she was, had to take matters in hand herself and sort them out. And that was when problems arose.

My Auntie Poldi: a glamorous figure, always ready to make a dramatic entrance. She had put on a bit of weight in recent years, admittedly, and booze and depression had ploughed a few furrows in her outward appearance, but she was still an attractive woman and mentally tip-top — most of the time, at least. Stylish, anyway. When Madonna's *Music* came out, Poldi was the first woman in Westermühlstrasse to wear a white Stetson. One of my earliest childhood memories is of her and Uncle Peppe sitting on my parents' patio in Neufahrn, Poldi in a bright orange trouser suit, beer in one hand, cigarette in the other, and everyone joining in the laughter she seemed to generate with her entire body, which erupted from her in inexhaustible gusts of mirth — interspersed with the smutty jokes and expletives that made me the star attraction of the school playground when I passed them on the next day.

Isolde and Giuseppe had met at a Munich television studio, where Poldi worked as a costume designer and Peppe was a tailor, an occupation which, for want of any other talent or aspiration, he had inherited from his tyrannical and hypochondriacal father, in other words my grandfather, who had likewise lacked any talents or aspirations — quite unlike *his* father, my great-grandfather Barnaba, that is, who, without being able to speak a word of German, had emigrated in the 1920s to Munich, where he set up a lucrative wholesale fruit business and became a wealthy man. But I digress.

Poldi and my Uncle Peppe had shared a grand passion, but alas, a few things went badly wrong. Two miscarriages, booze, my uncle's womanizing, divorce from my uncle, my uncle's illness, my uncle's death, the whole issue of the plot of land in Tanzania and sundry other unpleasant twists and turns, setbacks and upheavals of life had stricken my aunt with depression. But she continued to laugh, love and drink a lot, and she didn't simply take things lying down when they went against the grain. Which they always did.

Poldi had enjoyed being a costume designer, but in recent years she had more and more often lost jobs to younger colleagues. Television work had become scarcer, times harder, and Poldi had gradually fallen out of love with her profession. Stupidly enough, the disastrous venture in Tanzania had robbed her of almost all her savings. But then her parents died in quick succession and left her their little house on the outskirts of Augsburg. And because my Auntie Poldi had always hated the house and everything to do with it, nothing could have been more logical than to sell it and take herself off, together with the rest of her savings and her small pension, and fulfil one of her dearest wishes: to die with a sea view. And family for company.

The family in Sicily naturally suspected that Poldi meant to hasten her demise with a glass or two, given her depressive tendencies, and felt that this must be combated on every level and by all available means. When I say "family" I'm referring principally to my three aunts, Teresa, Caterina and Luisa, and my Uncle Martino, Teresa's husband. Aunt Teresa, who calls the shots in our family, tried to persuade Poldi to move in with them at Catania, if only for social reasons.

"Don't be daft, Poldi," Teresa lamented in her best Munich dialect. "Why would you want to live out there, all on your lonesome? Move in near us, then you'd always have someone to chew the fat and play cards with and you can do everything on foot. Theatre, cinemas, supermarket and hospital — everything's practically on the doorstep. We've even got a few good-looking policemen, too."

Not a chance, though. Poldi's private agreement with her melancholia stipulated a sea view, and a sea view was what she got, together with a breathtaking panorama from her roof terrace. The sea straight ahead and Etna behind — what more would anyone want? The only snag: with her bad knee, Poldi could hardly make it up the stairs to the roof.

A sleepy, friendly little town on the east coast of Sicily midway between Catania and Taormina, Torre Archirafi is unsuited to any form of tourist exploitation, gentrification or vandalism because of its coastline, which consists of massive, jagged volcanic cliffs. Or so one would think, anyway. This doesn't, in fact, deter the inhabitants from dumping their rubbish on the beach, making life as difficult for each other as possible, and, in the summer, shoehorning timber platforms and snack bars into the gaps between the cliffs. On weekends families and young people from Catania throng there to sunbathe, eat, read paperbacks, squabble, eat, listen to the radio, eat and flirt, forever bombarded by the thump of indeterminate bass rhythms and dazed by a miasma of coconut oil, frying fat and fatalism. And, in the midst of it all, my Auntie

Poldi. She liked the place, I've never known why.

Winters in Torre, on the other hand, are dank. A sea the colour of lead snarls at the projecting breakwaters as if intent on swallowing the whole town, and its moist, salty breath adorns every ceiling with black efflorescences of mildew. Air conditioning and feeble central heating systems don't stand a chance. My Auntie Poldi had to have the whole house whitewashed the very first April after she moved into the Via Baronessa, and again every year thereafter. Winters in Torre aren't much fun, but at least they're short.

For shopping one drives to nearby Riposto, or, better still, straight to the Hiper-Simply supermarket, where everything's on tap. All Torre itself has to offer is Signor Bussacca's little *tabacchi* for basic necessities, the BarGelateria Cocuzza presided over by the sad signora, and a restaurant even the local cats steer clear of. Torre Archirafi does, however, boast a mineral-water spring, and although the bottling plant down by the harbour was closed in the seventies, *Acqua di Torre* still means something to my aunts. Protruding from the side of the old building is a row of brass taps from which the inhabitants of Torre can still draw their own mineral water free of charge.

"What does it taste like?" I asked politely, the first time Poldi enthused about the public mineral-water supply as though speaking of a chocolate fountain.

"Frightful, of course; what do you expect? Still, local patriotism makes folk thirsty."

My Uncle Martino, who used to be a sales representative for a firm supplying banks with safes and cash registers, and whose knowledge of Sicily is second to none, spent a whole month driving Poldi back and forth between Syracuse and Taormina in search of a suitable house. My aunts had at least managed to persuade her to restrict herself to no more than one hour's drive from Catania, but no house fulfilled Poldi's requirements. She always found something to criticize, find fault with or deride. Fundamentally, however, she had only one rather esoteric criterion.

"It's quite simple, you know," Poldi once confided to me in a hoarse whisper. "I can always sense it right away: there are good places with good vibes and bad places with bad vibes, and there's nothing in between. It's digital, so to speak. It's the binary structure of happiness."

"The *what*?"

"Stop interrupting me all the time. I can sense it at once if a place is good or bad. It may be a town, a house, an apartment — no matter, I sense it at once. The energy. The karma. Whether the ice is thick enough, know what I mean? I can simply sense it."

But not in the case of any of the houses the aunts picked out for her. The ice was never thick enough, and even Uncle Martino became gradually demoralized by this — which is saying something, because he usually becomes perkier the longer he spends behind the steering wheel, spurning the air conditioning, never drinking a drop of water, even in August, and inhaling as much cigarette smoke as air.

I remember going on excursions with Uncle Martino when my first dose of sunburn prompted me to take a brief respite from the beach during the summer holidays. Excursions? Twelve-hour drives through a Dantean inferno, through air like molten glass, without water or air conditioning, in a Fiat Regata thick with smoke. If I wound down the passenger window the sirocco scorched and scoured my cheeks, so I preferred to go on inhaling tobacco fumes. Meanwhile, Uncle Martino talked at me without a break. He pontificated on Sicilian history, the source of the best pistachio nuts, Lord Nelson and the Brontë siblings, life in the Middle Ages, Frederick II, Palermo's Vucciria market, tuna shoals, overfishing by Japanese trawlers and the mosaics of Monreale. He commented on Radio Radicale's live broadcasts of debates in the Italian parliament. He lectured me on the Cyclops, the Greeks, the Normans, General Patton, Lucky Luciano and yellow silk scarves. On the only acceptable way of making a granita. On angels, demons, the *trinacria,* the truth about Kafka and communism and the relationship between physical stature and criminality in the male population of Sicily. His rule of thumb: the shorter the man, the more threatening and the more likely to be a Mafioso. That I scarcely understood a word didn't bother him. My Italian was appalling — in fact it was practically nonexistent apart from one or two helpful swear words and *che schifo, allucinante, birra, con panna, boh, beh* and *mah,* which constituted an adolescent's vocabulary on the beach. My Uncle Martino couldn't have cared less, even when I no longer had the energy to show any sign of life. He simply drove on, smoking, holding forth and becoming younger and more chipper by the hour, like a kind of Sicilian Dorian Gray. Between times, in the rare

15

moments when he briefly fell silent in order to light another cigarette, he would whisper his wife's name.

"Teresa."

Just like that, quite suddenly, as if she were somewhere nearby, possibly in the boot or under the back seat, and he had something important to tell her.

"Teresa."

There was no need to respond to this strange, affectionate invocation, and Aunt Teresa once assured me that she heard him call her every time, no matter how far away he was.

From time to time we used to pull up outside a bank in some shabby provincial town. There I would at last get a Coke while Uncle Martino drank a *caffè* with the bank manager, clinched a deal, or laid his expert hand on a safe door that had got stuck, whereupon it would miraculously spring open. He was full of professional tricks, was my Uncle Martino. One of them was looking for mushrooms, but he also showed me occult Templar frescoes in octagonal Romanesque churches, cool secret passages in Arabo-Norman castles and obscene stucco reliefs in baroque palaces — all of them discoveries made on his trips across Sicily.

No one knows the island better than my

Uncle Martino, but finding a suitable house for Poldi was a task that severely tested his fund of experience and local knowledge — indeed, his entire *savoir faire.*

"My tactic for the first few days," he admitted to me, "was to wear Poldi down and soften her up so she'd make her mind up quickly and buy a house in the neighbourhood. Driving around for hours, heat exhaustion, frustration — a war of attrition, in fact. But your Auntie Poldi is simply indestructible, a human tank. She cursed and groaned, the sweat streamed down her face from under her wig like beer from a leaky barrel, but she wouldn't give up. She's tough, that woman. *Madonna,* I tried everything."

"So how did you find the house in the end?"

"Pure chance."

He puffed at his cigarette in silence. I waited, saying nothing. Another form of attrition — one that never fails with Martino because he *wants* to speak, can't help unbosoming himself.

"*Beh.* All right, listen. Last day, late afternoon, we've already viewed five houses. I'm at the end of my tether and in urgent need of a *caffè,* so I take the next turning off the Provinciale."

17

"To Torre Archirafi."

"I told you, pure chance. We didn't have any house there on our list. We simply have a *caffè* in the little bar — you know, the one with the sad signora behind the counter — and I get chatting with some man about this and that. And Poldi? She's getting itchy feet again, wants to drive on, but I refuse to be bullied, need a break, order another *caffè* and go on chatting with the nice man. Poldi can't stand it any longer, storms out of the bar — and vanishes."

"Poldi vanishes? How do you mean?"

"*Madonna*, that's a figure of speech, of course. She just doesn't come back. After a while I get worried and go looking for her."

Cigarette stubbed out, another shaken out of the packet and ignited.

"But you can't find her," I prompted, trying to get him back on track.

"It's like the place has simply swallowed her up. So I accost a priest who's just coming my way and give him a description of Poldi. The reverend father promptly beams at me — he's already in the picture. Ah yes, the charming Signora Poldina from Munich. He also knows my name and all our family relationships, knows we're house-hunting and points out a former fisherman's house halfway along the street in which we're standing. And what do I see? A ruin, I tell you. Totally dilapidated — nothing but cats and lizards, ivy and ghosts — but when I go nearer I see Poldi already striding around inside the old volcanic stone walls and stamping her feet in high delight. 'The ice is thick enough,' she calls out when she sees me. 'This is it. This is a good place. Did you see the name of the street? Great vibes, really pure, positive energy.' Her exact words. 'This is my house,' she kept saying. It was no use arguing — you know what she's like."

"But was the house for sale?"

"Are you joking? Haven't you been listening?" Uncle Martino clasped his hands together as if in prayer and shook them vigorously. "A *ruin.* Needless to say, there was an old *Vendesi* notice stuck to the wall complete with phone number. The owner couldn't believe his luck when Poldi called him. The rest you know. She paid too much for that ruin, if you ask me. She'd have done better to invest in a better bathroom for you on the top floor."

I don't know if my Auntie Poldi paid too much for the house in the Via Baronessa, nor do I care in the least. Generous people can't be conned, and Poldi is the most generous person I know. She has never expected something for nothing or tried to beat someone down. Everyone who helped her got well paid, including the builders, the dustman and Valentino, and she always left a decent tip in the restaurant. It wasn't that she had money to throw around — she wasn't that well off — but it simply wasn't that important to her.

Anyway, the fact is, she scored a bull's-eye in buying that house. This was confirmed by my cousin Ciro, who's an architect and ought to know. In the course of the next year he restored the Via Baronessa house exactly in accordance with Poldi's wishes and her modest financial means. It was a narrow but genuinely handsome house situated one row back from the sea. Neither too small nor too big, it had three floors, a baroque balcony, a small inner courtyard and the aforesaid roof terrace with spectacular views of the sea and the volcano. Wedged into a shady side street behind the esplanade, it was painted bright violet and sunny yellow, with green shutters and a big brass plate announcing the name of the person who resided at No. 29 Via Baronessa: Isolde Oberreiter, my Auntie Poldi — plus, up in the attic every few weeks, her nephew from Germany. Like her ebony African idols and her pair of life-sized china poodles, I kind of belonged to the decor from the outset.

A year later the house was ready to move into, the Munich apartment empty save for a few wraiths of memories and the removals van bound for the Alps, the Apennines and Etna. In the meantime, Poldi's old Alfa Romeo was parked on Westermühlstrasse, tanked up and fully laden, waiting to set off on its last long trip. Waiting for me, too. Poldi was scared stiff of flying and couldn't be expected to drive that far on her own while sober, so the aunts had browbeaten me into chauffeuring her from Munich to Torre Archirafi.

"Your time will be your own," I was told on the phone by my Aunt Caterina, the voice of reason in our family. "You'll be independent, and you can write just as well down here with us, maybe even better."

Her subtext: since you're unemployed and work-shy anyway, and you don't even have a girlfriend although other men your age have long since acquired a wife and kids, you might just as well loaf around here. Who knows, maybe something will come of it.

Which it eventually did.

Between Munich and Torre Archirafi, however, I was faced with a thirty-four-hour drive in Isolde's overpowered 1980s Alfa equipped with roll bars, which she flatly refused to exchange for a more practical Panda and seldom drove anyway because you had to be certifiably sober to do so.

"We could always drive to Genoa and take it easy on the ferry over to Palermo," I suggested timidly, but Poldi just eyed me with scorn. My mistake. I should have known. If there was one phrase she detested from the bottom of her heart, it was "take it easy."

"Well, if it's too much for you . . ."

"No, no, it's all right," I grunted, and we puttered off, never doing over sixty miles per hour as we slunk across the Brenner Pass and trickled down the whole of the Italian boot past Milan, Rome and Naples, keeping to the autostrada all the way to Reggio Calabria. We devoured our first *arancini di riso* on the ferry between Scylla and Charybdis and got lost in Messina, where Poldi insisted on driving the final stretch to Torre herself. She revved the asthmatic Alfa and stepped on it. When we got to Torre I kissed the ground and thanked the Mother of God for my salvation and resurrection.

"Many happy returns," I sighed, because it was the very day my Auntie Poldi turned sixty.

My Uncle Martino and the aunts came to

Torre every few days to see how Poldi was getting on. The thing was, my aunts had a project: to keep Poldi alive for as long as possible, or at least to help raise her spirits. For Sicilians, *joie de vivre* rests on two pillars: good food, and talking/arguing about good food. Uncle Martino, for example, went to his temple, Catania's fish market, every day. Not a very entertaining place, more a kind of stock exchange where men lounge with tense concentration, checking the quality and price of the fish on offer and speculating on tuna belly meat or on whether a belated fisherman will turn up with a swordfish when everyone else's needs have been met and they can buy it more cheaply and fresher than fresh. This can take hours and isn't much fun, either. Alternatively, Uncle Martino will take Aunt Teresa mushroom-picking on Etna. He once drove all round the volcano to buy bread, and for eggs he goes to a car repair shop near Lentini whose owner's mutant hens lay eggs with two yolks. Granita is only to be consumed at the Caffè Cipriani in Acireale; *cannoli alla crema di ricotta* can only come from the Pasticceria Savia on Via Etnea in Catania. Once, when I praised the Pasticceria Russo in Santa Venerina for its marzipan, my uncle merely growled disparagingly —

then drove there with me at once to check on the matter *in situ* and subsequently commended me on my palate. Cherries have to come from Sant'Alfio, pistachios from Bronte, potatoes from Giarre and wild fennel from one particular, top-secret old lava field where — if you're in luck and the Terranovas haven't got there first — you can also find oyster mushrooms the size of your hand. *Arancini di riso* have to be eaten at Urna in San Giovanni la Punta and pizzas at Il Tocco, beneath the Provinciale and just beyond the Esso garage. The tastiest mandarins come from Syracuse and the tastiest figs — whatever their ultimate provenance — from the street vendor in San Gregorio. If you ever eat fish outside your own four walls, the only place to do so is Don Carmelo's in Santa Maria la Scala, which also serves the best *pasta al nero di seppia.* Life is complicated on an island imprisoned in a stranglehold of crisis and corruption, where men still live with their parents until marriage or their mid-forties for lack of employment, but no culinary compromises are ever made. That was what Poldi had always liked about Sicily, being inquisitive and sensual by nature. All she considered execrable was my uncle's taste in wine, for neither he nor the aunts were great drinkers. Sicilians in general drank little — a glass with their meals at most. This initially presented Poldi with a problem, until she discovered the HiperSimply's wine department and, later on, Gaetano Avola's vineyard in Zafferana. But I'm getting ahead of myself.

Poldi's day always began with a revivifying Prosecco. Then came an espresso with a dash of brandy, followed by a slug of brandy without the espresso. Sometimes, when in a more than usually melancholy frame of mind, she would walk to Praiola, a remote little pebbly beach. An enchanted place with water as clear as liquid cobalt, it was sprinkled with lumps of lava sculpted into black and rust-brown dinosaurs' eggs by the ebb and flow of the sea. She usually had it all to herself. In high summer it wasn't until later in the day that families came with their radios, picnic baskets, cool boxes, rubber rings and sun umbrellas and strewed the little beach with litter until, by October, it resembled a rubbish dump until it was scoured clean again by the winter storms. My Auntie Poldi would sometimes dip her feet in the limpid water, toss a particularly handsome dinosaur's egg into the sea in memory of my Uncle Peppe, fold her hands and say, "*Namaste,* life." Followed by:

"Poldi *contra mundum.*"

At eleven in the morning came the first beer, accompanied by Umberto Tozzi belting out the 1979 pop song "Gloria" at a volume that would have driven even Scylla and Charybdis insane. When my cousins came visiting we used to sing the song together, but substituting "Poldi" for "Gloria." You might say it became a kind of anthem.

Strangely enough, the neighbours never complained. Strangely enough, they took to Poldi from day one, toted her shopping home for her, carried out minor repairs in the house, accompanied her on her visits to officialdom and invited her to play cards. No matter what had gone wrong in my aunt's life, everyone felt good in her company. The neighbours called her simply Donna Poldina.

The neighbours: Signora Anzalone and her husband on the left, both elderly. The house on the right belonged to a Dottore Branciforti, a tax consultant from Catania, but he only came on weekends with his mistress or during the summer months with his wife and children, if at all. At the end of the street lived Elio Bussacca, who owned the *tabacchi* on the corner and eventually found Valentino for my aunt.

For the first few weeks after Poldi's move, everything seemed to be going according to plan. Having installed her old furniture, the peasant cupboards, her father's collection of antique weapons, her ebony African idols and her china knick-knacks, she raised a glass to the sea and the volcano in turn. Before toasting Etna, she always paid tribute to the mighty smoker by firing up an MS — a *morto sicuro,* or "certain death," as the Italians call that brand of cigarettes — to go with her brandy.

The heat seemed to drip off her like dew off a lotus leaf, although the sweat trickled down from under her wig.

Ah, that wig.

She had worn one for as long as I could remember. A huge black monster variously dressed in accordance with the prevailing fashion, it loomed above her head like a storm cloud. According to family legend, no one had ever seen what lay hidden beneath it. Even my Uncle Peppe had been vague on the subject. I suspect that Vito Montana was later privileged to peek beneath that holiest of holies, but he, too, preserved a discreet silence.

On the very first Sunday after moving in, Poldi invited the aunts, my cousins and me, still recovering in the attic guest room from our drive, to lunch. Roast pork with beer gravy, dumplings and red cabbage. In mid-July. In Sicily. We were welcomed with tumblerfuls of a dry Martini strong enough to send a Finnish seaman into a coma. While Poldi was inside thickening the gravy, alternately adding beer and drinking some herself, we huddled together under the only awning in the little inner courtyard like penguins in a storm. Still, lunch already smelt delicious. When Poldi finally emerged with a monstrous great leg of roast pork, bathed in sweat and explosively red in the face, I jumped to my feet in a panic.

"For goodness' sake, come into the shade, Poldi."

But my Auntie Poldi merely — as so often — gazed at me pityingly. "You think I came to Sicily to sit in the shade? I want sun, proper sun, sun with some oomph to it. *Il sole.* The sun is masculine in Italy, like the sea and the volcano, and they're what I came here for, so sit down, all of you. I'll go and get the dumplings."

It really was a poem, that roast pork — *la fine del mondo,* even in a temperature of forty degrees. My cousins, who regarded German cuisine with a certain scepticism, were hesitant at first, but after the first polite mouthful they tucked in. They still wouldn't touch the red cabbage, but no one was deterred by the heat.

"Hey," my Auntie Poldi said, out of the blue, "how are you getting back to Germany?"

I shrugged. "You can book me a flight any time soon."

She shook her head as if I'd said something extremely stupid.

"Don't you like it up there in the guest room?"

"Er, yes, of course."

"Doing any writing?"

"Uh-huh."

"Can I read some of it?" The last question I wanted.

"Well, not at the moment, Poldi. It's still in a state of flux. Work in progress."

I had rashly told her during the drive about my self-destructive plan to write a big, epic family saga spanning three German-Sicilian generations. A regular doorstop of a novel, full-bodied, juicy, masterfully told, full of twists and turns, replete with brilliant images, quirky characters, stubble-chinned villains, ethereal beauties, plenty of sex, amatory entanglements, escapades, scorching days and velvety nights, and abrim with historical strands running parallel to the plot. The only trouble was, I'd made no progress at all. Writer's block, total paralysis. I felt like Sisyphus within the first few feet. I had told Poldi all this between the Brenner Pass and Messina, and she'd merely nodded, being an expert on failure.

"I was only thinking," she said, "if you like it up there you could stay on. Or come here now and then — regularly, I mean, to write and do your research. It'd do your Italian good, too."

I sighed. "Thanks. No pressure, then."

But for some reason my Auntie Poldi wouldn't let the matter drop. "I just don't understand what more you want. Up there you have your own bathroom and your own peace and quiet. You can come and go as you please, and if something turns up on the *amore* front, you're welcome to bring her home any time."

That was all I needed. My aunts naturally endorsed the idea with enthusiasm — it meant they would have a family member on the spot to keep an eye on Poldi — and when Aunt Teresa invited me to lunch the following Sunday, I knew further resistance was futile. After all, I told myself, even a failure can feast his eyes on the sea — that's something, at least. And so I flew down from Germany once a month at the aunts' expense, lodged in the attic at No. 29 Via Baronessa, chafed at my mediocrity during the day, and in the evening, if my Auntie Poldi was tipsy enough, marvelled at her accounts of the progress of her investigations into Valentino's murder.

2

Tells of Valentino, of Poldi's ultra-private photographic project, of afternoons in Torre Archirafi, and of sad Signora Cocuzza. Poldi becomes anxious and is nearly killed by some palm trees. She snaffles something in Acireale and soon afterwards discovers a small but heavily guarded paradise, which has been bereft of a lion.

Valentino was a quiet, slim young man of not quite twenty. He was one of those Sicilian types in whom Sicily's Arabo-Norman heritage shows through: olive complexion, broad nose, generous mouth, blue eyes.

"A good-looking lad" was Poldi's verdict. "Just as sexy as my Peppe used to be. One could really take a shine to him." Believe it or not, despite her sixty years and ample figure Poldi was still in great demand, certainly to judge by the glances she got from the local menfolk. She had always been a hottie and a fan of men in general, especially men in dapper police uniforms. That became clear to me when she showed me the photo albums containing her collection. The fact was, Poldi had a hobby: photographing good-looking traffic cops from all over the world. Having travelled widely in the previous thirty years, she had filled five capacious albums with steam-ironed, uniformed masculinity from Alaska to Australia, Belgrade to Buenos Aires. All the photos were neatly dated and many bore names indicating that Poldi had become better acquainted with the custodians of the law in question. Tattooed Maoris in snow-white shorts posed for the camera, a moustachioed Sikh in immaculate khaki brandished his lathi, and mounted New York cops wearing mirrored sunglasses bared their teeth. It was a proud parade of dapper figures, well-pressed trousers and bristling moustaches. Canadian Mounties in their flaming-red full-dress uniforms, narrow-hipped Scots in black and white, short-legged Bolivians in olive drab and snappy berets, wistful Siberian youngsters in fur caps — my Auntie Poldi had snapped them all. But her favourite subjects were *Vigili Urbani*. At least half the photos were of Italian traffic cops in their white gloves and, in some cases, white tropical helmets.

"The handsomest ones are in Rome. By far. No comparison, absolutely unbeatable. Graceful as Nureyev, every last one of them. Their hand movements, their uniforms — perfect. But don't go thinking they'd ever smile. They never smile until they're off duty, as I know from personal experience. But here, look, I spotted a prize specimen in Taormina the day before yesterday."

On Wednesdays Poldi attended a language school belonging to Michele, a friend of my cousin Ciro's, so Wednesday was the only day of the week on which she stayed sober. Her Italian was quite sufficient for everyday use, but that wasn't good enough for her.

"Why the stress?" I once asked her. "Why bother, when you're planning to drink yourself to death?"

Clumsy of me, very clumsy, to voice my other aunts' suspicions so explicitly.

"What sort of idiotic question is that?" she barked at me. "Until you've mastered the *passato remoto,* my boy, keep your pearls of wisdom to yourself. Understand?"

At all events, Poldi had photographed an exceptionally smart *Vigile* in Taormina and planned to make his acquaintance at the next opportunity. He wasn't in the first flush of youth, with his neatly trimmed beard and moustache and little pot belly, but he wore his immaculate uniform with the enviable arrogance of a good-looking chump whose mamma still irons his shirts.

But back to Valentino. He wasn't a chump — although he still lived with his parents as a matter of course — but he hadn't managed to land a traineeship or a regular job. He really wasn't a stupid youth, as Poldi quickly realized. Like many young Sicilians, he coped by doing odd jobs and toyed with the idea of emigrating to Germany. Sicilians find it a cinch to emigrate for decades: bag packed, *bacio, addio* — and off they go.

Valentino helped Poldi with the minor repairs that became necessary soon after the renovation of her house. No disrespect to my cousin Ciro, but his builders had made a rotten job of the roof. When I went to change the bulb in the top-floor bathroom, the bowl shade tipped a Niagara of rainwater over me. A miracle I wasn't electrocuted.

Valentino could change fuses, put up pictures, repair the air conditioning and go shopping at the HiperSimply. He was a multi-talented youngster, and Poldi soon took him to her heart, in which, as everyone knew, there was plenty of room. She even gave him German lessons, not that the accent he acquired would have made him comprehensible outside Bavaria. But in any case the Germany project came to nothing, because early in August Valentino suddenly vanished without a trace.

Poldi waited a whole day for him to fulfil his promise to clear a blocked drain. She didn't take it amiss if someone stood her up once, but when she heard nothing from Valentino the next day and the day after that, and he failed to answer his mobile, she became puzzled, angry and worried in turn. It dawned on her only then how little she really knew about him.

She did know his surname, which was Candela.

But she hadn't the faintest idea where he lived.

Signora Anzalone hadn't even noticed Valentino's disappearance, and Signor Bussacca merely shrugged his shoulders.

"*Boh.* Where else would he be. He'll have hooked up with some girl. He'll turn up again sooner or later."

Poldi was neither reassured nor convinced by this.

"When was the last time you saw him?"

Bussacca thought for a moment. "Yesterday? No, it must have been the day before.

Or Monday. Yes, Monday. He bought a packet of Lucky Strike and fifty euros' worth of credit for his mobile phone."

Poldi remembered this. On Monday, after hefting the heavy pot containing the lemon tree onto the roof terrace, Valentino had opened a new packet of cigarettes, scratched a new telephone card and activated the voucher code via his mobile.

"Do you remember which phone company the *scheda telefonica* was for?"

"A TIM. The others had run out."

Recalling the blue and red card, Poldi felt puzzled once more, because Valentino had always charged his mobile with a red and white card before. It now occurred to her that he had also been in possession of a brand-new folding mobile that Monday.

"Why did he change providers?" she wondered aloud, but Signor Bussacca's only response was another *"Boh,"* which in Italian is short for "I don't have a clue."

"Where's the best place to go when you want information?" Poldi asked me later, only to supply the answer herself. "You go to the waterhole, because all the animals always go there, big and small alike. Predators or prey, they're all attracted to the water, and folk are no different. And where,

I ask you, is the waterhole in Torre Archirafi?"

"The old bottling plant, you mean?"

Poldi sighed. "I was talking figuratively."

"The bar?"

"*Cento punti,*" she exclaimed, and took another swig of her drink.

Poldi had long been a familiar figure in the Bar-Gelateria Cocuzza, of course, because that was where she partook every afternoon of a mulberry granita with cream top and bottom and a brioche on the side. Fragrantly, in a white caftan and gold gladiator sandals plus dramatic eyeliner and plenty of rouge, she used to sail into the bar like a cruise liner visiting a provincial marina — always around five, when the houses opened up after a long, sweltering afternoon and the whole town set off on its *passeggiata.* Since there were no shop windows to graze on, the promenaders would take a brief stroll along the esplanade before veering off towards the air-conditioned paradise of the bar like comets that have ventured too close to the sun.

No wonder, for wafting out of the bar's two ventilators from morning to night — except on Tuesdays — came a wonderful polar breeze laden with the promise of vanilla, almond milk, coffee and aromatic substances calculated to arouse ecstasy in anyone not made of stone. Outside in the square the Sicilian summer afternoon shimmered like a mirage, but the interior was dominated by the arctic hum of the ventilators and air conditioning, which dried off your sweaty armpits and made you forget the August heat for the duration of a gelato. Eight varieties of ices were displayed in creamy, glistening mounds alongside fresh cream cakes filled with wild strawberries, almond pastries, *cornetti,* brioches and marzipan fruit. Scenting the air at the far end of the counter were golden *arancini, pizzette* and *tramezzini,* and slumbering behind it, hidden deep beneath aluminium lids, were granitas and bottles of ice-cold almond milk — guarantees, in short, of a kindly god's existence.

However, this impression was dispelled as soon as you entered the bar and looked into the face of Signora Cocuzza, who sat behind her till with an expression of such sadness, it almost wrung your heart. How old was she? Nobody knew for sure. Fifty? Sixty? A hundred? She might have been a ghost. Frail and thin, she exuded a faint odour of mothballs and eternity. All Poldi had managed to discover was that her husband had died ten years earlier. By contrast, her two grown-up sons looked the picture of health, their August lethargy notwithstanding, as they lounged behind the bar with their plucked eyebrows, upper-arm tribal tattoos, delinquent buzz cuts and football strips.

Signora Cocuzza never smiled, and seldom spoke. She merely operated the cash register, handed you a voucher, contorted her face into a kind of rictus, and then went on staring into space as if every transaction cost her another vital spark. This couldn't fail to arouse Poldi's curiosity, which was why she patronized the bar for more than just its delicious granitas. She had spotted right away that Signora Cocuzza must once have been a very beautiful woman, but she could also tell that the decrepit creature was profoundly miserable — for, as I have already said, Poldi knew a thing or two about mental anguish.

"Forgive me, signora, but have you seen or heard of Valentino in the last few days?"

The question seemed to percolate through Signora Cocuzza's consciousness very slowly. She was still holding out the voucher for Poldi's granita.

"You know who I mean," Poldi persisted, taking her voucher. "Valentino Candela. The boy simply vanished into thin air three days ago. He may have turned up here in the meantime. Not that I'm worried."

Signora Cocuzza almost imperceptibly shook her head as if that alone cost her a superhuman effort.

"I'm sorry," she whispered.

And relapsed into silence. Loath to press her further, Poldi started to take her voucher over to the counter. But Signora Cocuzza wasn't finished yet.

"Donna Poldina . . ."

It was almost unintelligible — just a wisp of a voice. Surprised by this unexpected personal invocation, Poldi promptly returned to the till. She saw the sad signora take a ballpoint from the pocket of her apron — effortfully, as though it weighed a ton — and scribble something on a slip of paper. An address in Acireale.

"His parents," whispered Signora Cocuzza, handing it over.

Poldi thought for a moment. It was on the tip of her tongue to ask how Signora Cocuzza knew the address, but she left it at that for the time being. She merely thanked the woman, handed back the voucher and changed her order.

An afternoon in August, as already mentioned. This meant, first, that it was hot, and, second, that Poldi wasn't really sober.

Nevertheless, she gallantly piloted her Alfa to Acireale with, on the passenger seat, a kilo of gelato in a polystyrene tub prettily wrapped in floral paper and adorned with a bow. Acireale wasn't far — practically round the corner — but the winding, narrow Provinciale, enclosed on either side by high old walls of volcanic stone, proved a sore trial to Poldi in her condition. She had to keep swerving to avoid the lemon transporters that came thundering towards her. Just before Santa Tecla a lorry laden with mature palm and olive trees shot out of the gates of a big market garden. Poldi just managed to slam on her brakes in time. The lorry driver tooted her furiously, turned out onto the road and roared off. Poldi pulled up on the verge, breathing heavily, and stared at the big gateway with the neon sign beside it. It read:

PIANTE RUSSO

Damn nearly squashed by a load of palm trees, she thought, shaking her head. Some mess that would have been.

Although she didn't know her way around Acireale, Poldi found the address on the outskirts in double-quick time. She always found her way around wherever she was, from Jakarta to Lima, because she had an infallible trick: she kept asking directions. Regardless of the horns blaring behind her, she would pull up every hundred yards and question the first person she saw. This procedure was proof against misinformation from practical jokers, and Poldi always wound up at her destination with the precision of a satnav.

Maria and Angelo Candela were both under fifty but looked older. Unemployed for the last four years, they lived on social security and the little money Valentino brought home. Their small apartment smelt of cigarettes, onions and despair, but Poldi was quick to notice the flat-screen TV. Valentino's parents didn't even look surprised when she turned up on their doorstep so unexpectedly.

"Valentino has told us a lot about you, Donna Poldina," said Maria, hurriedly spooning the gelato into three sundae glasses. "I feel like we already know you quite well."

"Where is Valentino now?"

The Candelas exchanged a worried glance that wasn't lost on Poldi.

"We don't know," Angelo said in a low voice. "We haven't heard from him for three days."

"Does he often do this sort of thing?"

The Candelas shook their heads and spooned up their ice cream before it melted completely. Or, thought Poldi, to avoid having to reply.

"And you've absolutely no idea where he might be?"

Heads were shaken again and spoons tinkled against sundae glasses. Poldi didn't believe them. Meditatively, she licked her spoon. The chocolate and pistachio ice creams had run into each other; they tasted sweet and bitter and salty. Like tears and unfulfilled hopes, she thought. All at once, too, as usual in this country.

"Please don't misunderstand me," she said, mustering her best Italian. "I don't mean to interfere in your private affairs, but I can see you're worried. I'm worried, too. Because . . . well, he may be in trouble."

They both winced at the word "trouble." Something deep inside Maria seemed to break adrift. It came bubbling up to the surface in the form of an anguished sigh.

"It was when I heard that sigh, if not before," Poldi told me later, "that I knew Valentino was really up the creek in some way. I'm an expert on trouble and sighs like that, that's why. Red alert, know what I mean? I guessed his parents had already

44

given him up for lost, and that they wouldn't tell me anything more. *Omertà* and so on. That was when this idea popped into my head: that I had to find him — Valentino, I mean — and find him in a hurry. And that was the only reason why I pinched that little bit of mosaic."

Poldi resolutely laid her spoon aside and looked Maria in the eye. "Might I see his room?"

"Many thanks for the ice cream, Signora Poldi," Angelo said formally, "but it would be better if you left now."

Maria glanced sharply at him and rose to her feet. "But first, of course you can see the boy's room."

Valentino's room resembled that of any young man who still lives at home. An unmade bed, clothes scattered around, an ancient laptop hooked up to a game console, Ferrari posters and pin-ups on the walls. The place smelt of mothballs and weed. A magnificent cannabis plant was thriving in a pot on the window ledge.

While Poldi was looking around keenly, Maria lingered in the doorway as if afraid of disturbing the spirits that inhabited the room.

"That's a variety of cannabis you can't smoke," she said. "He only keeps it for decoration, because it's so pretty."

Poldi kept her thoughts to herself. On a chest of drawers she spotted some German textbooks, some Japanese mangas and a row of colourful little tesserae that glittered in the sunlight — bright shards of ceramic glazed on one side, none bigger than a fingertip. Lying at the outermost edge of these was a yellow crystal of the kind one can sometimes be lucky enough to find on Etna. Pretty to look at, it was a rhomboid prism about an inch across and growing on a porous stone. Poldi picked it up, and when she replaced it her fingers smelt faintly of sulphur. She took a picture of the little ensemble with her mobile phone, and whoops, before she knew it she'd surreptitiously snaffled one of the glazed shards. Unacceptable behaviour, but she'd acted on impulse — genetically programmed, as she put it to me. The thing is, there's something else one should know about my Auntie Poldi: her father had been a detective chief inspector in Augsburg. Homicide. Georg Oberreiter solved the Nölden case, as one or two people may recall, and even though Poldi had spent her life trying to slough off her parents, her parental home and her claustrophobic suburban background like a cat shaking water off its fur, it has to be

46

conceded that blood is thicker than water, Oberreiter blood included. Poldi was simply preprogrammed.

Maria accompanied her to the door. "Thanks again for the ice cream. If we hear anything from Valentino I'll call you at once."

"Perhaps you'll pay me a visit sometime — then we could have a little chat. I'd like that."

Maria shook her head and sighed again as only a mother can sigh who knows her child is beyond help.

"He used to work for Russo sometimes," she whispered. "At the *vivaio,* you know?"

Poldi remembered the lorryload of palm trees that had missed her by a whisker. *Piante Russo.*

"You mean the big tree nursery beside the Provinciale?"

Maria nodded. "Yes, near Femminamorta."

Femminamorta . . .

That triggered another vague memory. Diminutive and already half eroded by oblivion, it whirled around the convolutions of Poldi's brain and then, silent as a snowflake, drifted down to join her images of the last day Valentino was with her. Images of a nervous Valentino who was toting a half-full sack of cement up the stairs to the roof to patch a leak there. A somewhat dejected Valentino, she now recalled, who smoked too much, activated a brand-new mobile with a TIM card, and spoke of having to go somewhere that evening. Somewhere by the name of Femminamorta.

"Could you tell me where it is?"

Femminamorta wasn't easy to find, for it was neither a town nor a restaurant, so not signposted, but merely the unofficial name of an estate bordering the Provinciale and right next door to the Russo nursery. Since the lava stone wall beside the road obscured any view of the properties beyond it, and since there was no signpost and Poldi saw no one she could ask, she had to drive back and forth several times before she finally spotted the narrow entrance. From there an almost impassable farm track skirted the nursery's stone wall for several hundred yards. Beyond it sprinkler systems hummed and diggers roared as they transported mature palm trees to and fro.

Guided by Maria's description, Poldi sent the Alfa labouring over hundreds of potholes to an old archway wreathed in bougainvillea and flanked by two columns. Enthroned on one of them sat a sullen-looking lion guardant with a coat of arms featuring lilies in its paws. The lion on the other side was missing.

Beyond the archway lay a miniature paradise.

Femminamorta.

A somewhat dilapidated Sicilian country house from the eighteenth century, built of tuff and lime-washed pink, almost entirely swathed in bougainvillea and jasmine and set in the midst of a subtropical garden thick with palm trees, oleander bushes, hibiscus, and avocado, apricot and lemon trees. And, not far away in the background, with its flanks outspread like the wings of a dark guardian angel: Etna.

Not a soul to be seen. All the shutters were closed, but one upstairs window beside a sun-bleached sundial was open.

Poldi parked the Alfa and made her presence known. *"Permesso?"*

No answer.

Louder, then. *"PERMESSO?* . . . Hello?"

Still nothing.

Fair enough, thought Poldi. She went for a brief stroll through the enchanted garden. The wind rustled softly in the palm trees; house and garden were bathed in scintillating sunlight. There was nothing else to be seen or heard, as if the place needed to be roused from its slumbers. By a laugh, perhaps, because Poldi had realized at once that this was a good place — that the ice here was thick enough.

Some washing was hanging up behind the house. Poldi was about to call again when she was attacked, out of the blue, by a very angry, very large gander. Hissing, with wings extended, it darted out from under the washing on the line and menaced Poldi, who, in default of a walking stick, held the bird at bay with a barrage of Bavarian invective.

"Piss off, you miserable creature. If you think I'm scared of your antics, think again. Get lost, or I'll turn your liver into *foie gras.*"

Hisses on the gander's part, curses from my aunt. Attack, retreat, more hissing, more cussing.

"*Mon Dieu.* Who's there?" a woman's voice called from overhead in French-accented Italian.

"*Moi,*" Poldi called back.

The gander instantly calmed down.

A slim young woman had appeared on the balcony. Pale-faced, jeans, threadbare rollneck sweater with the sleeves rolled up, sunglasses, her short, dark hair tousled as if she'd just got out of bed.

"Every chain-smoking French film director's dream," Poldi told me later. "If you know what I mean. A total cliché — the quintessence of a nervous, incredibly capricious, unbearably lonely, ultra-sexy, Sartre-reading Gallic beauty."

"I get it," I said. "She wouldn't suit me, you mean."

"My, aren't you sensitive."

"Did you really say *'Moi'*?"

"Yes, of course. I pegged the accent spontaneously. I didn't have to think twice."

"Ah, vous êtes française?" the girl called down delightedly.

"No," Poldi called out in Italian, one eye on the now pacified gander. "But don't tell your macho goose."

The girl laughed and came downstairs. The gander withdrew to its lookout post.

"Mon Dieu, he is intimidating, isn't he? I suspect he even charges the dogs protection money." She spoke fluent Italian, but with a really strong French accent. Having eyed Poldi for a moment, she laughed again as if that brief inspection had proved thoroughly satisfactory, and extended her hand. "Valérie Raisi di Belfiore. Call me Valérie."

"Isolde Oberreiter. Poldi for short."

"What was that funny language you were speaking just now?"

"Bavarian."

"Ah, you're German."

"It's a bit more complicated than that."

"I'd never have known it from your Italian. But, *mon Dieu,* I'm the last person to judge. I've lived here since I was twenty, but everyone keeps telling me, 'Don't worry, signorina, another few months and your Italian will improve a lot.' " The girl laughed again — something she did almost as often as she said *mon Dieu.* Impulsively, like an old friend, she took Poldi by the arm.

"But why are we standing around out here? Would you like a coffee? Then you can tell me what friendly tide has washed you up on these shores."

Valérie led Poldi into the house, which was cool and shadowy and redolent of dust, books, mothballs and the luxuriant sprigs of jasmine she had distributed around the interior in numerous vases. Time seemed suddenly to slow as if compelled to find its way through scented oil. A dog barked somewhere, but that was all that could be heard of the outside world. The interior of the pink house, too, seemed timeless, abraded by the centuries but in almost pristine condition. The floor was tiled with pale terracotta and black basalt. Here and there, colourful mosaics glowed beneath the

52

worn carpets. The ceilings displayed shimmering floral ornamentation, pallid nymphs and their attendant fauns cavorting through tropical scenery, peacocks fanning out their tails, cranes soaring over misty landscapes, and patches of mildew. Huge krakens, dolphins and glittering goatfish cruised a mythical ocean populated by water sprites and sirens, and a lustful Cyclops leered down at my speechless aunt from behind the slopes of Etna.

"Well, tickle my arse with a feather," Poldi exclaimed in German. And, in Italian, "This house is sheer magic."

Delightedly, Valérie laid the espresso jug aside and showed Poldi a guest room that had once been the family chapel. Although plaster was flaking off the vaulted ceiling, luminous frescoes depicting the Garden of Eden and the expulsion of Adam and Eve could still be seen between the mould patches.

"Last year I had a dowser to stay," said Valérie. "A German who said he'd never detected such a charge of positive energy anywhere else."

Hanging throughout the house were gloomy old portraits of the former residents of Femminamorta. Melancholy youths, old men with spiteful eyes, and powdered belles encased in corsets and silken gowns.

"*Voilà,* my paternal ancestors, the Raisi di Belfiores," Valérie explained. "Bourbons, cowards, whoremongers and visionaries, heroes and poets, saints and ghosts — they're all there. Until 1861, when Garibaldi dispossessed and shot a random sample of them."

Poldi nodded. After all, she had seen *The Leopard* with Claudia Cardinale and Alain Delon some twenty times.

"Everything has to change so that everything can stay the same," she said, quoting from the film.

For the surviving Belfiores, however, change had meant growing more impoverished from generation to generation and, to prevent their old house from succumbing to the forces of gravity, selling off land bit by bit and — *mon Dieu* — taking up middle-class professions.

"I'll bet some of them still haunt this place," Poldi said, contemplating the portrait of a particularly disconsolate-looking ancestor.

"*Mon Dieu,* and how."

Since her German-Bavarian-Italian visitor was so obviously taken with the house, Valérie showed Poldi the adjoining wine cellar, an airless vault containing a big wine press of age-old oak, various brick basins for the fermenting must, and some old wooden casks in which a grown man could have stood upright.

"This was where the dowser detected the focus of the positive energy."

"It must be ages since any wine was made here, though." Poldi indicated the dusty casks and the rubbish and mattresses piled up behind the press. "A sad waste of all that positive energy."

"Oui, mon Dieu," said Valérie. "Originally this was all a wine-growing area. The Raisi de Belfiores only lived in Femminamorta once a year at harvest time. At the end of the nineteenth century there was an earthquake that brought half the ceilings down. My great-great-grandfather promptly quit the house for fear it would collapse, and he never set foot in it again. Nobody did so for a century after that. Then, in the 1970s, my father inspected the place and found it was relatively intact. All the earthquake did was dislodge some plaster."

"And the wine?"

Valérie shook her head. "After the Risorgimento the Belfiores gradually sold everything off, just to avoid having to do any work."

Poldi learnt that Valérie had inherited the

little estate from her father, who had left her mother shortly after her birth.

"They loved and hated each other. That kind of incandescent passion will destroy any relationship."

"An *amour fou,*" remarked Poldi, who knew a thing or two about such matters, thinking of my Uncle Peppe.

"I hardly knew my father, but when I heard he was leaving me this place I thought it was time I got to know him. So I learnt Italian and moved here. But, *mon Dieu,* we were going to have some coffee."

In the drawing room, some decrepit armchairs covered in faded upholstery were clustered around a coffee table piled high with a mixture of old tomes and tattered paperbacks. There were books everywhere: on the tables, in bookcases, in display cabinets and in the library, which, said Valérie, dated from the eighteenth century.

She produced some stale biscuits and an espresso so awful that Poldi marginally improved its taste with the contents of her hip flask. Valérie helped herself to five spoonfuls of sugar. Poldi was finding her more and more likeable.

Femminamorta, she learnt, was all that remained of the Raisi di Belfiores' once immense estate. In order to hang on to the house and keep the wolf from the door, Valérie rented the unused rooms to holiday-makers.

"Most of the surrounding land belongs to Russo."

Poldi pricked up her ears. "Do you know him?"

"*Mon Dieu,* I certainly do. He's been trying for years to talk me into selling Femminamorta."

"Is he married?"

"Divorced. He has a grown-up daughter who's about to get married." Valérie laughed. "We have quite a stable relationship, actually, though lately he's taken to adopting drastic measures. Did you notice the lion guardant at the entrance?"

"Yes, but its twin is missing."

"It certainly is. Russo denies it, but I know, of course, that he's behind its disappearance. An unmistakable warning that he's running out of patience." Valérie sprang to her feet abruptly. "But what am I doing, chattering away like this? Would you like to see another room before you decide? You can stay as long as you want — we'll agree on the rent in due course."

Poldi suddenly remembered the original reason for her presence and realized that it had been misunderstood. "I came looking for Valentino, actually. Valentino Candela — does the name mean anything to you?"

Valérie looked at Poldi for a moment as if she needed to adjust the focus of her gaze in order to see her visitor in a new light.

"Of course," she said cautiously. "Valentino. A good-looking fellow. Works for Russo, but he sometimes helps me in the house and garden."

"He's been missing for three days."

Valérie looked dismayed. "*Mon Dieu.* Now you mention it, I haven't seen him for quite some time."

"On Monday he told me he had something to do at Femminamorta that evening."

Valérie thought for a moment, then firmly shook her head. "Not here he didn't, I'm absolutely positive."

Poldi handed her the tessera she had pocketed at the Candelas'.

Valérie merely shrugged and handed it back. "Very pretty. But what's it got to do with Valentino?"

Poldi rolled the piece of mosaic around in her palm. "I don't know." Then, enlivened by coffee, brandy and an abundance of positive energy, she had an idea. "But I'd like to ask Signor Russo, preferably without having to give him much prior notice."

"I doubt if he'll see you." Valérie suddenly

smiled again. "But I can show you a short cut to his office building."

The narrow path that ascended a gentle slope from Valérie's garden traversed a small almond orchard before skirting a football pitch and a vegetable garden. Poldi could already make out the chunky, sand-coloured administration block bearing Russo's logo. Beyond it were rows and rows of palm trees on parade and, further away still, Etna. The setting sun had already imparted a pink and violet tinge to the volcano's plume of smoke, but it was still hot. After the cool interior of Valérie's house, Poldi had broken out in a sweat again, and perspiration was daubing grey shadows on her white caftan. Never a great walker at the best of times, my aunt cursed the heat and the dust that was ruining her slip-ons and besmirching the caftan up to knee height. To crown everything, two dogs — two scruffy mongrels — came lolloping towards her barking furiously. My Auntie Poldi was fond of dogs, especially little mongrels with pug faces and loud voices, so she couldn't resist clapping her hands and calling out, "Well well well, what's all this then?" Which, in mongrel-speak, meant, "Yes, that's right, you're welcome to jump up and scrabble me with your dirty paws." The two mutts, which needed no second bidding, left big, black smears of volcanic soil, humus and dust on her caftan. Then, before Poldi could curse, they scampered off in search of rats and more adventures.

Dusty, sweaty and grimy, Poldi was promptly intercepted in the lobby of Russo's palm-tree empire by two security guards in black tracksuit bottoms and sports shirts and ushered off the premises. "Very sorry, signora, but you need an appointment — no, nothing to be done without an appointment, Signor Russo's a very busy man — no, you *really* can't see him without an appointment, no, not even if you have come specially from Germany, send us an email or phone for an appointment with one of our garden consultants, they'll gladly call on you without obligation and give you an estimate, but you're also welcome to order online, have a nice evening, signora."

"I did tell you," Valérie sighed when Poldi returned, crestfallen, to Femminamorta.

The two mongrels, Oscar and Lady, were good-naturedly rollicking around her and biting each other's tails. Grumpy and thirsty, Poldi flopped down behind the wheel of her Alfa. She badly needed a beer to dispel the frustration and thirst that were warring within her.

Valérie came over to the driver's window. "Do you really think something has happened to Valentino?"

"I don't know," Poldi grunted wearily. "I simply want to find him before it does, know what I mean?"

Valérie nodded. "But Russo employs more than a hundred people. Why should he know where one of his part-timers has got to?"

Poldi was feeling really thirsty now. She needed a beer. Or two. Or something stronger. Most of all, she wanted it quickly, but she gave Valérie's question some thought.

"Know what it's like when you wake up in the morning and something is troubling you? An almost imperceptible change in the temperature? The wind has veered, the light is different, something is creeping up on you, the ice beneath your feet is creaking softly. Perhaps you had a bad dream that was meant to warn you, but you can't remember it. There's nothing left but this sense of unease that pursues you all day long, whispering unintelligibly in your ear."

Valérie stared at her.

"What I mean is, Valérie —"

The young woman made a dismissive gesture. "I think I get it. Would you care to accompany me to an informal little *serata* this evening, Poldi? The host is a cousin of my father's. He's a frightful bore, but his wife Carmela is a fantastic cook. She's recently been doing a show on Channel Five where she presents clever variations on traditional Sicilian dishes."

"Isn't there some young man who would give his right arm for the chance to escort you?"

Valérie laughed. "Maybe I'd sooner go with a woman friend. Besides, Russo is also invited."

Poldi beamed.

The *serata* proved to be rather less free and easy than expected because the host, Domenico Pastorella di Belfiore, known as Mimì, was a great admirer of the German poet Hölderlin.

3

Tells of Poldi's introduction to Hölderlin, of some less impoverished descendants of the Sicilian Bourbons, and of what there was to eat. In a fit of melancholy, Poldi really lets fly. When she's sober again she makes an unpleasant discovery and dials the wrong number.

Shortly before nine, when Valérie collected Poldi from Torre to chauffeur her to Acireale, the French girl was wearing a strapless, figure-hugging black dress and sneakers. Poldi, freshly showered, titivated and discreetly scented, had opted for a flowing, very low-cut red silk fantasy adorned with gold dragons, invested with a tasteful exclamation mark by an enamel yin-and-yang pendant. Quite unnecessarily, it should be added, but having been a costume designer she ought to know.

"A woman's supreme rule for success in

business," she told me later, "is: when the chips are down, show plenty of cleavage."

"Uh-huh," I said, unconvinced.

"Uh-huh be buggered. I was a costume designer with Bavaria Films and I should know. Get this — you, with your ripped jeans and navy-blue sports shirts: *always overdress,* that's what matters in life. Get it? Always overdress — Karl Lagerfeld told me that. It's an old theatrical rule: moderation is a sign of weakness. Get that into your fat head."

I think she only meant me well, even when she made me wear those Indian cravats that had belonged to my Uncle Peppe. Style-wise, though, I was on a different planet.

"You're always well dressed in a sports shirt," I said defensively. "I'm quoting Dad."

"Except, my boy, that your father had genuine style and personality."

She really did mean me well.

Valérie drove her Fiat Panda like a Formula One Ferrari. She roared along the winding Provinciale, headlights blazing, sounding her horn before every bend and seeming to consider the use of brakes a symptom of nervous debility. My Auntie Poldi, no longer sober and rather hungry, clung to the grab handle and tried to breathe calmly.

"The Pastorella branch of the Belfiores is the only one that wasn't strapped for cash after 1861," Valérie said blithely. "Uncle Mimì hasn't had to do a regular day's work in his life. He's been writing a book about Hölderlin for the past thirty years."

"Good for him," groaned Poldi.

Valérie described her uncle as a *leone di cancello,* or paper tiger. Poldi, rather preoccupied with trying not to faint, gathered only that Mimì's great-grandfather had managed to do some kind of deal with Garibaldi that stripped the Pastorellas of only half their assets — roughly the equivalent of half of Bavaria and all its castles. Since then the Pastorella di Belfiores had survived by selling off the remains of their estates: a parcel of land here, a vineyard there, a country house here, a cottage there, a hectare here, a hectare there. There was enough to spare. By Valérie's reckoning, the sheer quantity of land and buildings would suffice for another generation. Then it would be *finita la commedia,* but since Mimì and Carmela were childless they had no need to concern themselves with questions like the finite nature of natural resources. Mimì much preferred to think of Hölderlin, or, better still, to pontificate about Hölderlin, preferably to unexpected German guests. However, Poldi didn't know that at this stage.

The drive ended in the centre of Acireale. Just behind the cathedral, plastered with advertising posters, was a high but unremarkable wall with a plain iron gate set in it. Paved with basalt cobblestones, the narrow one-way street was barely wide enough for a car and only dimly illuminated by isolated sodium lights — not a place Poldi would have associated with baroque splendour.

But Valérie rang the bell beside the iron gate, which automatically opened at once. Even Poldi caught her breath for a moment at the sight of what lay beyond it.

Immediately inside was a formal garden with neatly manicured hedges, flowerbeds and an illuminated fountain.

"Mimì claims that Goethe spent the night here on his tour of Italy and wrote a poem about it. Don't ask me which one — he's bound to tell you."

An avenue of carefully espaliered orange trees lit by LED floodlights culminated in a U-shaped baroque country house which was also bathed in bluish radiance by ground-mounted floodlights. As if that were not enough, big torches were burning on either side of the entrance. Poldi was amazed at

66

how secluded this mansion was. Unlike Femminamorta, however, it had about as much charm as the HiperSimply car park. She also doubted whether Goethe had really overnighted or written a poem there.

But Hölderlin, not Goethe, was the prevailing spirit in the Pastorella household, and Poldi encountered him as soon as she crossed the threshold. She glimpsed the shadowy form out of the corner of her eye as it almost soundlessly darted towards her out of the gloom.

My aunt was fond of dogs, as I have said.

With one exception: dogs with sharp muzzles, slit eyes and bat-like ears — long-legged, glossy black packets of muscle. Poldi considered them the embodiment of malignity.

The Dobermann suddenly materialized in front of her. An adult male with enormous balls, it came up almost to her chest. Its growl was so spine-chilling that Poldi's scream died in her throat and all that emerged was a strangled squeak. She stood rooted to the spot.

So did Valérie, but she recovered herself in an instant. "Shush, you brute," she cried. "Shush, 'Ölderlin. Piss off."

The Dobermann had no intention of doing so. On the contrary, it bared still more of its immaculate teeth and tensed its muscles in readiness to spring at their throats. Poldi felt sure her time had come, and for one brief moment she found that prospect a lousy idea.

"But you don't mind dying of cirrhosis of the liver, eh?" I blurted out later, when she was telling me the whole story.

"Now you're talking like Teresa. You don't know the meaning of genuine despair."

"Carry on, I'm listening."

"No, you aren't, you keep on interrupting me. You were like that as a boy. Know what your father said to me once? It was lucky you didn't speak better Italian, or you'd talk us into the ground."

"So why are we sitting here, then?"

"Because hope is the last thing to die," said my aunt. Which brought us back to the subject of death, hope and Hölderlin.

"Hölderlin. Sit."

Salvation appeared in the shape of a white-haired gentleman with slender hands, dainty gestures and a mellifluous voice.

Hölderlin responded to his command as if Jupiter himself had spoken. He throttled back his growls from volume ten to three, lowered his bat-like ears and meekly sat down on his huge balls.

"Beg your pardon, my dears," the master

of the house said softly, fondling the Dobermann's head. "Hölderlin is in his *Sturm und Drang* mode, but he's really such a sensitive soul."

Mimì kissed Valérie lightly on both cheeks before turning his full attention to Poldi. Or rather, to her cleavage.

"You must be Donna Isolde," he said in German, and kissed her hand. "Delighted to make your acquaintance."

"Poldi. Plain Poldi," replied my aunt, who was gradually recovering her habitual composure.

"But how mundane that sounds for such a" — Mimì gulped — "for a beauty such as yourself, signora. Where have you sprung from?"

"Torre Archirafi. Via Munich."

"Ah. Munich isn't far from Hölderlin's Tübingen, is it?"

"Just around the corner, so to speak."

Mimì beamed at Poldi and offered her his arm. "Are you fond of Hölderlin?"

Poldi squinted at the Dobermann, which was just trotting off with a blasé air. "Well, we've had a rather difficult relationship up to now."

"Trust me, Donna Isolde, I shall open your eyes to a new cosmos."

Without paying any more attention to

Valérie, Mimì led my Auntie Poldi into the house and introduced her to his wife. Carmela looked a good thirty years younger than him, but Poldi wasn't entirely sure because she'd obviously had a few things tweaked. Her retroussé nose, slightly bee-stung lips and host of dimples didn't really go with her otherwise classically Greek physiognomy. Her nails were perfectly manicured, her figure was eloquent of great self-discipline, and she spread her fingers every time she gestured, activating a whole orchestra of bangles, chains and earrings. Poldi's idea of a hands-on cook had been rather different.

What a day it had been, she thought. Relieved to catch sight of a young Moroccan in red livery padding around with a tray full of colourful *aperitivi* as if duty-bound to protect them, she made a beeline for him. Having sunk two in quick succession, Poldi took a third to be on the safe side and then felt sufficiently refreshed and fortified to cope with the rest of the evening.

Enchanted by his unexpected German guest with the spectacular bosom, Mimì led her around, patted her hand, squinted down her décolleté and introduced her in a whisper to the dozen-odd guests who had already assembled in the drawing room. Bent-backed old gentlemen in grey suits and tiny, elegantly dressed ladies, most of whom were the wrong side of eighty. The sight of them reminded Poldi irresistibly of dried figs and candied fruit. However, the main focus of her attention was the man facing her, who never took his eyes off Valérie.

My aunt had pictured Italo Russo quite differently — more like the typical, greasy Mafioso familiar from movies and TV, with a pot belly, pencil moustache and oily hair, wearing shirtsleeves and braces. Uncle Martino had told her that slovenly dress was part of the typical Mafia look, and that the bosses of Cosa Nostra made a point of neglecting their outward appearance in the extreme, but I think that's just a postwar myth.

Poldi was, in fact, confronted by a tanned, good-looking man wearing jeans and an orange sports shirt. He was in his mid-fifties, with no tummy to speak of, but was shaven-headed and endowed with a pair of pale, darting, lizard-like eyes that missed nothing and radiated serene self-confidence. It was as if Russo owned the house and everything in it — or would very soon do so. Despite herself, Poldi couldn't help picturing him in police uniform. The other guests and Mimì treated Russo with the utmost respect, but one of them overdid it. A man in his mid-forties, he bore a closer resemblance to Poldi's Mafioso stereotype: swarthy, ill-shaven, thickset, collar sprinkled with scurf. He munched grissini and nuts the whole time, picked his teeth with his thumbnail and followed Russo around like a dog.

"Who's that greasy character?" Poldi asked Valérie in a whisper.

"Corrado Patanè, a building contractor from Riposto."

"Why's he fawning over Russo like that?"

Valérie shrugged. "Probably hoping for a contract if Russo expands his empire further. Smarmy but harmless."

Instinct told Poldi otherwise, but she pushed between the two men and shook Russo by the hand. "Well, what a coincidence, the two of us meeting here. I needn't have gone to the trouble of getting myself so rudely ejected by your gorillas this afternoon when I asked to see you."

Russo grasped her hand and looked her keenly in the eye. "I'm sorry if you had any unpleasantness, but we maintain strict security measures."

"In case someone runs off with a palm tree?"

He smiled. "What did you wish to speak

to me about?"

"I simply want to know where Valentino is. Valentino Candela, who works for you."

"Ah yes, you're the German signora Valentino sometimes goes shopping for, aren't you? Delighted to meet you in person. Valentino is a great admirer of yours."

"Oh, did he tell you that? Then you surely must know where he is."

Russo remained calm. If he was nervous, he didn't betray it by so much as the bat of an eyelash.

"I'm afraid I'll have to disappoint you there, signora. Valentino hasn't turned up for work for the last three days. My foreman called his parents, and they had no idea of his whereabouts either. But *bene,* if he doesn't want to work, nobody's forcing him."

"You sound a little piqued."

Russo smiled again. "Valentino is a boy with a lot of potential. A shame he isn't a bit more reliable."

That appeared to conclude the conversation as far as he was concerned, because he turned back to Patanè, who was standing beside Poldi and eyeing her nervously.

"Perhaps you know the whereabouts of Femminamorta's missing lion?" Poldi persisted, but Russo seemed equally unperturbed by this question. He merely turned to Valérie with a look of surprise.

"*Is* one missing, signorina? That's most regrettable."

And that was the end of that, because Carmela clapped her hands and said, "Dinner is served."

Instantly, like stampeding cattle, the guests trooped into the dining room. Mimì seized Poldi's hand and gallantly steered her to the head of the table. "Sit beside me, Donna Isolde. I must tell you all about my Hölderlin biography."

Poldi saw Patanè practically barge an elderly lady aside in order to sit next to Russo. She would have liked to continue questioning the latter, but she had no chance to do so for the next two hours, which were devoted to food. The menu:

Risotto ai fiori d'arancio Timballo di pasta
   ripieno di ragù Frittata di mascolini
Caponata
Sorbetto di olio d'oliva Involtini di pesce
   spada
Sarde a beccafico su finocchio selvatico
   Cassata della nonna
Formaggi e profumi della Sicilia

Meanwhile, two liveried Moroccans tirelessly bore in trays, terrines and dishes as if producing them from some inexhaustible subterranean cornucopia of delicacies. Involuntarily reminded of the effort it cost her to slave over a simple leg of roast pork, Poldi was filled with admiration for Carmela, who had cooked all this yet looked as fresh as a spray of orange blossom at dawn.

Twelve guests, as already mentioned, but food for thirty. The wine, however, sufficed for only four. This aroused a certain measure of dissatisfaction in my aunt, though she did find it amusing when four-legged Hölderlin stuck his head in Russo's crotch and refused to budge. Russo didn't budge either.

"I've had Dobermanns for fifty years," Mimì whispered to Poldi, "and I named each of them Hölderlin."

"A form of immortality in itself," she said, before she could stop herself.

Valérie nearly choked.

Mimì clapped his hands in delight. "Bravo, Donna Isolde. At last a kindred spirit who can see into the depths of my heart."

Hölderlin-wise, this dispelled the last of Mimì's modesty and restraint. *Forza* Hölderlin. Hölderlin ruled the waves. Leaning over Poldi like a junk in a gale, Mimì spent the whole evening raving to her about his idol from Tübingen, recited his hymns, patriotic poems and *Hyperion,* and expatiated on the poet's insanity (which Mimì disputed), his many years of seclusion in a tower, and the Masonic conspiracy that lay (in Mimì's view) at the root of this.

"I can prove, Donna Isolde, that Hölderlin's poems reveal arcane knowledge of great antiquity. Encoded, of course. Hölderlin was not only the greatest German poet, but also a cryptological genius. I'm on the verge of deciphering his code and thus of revealing a truth that will shake the world to its foundations."

"Is there any more wine anywhere?" Poldi cried out in despair, wondering what the hell she was doing there. Mimì continued to blather incessantly. The other guests looked relieved to be able to concentrate entirely on their dinner. Beside her, Valérie merely picked at her food for form's sake and did her best to ignore Russo, who spent the whole time eyeing her across the table. Unable to get properly drunk on such a paucity of wine, Poldi couldn't help wondering what, if anything, had gone on between them. Patanè, who never took his eyes off Russo for a moment, munched, chewed, grunted, sighed and belched without a break, spoke to nobody else, and took not the slightest trouble to feign polite interest in the other guests.

When inebriation simply refused to supervene for lack of wine, my aunt became first sentimental and then melancholy. A familiar shadow descended on her soul like a heavy velvet curtain beneath which one could sleep or suffocate. Preferably both. Poldi thought of her Peppe, of the house in Tanzania, of all the people, things and hopes she had lost. Of the countless times she had stuck in her oar and ruined everything. She thought of Valentino, who was very probably in bed with some girl, and it seemed to her that today had been nothing but a bloody awful, shitty waste of time. She heard Mimì's voice beside her. He had risen to his feet and was declaiming a Hölderlin poem, first in German and then in his own Italian translation. It ended: *"Nought am I now, my love of life is gone."*

The words pierced Poldi to the core. Direct hit; sunk. She felt Valérie's hand on her arm.

"Poldi? Everything all right?"

"Of course. Why shouldn't it be?"

"You're crying."

"No I'm not."

"You most certainly are. You're trembling."

77

Poldi noticed only then that everyone was staring at her and that Valérie was holding out a handkerchief.

"Thanks," she sniffed. She blew her nose and promptly felt a trifle better. She turned to Valérie. "Would you mind driving me home, please?"

So much for that evening. In order to draw a line under it, Poldi spent the whole of the following day lying in her darkened bedroom in the Via Baronessa with a bottle of vodka, drinking and wallowing in self-pity. She heard children romping around and neighbours chatting, heard laughter and squabbles, the blatting of Vespas and the babble of quiz shows, heard the sea murmur and the day expire with a long, exhausted sigh. She didn't go out, didn't answer the door, didn't answer the phone; she just drank, hoping that her liver and heart would soon give out and finally shut up shop.

But they didn't. They simply soldiered on. They knew better.

Having boozed for a day and a night, my Auntie Poldi was promptly afflicted with insomnia because her liver was working overtime to metabolize all the alcohol. Thanks to that and a full bladder, she was roused between three and four in the morning by a recurrence of thirst, which assailed her like an angry, neglected lover. Poldi would normally have taken half a diazepam and slept till noon, but this morning she didn't. She'd been woken by a dream accompanied by an ugly metallic noise, but she couldn't remember what it was about, only that a heavy, immovable shadow had been resting on her chest. Restlessly, she tossed and turned in her bed but drank only water and took two aspirin, then got up shakily and made herself some coffee. She ate two slices of toast, watered the plants in the courtyard, and ate another two slices of toast. The trembling and the aftermath of the nightmare were slow to subside. At around five, in the first pale light of dawn, she couldn't stand it any longer. She got dressed and drove to Praiola to toss a pretty pebble into the sea in memory of Peppe and, perhaps, to have a little dip in the light of the rising sun.

Her plan came to nothing.

She caught sight of the figure as soon as she parked the car. Seemingly poured out like liquid on the rounded volcanic rocks, it was just a shadow in the half-light, just a dark patch forgotten by the sea, like jetsam. Not a sound to be heard but the buzzing of flies and the splash of wavelets on the shore as if the sea itself were not yet properly awake. Somehow, Poldi already guessed what had woken her.

And what she would very soon see.

Cautiously but resolutely, she made her way over the big, rounded boulders and approached the figure on the beach as if loath to wake its owner. He was so young, after all, and young men need plenty of sleep.

"Valentino?" Her voice sounded hoarse, like the mewing of a kitten.

Valentino was lying stretched out on his back. Poldi recognized him at once by the *trinacria* tattooed on his left forearm, the Sicilian symbol consisting of a three-legged Gorgon's head. She wouldn't, however, have been able to recognize him by his handsome Arabo-Norman face because someone had blown that away at short range with a lupara, a sawn-off shotgun. When Poldi came nearer a cloud of flies rose from the remains of his head.

With a groan, she knelt down beside him. Just crouched beside the corpse, whimpering softly as if that age-old song of grief could bring him back to life. The big pebbles hurt her knees, but she scarcely felt the pain. She grasped his left hand, which was as cold and hard and dry as the stones on the beach.

"Oh, Valentino, why did you never say a word?"

She fondled his cold hand and stared at the sea and the rising sun, to avoid having to look at him. It wasn't her first dead body and she wasn't easily shocked, but the sight of that mangled face affected her deeply. She turned her head away and tried to concentrate on his hand, on his dirty finger-nails and the familiar tattoo.

At length, however, she forced herself to look.

"That was when I made Valentino a promise," she told me later. "An almost automatic process was at work, that's why. It was genetically conditioned."

"You mean a kind of . . . criminalistic hereditary reflex?" I asked, remembering the psychology course I'd dropped out of.

"Bullshit. It was the hunting instinct." She looked at me. "Either you've got it or you haven't."

Valentino's face looked really awful. The eyes, nose and mouth were scarcely distinguishable — just a gory mush of shredded flesh and bone fragments — but Poldi took a careful look in spite of the flies and her urge to vomit. The blood had already congealed. She carefully raised the head a little, then gently laid it down again. After hesitat-

81

ing for a moment — she drew a deep breath — Poldi bravely felt in his trouser pockets. The left-hand pocket yielded nothing but some reddish grains of sand, but in the other she found a few coins and, among them, a little piece of mosaic like the one she had purloined from his bedroom: a glazed, cobalt-blue ceramic fragment the size of a cent. After a moment's thought she pocketed the tessera and stuffed the small change back in Valentino's trouser pocket. She didn't find his mobile phone.

Poldi knew it was time to call the police, but first she examined the immediate vicinity of the corpse. Not until the sun had almost climbed above the skyline did she return on trembling legs to the car, where she'd left her mobile, and dial 112.

Which meant that she had misdialled in her agitated state of mind, because instead of calling the Polizia di Stato, who answer to 113 and are responsible for homicide, she had called the Carabinieri, who are only semi-responsible for such cases.

The Italian state maintains a Babylonian multiplicity of police forces: Polizia di Stato, Carabinieri, Guardia di Finanza, Polizia Penitenziaria, Corpo Forestale dello Stato, Guardia Costiera, Polizia Municipale (Poldi's *Vigili Urbani*), the Presidential Corazzieri, Polizia Provinciale and Polizia Locale. Plus various special units dedicated to combating terrorism and the Mafia and protecting the state, nearly all of them subordinate to different ministries.

They almost defy comprehension — except, of course, by Poldi, with her lifelong expert knowledge of uniformed masculinity.

The Carabinieri, or Italian gendarmerie, tend to operate more in rural districts and are nationally reputed to be a catch-all for village idiots and knuckleheads in general. This may be to do with their full-dress uniform, which would grace an operetta with its silver epaulettes, scarlet-lined cape and monstrous bicorn hat, the *lucerna*. The Carabinieri will accept anyone, so it's said, which is why they are the favourite butt of schoolboy jokes. One classic example: Why do carabinieri always patrol in threes? Well, one can read, one can write, and the third is to keep an eye on that pair of dangerous intellectuals. An absolute scream, no? Or this one: Two carabinieri are on guard in the street. One says, "Look, a dead seagull." The other looks up at the sky and says, "Where?"

But this is all malicious nonsense, of course, because the Italian police are no less professional than those of any other country.

It should be pointed out that the Carabinieri are in competition with the Polizia di Stato. Actually, it's a nice, democratic idea to protect the country from an overly powerful police force by getting one type of police to keep a check on the other. Except that in practice it leads to squabbles, arguments over spheres of responsibility and delays. This was precisely what happened on the beach at Praiola, because soon afterwards Poldi noticed her mistake and dialled 113 as well.

Ten minutes later an Alfa Romeo zoomed up, and out jumped two carabinieri in dark-blue uniforms with snappy red stripes on their trousers. The older of the two had wrinkled, care-worn features. The other, who looked as young as a new-laid egg, had plucked eyebrows and a neat fringe of beard adorning the edge of his jaw.

Poldi, who had retired to her car, gave them a weary wave.

"Was it you who called us?" yelled the older man.

"Yes." She indicated the shore. "His name is Valentino Candela."

She watched the young policeman picking his way over the boulders.

"Your colleague should be careful not to trample on any clues."

She saw the youngster bend over the body and recoil in horror, then put his hands over his face and turn away.

"Oh my God," he called. "Madonna, how frightful."

The older policeman looked irresolute for a moment. Then, after glancing in turn at his horrified colleague and the bewigged woman in the old Alfa with the Munich licence plates, he reached for his holster.

"Kindly get out of the car, signora. Very slowly."

"I'm sorry?"

"You heard me."

"Surely you don't think I —"

"I won't say it again," he said. And then he did. "Get out." With a sigh, Poldi got out with her hands raised, one of them holding her ID. She remained standing beside the car.

"Step away from the car, signora . . . Good, that'll do."

"That was just how I found him lying there."

"Name?"

"I told you, Valentino Candela."

"No, *your* name."

"Isolde Oberreiter."

"German?"

The young policeman was tottering back

across the beach. Poldi saw he was weeping. She felt sorry for him.

"Yes, German, but resident in Torre Archirafi."

The young officer stared at her while the older man peered into her car. "When did you find the deceased?"

"Half an hour ago."

"What were you doing here all on your own?"

"I came for a swim."

"What, at this hour?"

"I'm German. We do these kinds of things."

The two carabinieri seemed to think this made sense. They checked Poldi's ID and carefully noted down her name, letter by letter, and likewise the licence number of her car. She was just about to ask them whether it wasn't high time they sent for forensics and informed homicide when a Polizia di Stato Fiat came roaring up and the whole performance was repeated from scratch.

Two officers got out, one younger than the other. The former shuffled down to the shore and inspected the corpse, reacted accordingly and returned in tears. In the meantime, the older man sparred with his carabiniere colleague.

"Franco. What the devil are *you* two comedians doing here?"

"I might ask you the same question, Pippo."

"We received a call."

"So did we."

"Did you call us, signora?"

"Yes."

"You see? You two losers can push off. This case is ours."

"What number did you call, signora, one-one-two or one-one-three?"

"Both."

"Both???"

Dismayed silence.

"Holy shit."

"So what now?"

The four policemen stared uneasily at Valentino's mutilated body.

"No problem," said the older state policeman. "You were here first. We'll beat it."

"Hey, not so fast, Pippo. You can have the case."

"Oh, sure, that would suit you fine, wouldn't it? Okay, Marco, let's go."

Beckoning to his young colleague, the older state policeman turned to go.

"She knows the murder victim," cried the older carabiniere, pointing to my aunt.

The state policeman spun round and

stared intently at Poldi as if to show the carabinieri how to launch a preliminary attack. "Did you shoot him, signora?"

"No."

"How did you know who he was?"

"By the tattoo on his arm."

"Aha. And where did you know him from?"

"Valentino — his name is Valentino Candela. He helped me in the house occasionally. He'd been missing for four days."

"I see. And what were you doing down on the beach so early?"

"Going for a swim."

"A swim?"

"She's German."

"I see."

A pensive silence.

"A fine mess, eh, Pippo?"

"You could call it that."

"Are you thinking what I'm thinking?"

"Yes. Haven't seen anything like this since 1988."

"Did you touch anything, signora?"

"I held his hand."

"You did *what*?"

"Held his hand."

"Why the devil did you do that?"

"Because . . . because I felt sorry for him."

Even Pippo and Franco seemed to find

this logical. The two younger policemen didn't utter a sound. Still in shock, they stood there smoking while their elders conferred.

"We must call forensics and homicide."

"Yours or ours?"

"Both."

Irresolutely, they stared out to sea past Valentino's corpse.

"What a mess."

"Just like 1988."

"What was his name?"

"Valentino Candela."

"No, I meant in 1988."

"Totò Scafidi."

"Totò the butcher, that's right. Horrible business. With a lupara, too. Blood everywhere."

Poldi surmised that she wasn't needed for the moment. Somewhat tremulous and suffering from a slight headache, she went back to her car. She badly needed a drink.

"You realize, signora, that you may have disturbed a lot of evidence."

"This wasn't the crime scene, in any case," Poldi said irritably, "as I'm sure you've noticed."

"Only the perp could know that," cried Marco, the young state policeman, and the two older officers instinctively reached for their guns.

"Stand still."

"Don't move, signora."

"Oh, pipe down, laddie," Poldi growled in German, adding, in Italian, "I'm going home now; I've had enough. You've got my address and everything."

"You're going nowhere."

"You're a murder suspect."

"Like an echo, those two," my Auntie Poldi told me later. "Like a crotchety old married couple. You know, sometimes I'm glad Peppe and I didn't grow old together. When I look at couples like that, I'd sooner have topped myself."

She reached for the whisky bottle, but I jerked it back out of range.

"So you were suspected of murder," I said to distract her. "What happened next?"

"Well, the dickheads simply kept me there till homicide arrived. Which turned out to be an advantage in the long run."

"Because that was how you got to know Montana?"

"You're always so impatient. If the stories you write are as breathless, you mustn't be surprised if your readers get stressed and give up. Calm equals strong, in sex as in art."

" 'All styles are good except the boring

kind,' " I lectured in return. "Voltaire."

Poldi took a pull at her drink and gave me a long look. "You don't believe me, eh? You think I'm lying — you think I made it all up, don't you?"

No, I didn't think that. And even if I had, what then? "So you were a murder suspect," I said.

4

Describes how Poldi is questioned by a detective chief inspector with beautiful eyes and demonstrates that she herself is an expert detective. Rumours take shape in Torre Archirafi and Poldi forms a preliminary suspicion. Subtle eroticism notwithstanding, the policeman proves to be a tough nut. Poldi jousts with death, reaches a decision and receives an initial clue to the murder motive.

It quickly became hot on the beach at Praiola. Poldi continued to sit in her car, cocooned in a bubble of heat, stupidity and fluttering scene-of-crime tape. Sweating, she watched men in paper overalls cordoning off the beach, spraying marks on rocks, planting little flags and taking photographs. All these procedures were carried out as slowly as if they were taking place on a peak in the Himalayas. The forensic medical examiner scraped something from beneath Valentino's fingernails, dropped it, looked for it feverishly and rediscovered it on a rock. Peering around with a furtive air, he hurriedly inserted it in a glass vial. Poldi sighed.

Having been familiar with the course of police investigations from an early age, she waited patiently for homicide to arrive so that she could finally dispel any misunderstandings and be permitted to drive home. But they took their time. Instead, more carabinieri and state police turned up to keep the first inquisitive spectators at bay or simply to chat together and cast suspicious glances at my aunt. The approaches to the beach became choked with patrol cars.

No one brought Poldi any water or asked her any more questions, not even the two young policemen who were detailed to guard her and had confiscated her car key for safety's sake. They simply stared at her and left her to sweat.

"You might at least give me a cigarette, boys."

After exchanging a glance, the young pups eventually offered her an MS. From their manner, she might have been a prisoner on death row.

Poldi shut her eyes against the sun and

smoked, thinking of Valentino and her brief preliminary investigation, which seemed to indicate that she was the last person to see Valentino alive. Apart, of course, from the murderer.

A shadow fell across her face.

"Signora Oberreiter?"

A man in a pale-grey suit was standing beside the car. Possibly a trifle short for Poldi's taste, he was wearing the grumpy expression of someone attempting to give up smoking. The beginnings of a tummy, but thoroughly fit in other respects, aquiline nose, dark hair not cut too short. A face like a Greek god cast in bronze, beard and moustache flecked with grey. A face devoid of fatigue. An angry little furrow between the eyebrows offset by laughter lines around the eyes. Hands like a pianist's, slender but strong, with the curving thumbs indicative of willpower. Poldi was something of an expert on these things.

"My name is Vito Montana. I'm heading this investigation." The man held up his ID card. Poldi saw a passport photo and the words *Commissario Capo.* A detective chief inspector. "I should like to ask you some questions."

"What outfit do you belong to, commissario?"

"State police." The commissario indicated Poldi's Alfa. "I used to have one of these."

"I didn't kill Valentino."

Montana nodded as if this had long ceased to be an issue. "Any idea who it could have been?"

Poldi shook her head and eyed Montana's hands.

"Ring?" asked my Aunt Teresa, pragmatic as usual, when Poldi gave her a detailed description of this first encounter.

"Absolutely not. And his eyes," sighed Poldi. "Bright green and always on the move. But quite unlike Russo's. Not so . . . predatory. More observant, more receptive — you know, more interesting."

Teresa, Caterina and Luisa nodded. They knew a thing or two about beautiful eyes.

But Poldi immediately detected something else in the inspector's eyes: profound sorrow despite the laughter lines that belied his grumpy manner. She put him in his late fifties, so by no means too young for her. And although he wasn't, alas, in uniform, one thing was clear from the start: the man appealed to her. This was also the moment when a kind of hunger, a painful ferment in her epicentre, spread rapidly and set everything ablaze.

"You come from Munich?"

95

"I'm sorry?"

"You're from Munich?"

"Er, yes, originally, but I live at 29 Via Baronessa in Torre Archirafi. I must change the registration on my car."

She surreptitiously adjusted her wig, squinting in the rearview mirror and cursing herself for not wearing any make-up.

"What brought you to Sicily?"

"Love," she said spontaneously, and Montana smiled. He produced a small notebook and turned over a page. To Poldi's regret, she could no longer see his eyes.

"You were acquainted with Valentino Candela?"

"He sometimes ran errands for me."

"And you come here to swim every day?"

"For my figure's sake — I'm not twenty any more. That's to say, no, not every day."

"But today."

Montana made a note with his strong, willpower-laden hands.

"Why do you believe this isn't the scene of the crime?"

"Heavens, surely you must have noticed."

"Noticed what?"

"Well, there's hardly any blood beneath his head and none round about, either. There'd have to have been blood everywhere

96

with a killing like this. Like the Totò Scafidi case."

Montana looked up from his notebook. Much to Poldi's regret, he wasn't smiling any more.

"You think this murder is somehow connected to that of Totò Scafidi?"

Poldi sighed. "That was just an incidental remark."

"Perhaps you'd better refrain from making incidental remarks, signora. Did you remove anything from the victim's body or its immediate vicinity?"

Poldi stared at the cobalt-blue piece of mosaic that had been lying, clearly visible, on the dusty dashboard all this time, like a little jewel. She resisted the impulse to pick it up, but only with the greatest self-control.

"No."

Montana looked out across the beach, thinking hard.

"Perhaps Valentino was killed near the water's edge and deposited further up later on. The tide would have washed all the blood away."

"Unlikely," said Poldi. "There's hardly any tide here, and there are no salt-water marks on his clothing."

Montana drew a deep breath. "You come here this morning for a swim, find an appallingly mutilated body, recognize the young man by his tattoo, hold his hand, and then examine the corpse for clues."

Poldi said nothing.

Montana took another look at his notes. "Valentino had been missing for three days?"

"Four, counting today. Since Monday."

Montana wrote "Monday" and ringed the word.

"And you were worried?"

"Yes."

"Why?"

"Because you worry when someone who is normally reliable suddenly disappears and doesn't answer his phone."

"Had something happened between the two of you?"

Beautiful eyes or no, Poldi was getting sick of being questioned.

"Certainly not," she snapped. "I'm just a caring person. It comes naturally to me."

"To search a murder victim?"

"*Madonna,* commissario, what the hell are you getting at?"

The chief inspector gave Poldi a long, long look that pierced her to the marrow. Then he handed back her car key. "Thank you, Signora Oberreiter. That will be all for now. I have your address in Torre."

Their fingers briefly touched as the key changed hands. Poldi gave a start.

"Number Twenty-nine Via Baronessa," she purred. "It's easy enough to find."

"I hope you aren't planning to leave the island in the immediate future?"

He looked at her again, his bright eyes sad despite the laughter lines.

Poldi smiled at him and started the car. "That would be extraordinarily stupid of me, commissario."

"You chatted him up," I exclaimed when she told me about it later. "You find a dead body and flirt with the chief investigator. You're simply —"

"Shameless?"

"No, totally cool."

Poldi smiled, looking flattered. "I had to lay a little scent mark, and nothing is more appealing to a detective than a mixture of half-truths and subtle eroticism."

"What made you so sure Montana would soon be ringing your doorbell?"

"Why, I pegged him as a real pro right away. One day at most, I told myself, and he'll discover that I went looking for Valentino. And what does that mean?"

I didn't have a clue.

"He'll know that I was one of the last people to see Valentino alive," she explained.

"And that I may know more than he does."

That figured.

Within a few hours Torre Archirafi was enveloped in a fog of rumours, a toxic aerosol of conjectures, remarks hastily cut short, half-truths, whispered names, meaningful glances and eloquent silences. My aunt's name did not, however, crop up amid these nebulous rumours, a circumstance Poldi attributed to the handsome commissario, who had clearly enjoined the whole police force to silence. She did not delude herself that something wouldn't leak out sooner or later, but until it did she might be able to glean some information while feigning dismayed ignorance.

Although no clear picture emerged from the rumours, everyone in town seemed to associate Valentino's death in some way with his activities for Russo.

"Simply . . . blown . . . away," Signor Bussacca whispered to Poldi next morning, when she went to replenish her supply of cigarettes and buy a copy of *La Sicilia,* which had splashed the murder on its front page. "The whole head. A ghastly mess. Blood everywhere — lashings of it."

Gossip was the last thing Poldi felt like that morning. She was feeling thin-skinned and irritable, but her curiosity was stronger than the impulse to get back into bed and ignore the world.

"You mean you saw it?" she asked with simulated horror.

"Not personally," Signor Bussacca was forced to concede, "but I've got a close acquaintance in the Carabinieri."

"It's awful, simply awful." Poldi mopped her perspiring brow. "He was such a nice young man. Who would do such a thing?"

Signor Bussacca glanced around and leant towards her. "My close acquaintance in the Carabinieri isn't supposed to talk about it, but . . ." He cleared his throat and hesitated, as if to satisfy himself of my aunt's discretion.

"Not a word," Poldi whispered back.

"Officially, of course, all lines of inquiry are being explored. The fact is, however, my friend in the task force hinted at the existence of some definite leads."

Bussacca straightened up as if he had already said too much.

"What sort of leads?"

He raised his hands. "Well, the murder weapon, Donna Poldina. A lupara. That says it all, surely."

"You mean Valentino was murdered by Cosa Nostra?"

Bussacca gave an almost imperceptible

start, as though bitten by a mosquito. "The Mafia, Donna Poldina, is just an invention of the fascists in the north."

Poldi nodded and thought for a moment. "Let's assume, purely theoretically, that Valentino was murdered by a relatively unimportant criminal organization that traditionally kills traitors and competitors with a sawn-off shotgun. Why should it have done that? Valentino was such a nice young fellow."

"*Boh,*" Bussacca exclaimed, spreading his hands in a gesture of utter ignorance. "Perhaps he wasn't what he seemed — perhaps he knew too much."

"About Russo, you mean?"

Bussacca gave another shrug. "I mean nothing. Nor do I subscribe to rumours."

All at once, Death had entered my Auntie Poldi's life once more. He had sneaked up on her from behind, shouted "Boo" and laughingly reminded her of his power and the expiry of her own deadline. All at once there he was again, the jack-in-a-box, the capricious djinn whose embrace she had yearned for so ardently, wanting him at last to bring the curtain down on this lousy farce of a life. To request the audience to refrain from applauding and leave the theatre quickly — that had been her aim: to take the whole messy business into her own hands and, having got pleasantly sozzled to the accompaniment of "Gloria" and the sound of the sea, to let herself glide over to the other side, where my Uncle Peppe might still be waiting for her.

But all at once Death was there and laughing at her.

"This isn't fair," she shouted.

Death merely brushed that aside. "Come off it, Poldi. Did you really think you could trick me — simply overtake me on the right? I thought we'd settled that."

"But why Valentino? What a waste of youth and *joie de vivre*."

"Pff." Death just shrugged his shoulders and made a tick on his to-do list. "It all went off according to plan."

But that, of course, was no way to treat my Auntie Poldi. Not even Death could get away with that.

"You can kiss my ass," she yelled. "If you don't keep your agreements, neither will I, okay?"

Death looked puzzled for a moment and re-examined his to-do list, then tapped his clipboard pedantically. "In the first place, my dear Poldi, there's nothing here about any agreement, and secondly —"

That was as far as he got, because Poldi booted him hard in the backside. Then, in order to get the suspension of her contractual relationship with Death endorsed by higher authority, she did something she very seldom did: she prayed.

Although she went to the church of Santa Maria del Rosario every Sunday, this wasn't because she was a believer. She went because she liked chain-smoking Padre Paolo and because the Madonna beside the altar looked so heart-rendingly sad — the very epitome of sorrow. Moreover, my Auntie Poldi liked the smell of incense and joined in the hymns enthusiastically, especially as she found the Italian words less annoyingly idiotic than the German. Besides, going to church on Sundays was simply a part of Torre's social life. Your granita somehow tasted better afterwards. And anyway, atheist or not, Poldi simply thought it behooved her to say a prayer for Valentino, who had always worn a crucifix on the chain around his neck.

So that Sunday my Auntie Poldi sat in the front pew dressed all in black with a lace shawl over her wig like a Mafia widow in a B feature, and asked the Almighty to accept Valentino's soul and persuade Uncle Peppe to wait for her a little longer.

The same afternoon, as expected, Poldi received a visit. She had just cut a photo of Valentino out of *La Sicilia* and pinned it to a corkboard on her bedroom wall when the doorbell rang.

Montana was still wearing the same suit, but he and the suit were looking rather crumpled as though they had both been through a lot in the last day and a half. Poldi, who was still attired in black, feigned surprise and invited the policeman in.

"Some coffee, commissario?"

A momentary pause. Then, "Please."

Montana surveyed his surroundings while Poldi was in the kitchen making coffee. He noted the half-full bottle of brandy, cast a fleeting glance into the bedroom, and inspected the ebony idols, decorative spears and crudely carved masks in the living room.

"Have you been to Africa a lot?"

"No," lied Poldi, because she preferred to gloss over that chapter in the novel of her life.

Montana turned his attention to the collection of antique firearms. "Quite an arsenal you have here."

"From my father," Poldi called from the kitchen. "It doesn't include a lupara."

"Can they be fired?"

"What? Of course not — they've all been officially deactivated."

"Are you a good shot?"

"Fair to middling. But in any case, Valentino's murderer didn't need to be a marksman."

With a sigh, Montana sat down on the sofa. He noticed the copy of *La Sicilia* with the excision in it.

"Mind if I smoke?"

"Feel free, commissario."

Poldi heard the click of his cigarette lighter. She could sense that he was watching her through the kitchen door. Unobtrusively bracing herself, she presented his laser-beam gaze with her best physical assets and imagined it was his hands.

"Are you married, signora?"

"I used to be. My husband died many years ago."

"Oh, I'm sorry, I didn't mean to —"

"You didn't. How about you?"

"It's complicated."

Complications were another field of Poldi's expertise. She emerged from the kitchen with the coffees and some colourful little marzipan fruit she'd bought from Signora Cocuzza, just in case.

"I like complications. How complicated are yours?"

Montana cleared his throat. "When did you move here, signora?"

"Poldi. Call me Poldi. Just over a month ago."

"And you seem to know everyone in the locality. Wherever I go, you were there before me."

"I'm the communicative type."

"Your Italian is pretty good."

"Apart from my accent, you mean? Thanks. I get by."

"When did you learn it?"

"Oh, over the years. My husband was a Sicilian."

"From this area?"

Poldi sat down on the sofa beside Montana. She had to restrain herself from crowding him.

"In a manner of speaking. He was born in Munich and only spoke Bavarian and Sicilian. We often spent the summer here with his sisters, and I sometimes came to Italy on business."

Montana was smoking his cigarette like calm personified. Poldi half welcomed and half resented this, because she would have preferred him to be a trifle nervous in her presence. She was accustomed to a different reaction.

"You've created a fine old mess, signora,

do you know that? You called the Carabinieri *and* the state police, and the result has been a squabble over spheres of responsibility."

"I thought *you* were heading the investigation."

"Yes, but I have to keep those idiots permanently in the loop. Still, that's not your problem."

Montana stubbed out his half-smoked cigarette and sank his teeth into a dark-red marzipan cherry as plump and authentic-looking as the real thing.

"Mm. This *pasta reale* is really fresh."

"Glad you're enjoying it. There's no one I like better than an appreciative guest."

My Auntie Poldi was adept at subtle eroticism. She also liked to get straight to the point.

"Now then, commissario, have you found out anything new?"

Montana took his time. He ate the rest of the cherry and sugared his coffee.

"Why didn't you tell me you'd made inquiries about Valentino?"

"Oh, because I failed to discover anything. Certainly no more than you have since yesterday."

"How would you know?"

"Take it as a compliment. I'm sure you've interviewed Valentino's parents and Russo, haven't you? Do you know where Valentino was killed? Were there any clues on his body?"

Montana briefly swirled his coffee cup and downed its contents in one. He was wearing an open-necked shirt, and Poldi glimpsed a well-tanned chest. Hirsute but not too hirsute and sprinkled with a few white hairs, it seemed to whisper sweet nothings to her. She imagined herself unbuttoning his shirt and conducting some gentle preliminary research at first hand, then pulled herself together.

"What about the red sand in Valentino's trouser pocket? It came from Russo's nursery, didn't it?"

"So you *did* rummage in his pockets."

"I only looked while I was holding his hand. Well?"

Montana shook his head and eyed her suspiciously.

"Russo's hiding something, don't you think?" Poldi persisted. "Does he have an alibi for the time in question?"

"I think *you're* hiding something from me, Signora Oberreiter."

"Poldi. Just Poldi." She was now sitting so close to Montana she could have grasped that strong, shapely hand of his. She was on the point of owning up about the two pieces of mosaic, but she felt it would only have got her into more trouble. It wasn't that my Auntie Poldi ever ran away from trouble, but something else held her back: an instinctive restlessness that had dominated the Oberreiter family for generations, taking hold of the entire body and arising whenever the wind changed — whenever the world went awry and called for adjustment and correction. That was when my Auntie Poldi experienced a kind of tug in the guts, an unpleasant tightening of the skin like sunburn, a change in her general well-being — a kind of atavistic wanderlust that could be cured only by setting off at once into the unknown, and it grew worse the longer departure was postponed.

It was the hunter's instinct.

Perhaps Montana had noticed that fever in my aunt's eyes, that particular form of hunger he recognized from his own experience and that of some of his colleagues.

"So you've nothing more to tell me?" he persisted.

Poldi leant forward, cursing the fact that she was still wearing her high-necked churchgoing dress.

"No," she said in a low voice. She could smell Montana's aftershave. A whiff of sandalwood, khus-khus and tobacco laced with a hint of sweat — a mixture that demanded almost inhuman self-control from her.

Montana cleared his throat but did not move away. He picked up the newspaper and tapped the spot where Valentino's photograph had been. "I'd like to make something clear, signora."

"Poldi."

"Keep out of this. I've got enough on my plate as it is."

Poldi was galvanized. "You mean," she exclaimed, "I've stirred up a hornet's nest, and now you're being pressured into sweeping something under the carpet. Who is it? Russo?"

"You know," Montana said with a sigh, "I hate it when someone obstructs me in my work, so keep out of it. I mean that in the friendliest way, do you understand?"

Poldi looked at him and nodded.

"I understand."

"No playing Miss Marple, are we agreed?"

"We'd make such a good team, though."

"Are we agreed? If not, I'll have to come and see you again."

My Auntie Poldi construed this as an invitation, and as a definite indication that a terrible battle was raging within Montana's splendid, hairy chest between the inner demon of the steadfast, lonely sleuth and the inner demon of passion. And Poldi knew a thing or two about inner demons and passion.

"I agree," she said with a smile, resting her hand on his. "But only if you at least answer me one question: who was the last person to see Valentino alive?"

Montana withdrew his hand. "To date, signora, it's still you." He looked at his watch, rose stiffly to his feet and handed Poldi his card. "In case something more occurs to you."

"Why in such a hurry, commissario? It's Sunday. Some more coffee?"

"I've a murder to solve." In the doorway he turned and looked at Poldi. As before, his gaze seemed to pierce her through and through.

"Thanks for the coffee. And . . . welcome to Sicily."

"And that was all?" Aunt Luisa asked that evening. "You let him go, just like that?"

"What was I supposed to do, handcuff him? Don't worry, though. Signor Adonis took the bait. I've got a feel for that sort of thing."

"You really ought to keep out of it," said Aunt Teresa.

"You'll only make trouble for yourself," warned Aunt Caterina.

"Fiddlesticks," cried Aunt Luisa, who was more enterprising. "*Forza* Poldi."

My aunts are vernal creatures. Ever beautiful, ever in bloom, a trifle sensitive and reserved if there's a cold wind blowing, but brimming with laughter and confidence at the least sign of a thaw. Always ready to render assistance, to bestow consolation, to give pleasure, to feed cats, to love and enjoy, to bring up grandchildren, to protect sisters-in-law from themselves, or to cook their nephew a dish of spaghetti. Teresa, Caterina and Luisa had grown up in Munich, but during the 1970s they met their husbands while on vacation in Sicily and soon afterwards moved back home with my grandparents. Only my father and Uncle Peppe stayed behind in Germany, but they are both dead. The aunts are my only remaining relations on my father's side.

They're all very small, those three vernal creatures, and all born under the sign of Taurus, so they're contented, patient women and sensual pragmatists who appreciate good food and nice perfumes, harmony and solid prosperity. They love life. What they hate, on the other hand, is change, turmoil and unreliability. If someone shoves them around too much, lets them down or gets on their nerves, they can really lose it. That's when the fun stops and it's time to take cover. Where men are concerned, though, they have a slight penchant for unreliable adventurers and twinkle-toed eccentrics. Take Uncle Martino, for instance, who wasn't taking part in the conversation but getting ready to barbecue half the fauna of the Mediterranean clad only in a pair of ancient shorts.

"What does a commissario like that earn, does anyone know?"

"What did he smell like?"

"And he liked the marzipan, you say?"

"A creased suit means nothing. It's the shoes that matter — they're always worth a second look."

"His business card isn't very impressive."

"I used to know a Montana family from Lentini. Nice folk. Lawyers, some of them."

"Heavens, Poldi, don't be so secretive."

But Poldi was thinking of Valentino and the morning when she found him on the beach — when she hunkered down beside his corpse, held his cold hand and made him a promise: that she would do all in her power to find his murderer. And she already had a suspicion.

"I mean," she muttered to herself, "who

murders someone with a lupara these days?"

But the aunts would have none of this.

"Whenever you Germans say 'Sicily,' you really mean the Mafia," Aunt Caterina cried indignantly. "You're positively obsessed with the Mafia. No, worse than that: you're in *love* with the Mafia — you romanticize it like everything else."

"As if there aren't criminal gangs elsewhere in the world," Aunt Luisa chimed in.

"The Mafia," Aunt Teresa stated categorically, "is just an invention of North Italian fascists designed to give us southerners a bad reputation."

But that wouldn't wash with Poldi, of course.

"Come off it. Why do I read the M-word in every edition of *La Sicilia*?"

"Anyway," Aunt Teresa said stoutly, "even in Italy the police are still responsible for murder inquiries."

"But I can at least keep an eye on the signor commissario and see he doesn't go astray."

"Talking of going astray," said Caterina, pointing reproachfully at a big wooden crate in the courtyard, which was overflowing with empty beer, wine and spirit bottles, "did you drink all those in the last week?"

Poldi sighed, because now she had to

come clean. This was serious.

"I had a drink or two the day before yesterday, but most of them I poured down the drain," she said deliberately, but with a slight tremor in her voice. "The thing is . . ."

She harrumphed, drew a deep breath, braced herself and spoke the fateful words.

"I'm on the wagon."

Luisa, Caterina and Teresa stared at her in disbelief.

"For the time being," she added quickly. "It's just that I need a clear head and sweet breath at the moment."

Universal delight. The aunts beamed.

Aunt Teresa sat up a little straighter. "How can we help?"

Her sisters nodded enthusiastically. It should be explained that all three of them are ardent fans of police procedurals and, thanks to satellite television, cast their net widely.

Poldi looked surprised. "What about, 'Even in Italy the police are still responsible for murder inquiries'?"

Teresa dismissed this objection with a brusque gesture and spread her fingers while speaking, as she always did when important matters were under discussion. "You may not have been able to save Valentino's life," she said firmly, "but we can at least save *yours.*"

Although Poldi hadn't asked to be saved, she was touched by this suggestion. Besides, she really could use some help, so she fetched the two little pieces of glazed ceramic from her bedroom and deposited them on the table.

"Where might these have come from?"

The aunts inspected the tesserae but were no wiser.

"Amore," Aunt Teresa called through the window.

Rather sweaty, with sooty hands and a cigarette in the corner of his mouth, Uncle Martino came shuffling in. Having donned one of the three pairs of reading glasses suspended from chains round his neck, he scrutinized the ceramic fragments with the air of a jeweller offered some trashy items from a flea market. He weighed them in his hand, held them up to the light and eyed them closely from every angle.

"They're fragments of old tiles," he mumbled eventually. "Pretty old, I'd say. They don't produce glazes like that these days. That luminosity. That blue. I guess they were parts of a floor or a wall. Or a mosaic."

"You can tell that, can you?" Poldi exclaimed in surprise.

Uncle Martino nodded.

"Hm."

"Have you seen that sort of thing before?"

"Hm."

"Where?"

Uncle Martino shrugged his shoulders. "In old palaces and country mansions. Common folk couldn't afford such things. They'd cost a fortune even today."

"I thought you said no one produces them any more."

"I meant the old originals, of course. People who *can* afford it get old tiled floors laid in their new houses. The tiles have to be carefully removed from some old palace, of course."

Poldi didn't catch on right away. "You mean there are people who sell their precious old tiled floors?"

"Sell them? Most of them are stolen while the houses are empty. Some professional gangs can strip a whole floor in a night."

With this subject in mind, my Auntie Poldi visited her new friend Valérie at Femminamorta the next morning.

"I've been worried about you," Valérie cried in relief as Poldi got out of her car. "Where have you been? I called you heaps of times."

"I was in a bad way," Poldi said apologetically.

"*Mon Dieu,* I can imagine. It's really awful. Is it true that *you* found Valentino on the beach?"

So word had leaked out.

"How did you know?"

"From Turi, one of Russo's workers. His nephew Alfio is in the Carabinieri — he was first on the scene. After you, I mean."

"Has a Commissario Montana called on you already?"

"A good-looking, oldish man? Yes, yesterday. Why?"

"He's not as old as all that, but never mind. Did he ask about me?"

"Yes, indeed. He wanted to know exactly how we met, but I don't think he suspects you. He seemed more . . . interested, if you know what I mean."

"How about you?"

Valérie laughed. "I don't think he suspects me."

"I mean, do you think I killed Valentino?"

"*Mon Dieu,* no."

"You hardly know me."

Valérie looked at Poldi. "Believe me, Donna Poldina, I think you might be capable of a lot of things, but murder? Never."

Poldi drew a deep breath. A gentle breeze

119

laden with a faint scent of rosemary and hibiscus was rustling the bougainvillea that trailed halfway across the house. Turning her head a little, Poldi caught sight of one of Valérie's friendly mongrels dozing under an avocado tree in the garden. Turning a little further, she saw the sea glittering below. Valentino was dead, but here, at this moment, everything was filled with promise, imbued with life. The sheer, overwhelming superabundance of it was unbearable. But that was Sicily.

"Poldi? *Mon Dieu,* are you crying again?"

Poldi shook her head. "No, I was only thinking it's time we called each other *tu.*"

Valérie smiled. "How about some coffee?"

It tasted as frightful as ever, like burnt rubber gaskets. Poldi would have liked to lace it with some brandy, but she was determined to remain stone-cold sober during her investigations, so she copied her new friend and sweetened it with five spoonfuls of sugar. Quite apart from the undeniable awfulness of Valérie's coffee, coffee-drinking in Italy is nothing like the activity portrayed in television commercials. It has nothing to do with coffee as a *beverage,* only with sugar. Coffee is merely a hot, aromatic, caffeinated liquid designed to dissolve sugar, so you don't need much of it. It can be small as long as it's strong, but sweetness is paramount. That's why many baristas mix coffee and sugar in the filter itself. There's nothing more bizarre to a Sicilian than drinking an espresso without sugar. Mind you, having a cappuccino after lunch and cycling along the Provinciale are probably considered more bizarre still.

Valérie regarded my aunt attentively over her coffee cup. Poldi showed her the pieces of glazed ceramic. "You aren't by any chance missing the floor these came from?"

Valérie shook her head, but she seemed to get the point. "No. I'm missing a lion, though."

"Exactly when did it disappear?"

Valérie thought awhile. "I noticed it was gone on Wednesday. Why are you interested?"

"Do you still assume it was a warning from Russo?"

Valérie shrugged her shoulders.

"Looking at it from another angle," Poldi persisted, "what would a lion like that be worth on the open market?"

"*Mon Dieu,* I've no idea. A couple of thousand euros, maybe? Are you going to tell me what this is about?"

The shaggy mutt beneath the avocado tree stretched and got to its feet. It gave Poldi a pathetically mournful look, shook itself briefly and trotted off as if that said it all. Poldi felt a familiar itch beneath her wig and drew a deep breath.

"I may have an idea why Valentino had to die."

5

Tells of Poldi's tenacity and of how she follows up her original suspicion. In this connection, she finds it useful to resort to behaviour she often engaged in at anti-imperialist demos in the distant past. She has an unpleasant encounter and takes a photograph in Taormina. Vito Montana wears a smart suit and is at pains to present a *bella figura* at all times.

"Why Russo?" Valérie asked uneasily.

"It's obvious," said Poldi. "One, Valentino probably belonged to a gang that looted old country houses. Two, Valentino worked for Russo. Three, Russo wants to put you under pressure, so he stole your lion."

"That's only a suspicion, though. I can't prove anything."

"But just assume it's true. Russo would need trustworthy henchmen like Valentino."

"But, *mon Dieu,* why should he have

murdered him?"

The question of motive was a sore point with Poldi, who dodged it like a police press officer.

"Well," she said, "our inquiries are still at a very early stage."

"*Our* inquiries?"

"Commissario Montana's and mine. Does Russo have a son as well as a daughter?"

"No."

"Ah, I knew it."

"I don't understand, Poldi."

"Look, that night at your Uncle Mimì's, Russo said something significant: that Valentino had a lot of potential. He seemed positively hurt, as though the boy had disappointed him in some way. I suspect he was fond of him — he may even have regarded him as a son. What if Valentino let him down badly over something and he blew a fuse?"

"I'm afraid you're getting carried away, Poldi."

"Just wait and see."

It was no use arguing. Resolutely, Poldi marched across Valérie's garden and invaded Russo's arboreal empire for a second time, intent on questioning his workforce. In an exalted, forensic frame of mind, she strolled, as if blown there by some capricious gust of wind, through the orderly ranks of palms, olive groves, lemon trees, bougainvilleas, oleanders and strelitzias. She was so busy nodding affably in all directions, she narrowly missed being run over by a mechanical digger. *"Mizzica,"* the driver swore at her in Sicilian. *"L'occhi su fatti pi taliari."*

Poldi found this neither comprehensible nor impressive.

"Good morning. Lovely day, isn't it? What a nice machine you've got there — you must be the foreman. Tell me, did you know Valentino?"

Without a word, the driver put his digger in gear and stepped on the gas again. Poldi was enveloped in a cloud of dust as it roared past her.

"Hey, wait," she cried in vain.

Next attempt: two young workmen repotting palm shoots.

"Good morning. My, you're good at that. How quick you are — very impressive. Have you worked here long?"

They merely stared at her in silence. Undeterred, she pressed on.

"Did you know Valentino?"

"The guy with the *trinacria* tattooed on his arm?"

"Yes, that's him. Valentino Candela. Terrible, isn't it? What was his relationship like with your boss?"

A brief exchange of glances, then they turned away as if in response to a command and simply plodded off, leaving Poldi standing there.

"Hello? Signori. Please don't walk off."

Next attempt: an elderly workman pruning some young olive trees. Poldi noticed that one of his little fingers was missing.

"Good morning. Please excuse me, but I think I've lost my way."

"Where did you want to go?"

"To see Signor Russo."

"The boss is bound to be over there in the main building. But you'll need an appointment, signora."

"Thanks, very nice of you. Hey, isn't it awful about Valentino? They say he was like a son to Signor Russo."

That was as far as she got.

"Signora?"

Poldi turned to see the two security guards familiar to her from her previous visit. They were still wearing identical shades, the narrow, wrap-around sort that resemble reptilian eyes.

"Kindly come with us."

"Where to, if I may ask?"

"Off the premises."

"Is it forbidden to have a little chat with someone? This is plain ridiculous."

126

"You're trespassing on private property, signora. Please don't make any trouble."

"Who's making trouble? Only you two comedians, that's who."

The men looked like twins. They seemed rather uneasy, but a job was a job. One of them stepped forward and touched Poldi on the arm in an attempt to get her to move at last and come with them. "Please, signora."

But no one did that to my Auntie Poldi. In the grip of old reflexes, she fiercely wrenched her arm away. *"Let go of me,"* she yelled at the two shades. *"How dare you. This is deprivation of liberty. Help! Heeelp!"*

She was giving vent to her wide experience of demos. Too young for the Munich riot of 1962, there was scarcely a demo in which Poldi had not taken part after 1968, when she turned sweet sixteen. She marched everywhere against state tyranny and the Shah, emergency legislation and the arms race, chanted in favour of women's rights, sexual liberation and equality of education, and slept with revolutionaries, rock stars, honest biology students, budding terrorists and future government ministers. Until the mid-1980s she had regularly participated in peace marches and sit-ins against NATO's "double-track" decision, Pershings and dumping sites for nuclear waste, chained herself to railings and thrown flour bags at politicians. So it might be said that my Auntie Poldi had some experience dealing with the forces of law and order.

Yelling alternately in Italian and Bavarian, she went berserk like a dervish on khat or Rumpelstiltskin on a *caffè doppio ristretto*. The scene she made did not fail to have an effect on the two security guards, who stood rooted to the spot, staring in astonishment at my fiercely gesticulating, loudly vociferating aunt, and only half-heartedly fending off her furious blows.

Russo's workers, who had rapidly gathered around the scene of the action, anxious not to miss anything, were highly entertained by all this. No one laid hands on Poldi and no one made any further attempt to hustle her off the premises. She had won.

However, it wasn't long before she ran out of breath and had to abandon her antics. It should be borne in mind that Poldi was no longer sixteen, but sixty. So she automatically ceased to be a virago and became an older woman, perspiring and rather breathless. She was fully aware of this, of course, but before she allowed the security guards to lead her away, she turned and sketched a curtsey to the workmen around her. My

Auntie Poldi knew how to quit the stage: namely, to a round of applause.

"*Mon Dieu,* what happened over there?" Valérie exclaimed when Poldi returned to Femminamorta, exhausted but not dissatisfied. "I heard you shouting. And then, applause?"

Poldi straightened her wig and looked Valérie in the eye. "That, my dear, was only the start. I shall repeat the procedure every day until someone bloody well talks to me."

"Did Russo appear?"

"Afraid not, but give me time. Hey, do you think I could have a glass of water? Or maybe a little *prosecchino* for my nerves?"

"I thought you were supposed to be on the wagon," I said when Poldi told me about this later.

"Oh, come on, *one* little Prosecco isn't a *drink.*"

"Er, no?"

"No. Look at it this way. Mick Jagger and Keith Richards used to drink and smoke grass till it came out of their ears, but now they're all clean and teetotal, eat their muesli like good boys and don't touch alcohol any more. Only champagne."

As threatened, my Auntie Poldi went back the next day and repeated the procedure.

She began by strolling around Russo's property for a while, then chatted to a few of his workers. Then the security men turned up. Having performed her little routine once more, Poldi meekly allowed them to remove her from the premises. It was a reprise of the previous day, but with one minor difference: Russo's workers spotted my Auntie Poldi from afar and waved to her, gleefully awaited her performance and sent her on her way with loud applause. Poldi graciously acknowledged this, waving and blowing kisses in all directions. But Russo didn't appear.

The following day, Wednesday, she had to suspend her investigations in order to attend her usual Italian lesson with Michele in Taormina. She couldn't possibly play truant for two reasons:

(a) Michele himself; and

(b) the *Vigile* she'd recently photographed.

Although Michele was definitely too young for Poldi's taste, being in his mid-thirties, she had no intention of missing a chance to feast her eyes on him.

Far be it from me to be envious of Michele. He's a good friend of mine; he's amusing and a first-class teacher and businessman. He likes classical literature and gypsy swing, has seen something of the world and is on the introverted side. But appearance-wise, even an average sort of guy who has turned out more or less okay is a dead loss compared to Michele, and that's a bit hard to cope with. Because Michele looks like a top male model, like a heroic figure dreamt up by one of Mussolini's sculptors. I'll say no more. Michele didn't choose his personal appearance, nor did he parlay it into a profession; he founded a language school. No disrespect to Michele, but his courses were attended almost exclusively by (discounting Poldi) anorexic Scandinavian girls whose languishing eyes construed his every gesture as erotic. Or so I imagine.

Anyway, Poldi never missed her Wednesday Italian lesson. She took advantage of the lunch break to go for a little walk through the old quarter of Taormina in search of the *Vigile* she'd recently photographed, hoping to make his acquaintance. She failed to see the traffic cop, but sighted Italo Russo and Corrado Patanè instead. They were seated at a small table outside the Wunderbar Café on the Corso Umberto, deep in conversation and leafing through some illustrations in a transparent folder.

It didn't take Poldi long to decide what to do; her Oberreiterish instincts simply took over. She threaded her way nimbly to the café through a bevy of tourists, sneaked around behind the two men's table and sat down a little to one side, where she had a good view of the table and Russo wouldn't see her unless he turned his head at least ninety degrees. She wasn't afraid Patanè would spot her because his attention was so exclusively focused on Russo.

From where she was sitting, Poldi couldn't make out the pictures in the transparent folder, but she tried to take a few unobtrusive snaps of them in the hope that subsequent processing in a computer would reveal more, the way it always does on TV. In order to do this, however, she had to stand up again. This, in turn, seemed to indicate to a German couple in practical, functional clothing that her table was free. They at once made a beeline for it, pushing past Russo and Patanè and leaving a turmoil of apologies and jogged chairs in their wake. The man's rucksack caught in Patanè's chair and almost tipped it over. Poldi had only just sat down again and stowed the camera in her handbag when she saw Patanè jump to his feet, spilling his coffee over the transparent folder. Patanè swore and the German vacationer mumbled an apology. That would have been that, had not Patanè caught sight of my aunt and promptly recognized her. He stared at Poldi for an instant, then nudged Russo and pointed in her direction.

She could detect no emotion on Russo's face other than momentary surprise. He simply looked at her and came over to her table.

"Our paths seem to have crossed a lot in recent days, signora."

"Often but far too seldom, alas," Poldi trilled.

"And you've been making such efforts to impress me, haven't you?"

"Well, have I? Impressed you, I mean?"

Russo's tone changed abruptly.

"What exactly are you after, signora?"

"Just a few answers on the subject of Valentino."

"I'm afraid I must disappoint you, signora. I must also ask you to discontinue your performances on my property. Otherwise . . ."

"Otherwise?"

Russo drew a deep breath. "It's hot in August, signora, and the ice is thin."

"Eh?" I exclaimed when my aunt described the confrontation later.

"Those were his actual words."

"So what did they mean?"

"You mean you don't get it? It was a straightforward death threat."

"As straightforward as a corkscrew, more like."

"You simply don't have a feel for criminality, my boy. Me, I naturally interpreted it as an unvarnished death threat, and as things turned out not long afterwards, I was barking up the right tree."

Poldi's father, Detective Chief Inspector Georg Oberreiter, had taught her that the success of any police inquiry depends on two things: notebooks and corkboards. She had also learnt from her father that nothing is more dangerous to an investigation than preliminary theories to which one clings for too long although the facts have long been pointing in another direction — a classic pitfall besetting inexperienced doctors, motor mechanics, palaeontologists and detective inspectors alike. Poldi kept the danger of the preliminary hypothesis at the back of her mind, but until something better presented itself she steadfastly and doggedly continued to pursue her original suspicion.

First, however, she bought herself a notebook in which she recorded every lead, every clue, every name, every phone number, every fart — absolutely every last thing.

The most important leads she neatly transferred to a card index and pinned up on the wall of her bedroom, together with photographs, newspaper articles and a map of Sicily. Any items she believed to be connected in some way were linked with lengths of coloured wool. Thus her bedroom wall gradually sprouted a peculiar species of lichen, an autonomous creature that whispered unintelligible things to Poldi when she went to bed and when she woke up. One day — of this she was firmly convinced — that creature on her bedroom wall would tell her, point-blank, who had murdered Valentino. Until then she must simply feed it well, ask questions and keep her ears open, make a nuisance of herself and kick up a fuss. My Auntie Poldi was particularly good at this last activity.

Uncle Martino combed the Internet and the local newspaper archives for reports of art thefts and thefts from construction sites and brought Poldi masses of material, which she conscientiously pinned to her corkboard. When she looked at it at night, she seemed to be staring into an abyss that threatened to engulf half of Sicily, so much was being stolen from the island's palatial country houses. Even though she eschewed the M-word as far as possible, she felt there was only one conclusion: that a well-lubricated criminal machine must be behind it all. Headed by Russo.

Her problem was how to make the contents of the transparent folder fit this hypothesis, because the photograph she'd taken simply failed to enlighten her. My cousin Samuele, the computer salesman son of Aunt Luisa, had casually waved the magic wand of commercial image enhancement software over the photo. He enlarged it, adjusted the focus and contrast, lightened the shadows a little, and — bingo — one could more or less make out what Russo and Patanè had been studying with such interest. But only more or less, because the image remained badly pixelated like a photograph of a galaxy on the outskirts of the universe, and required no little imagination. With the best will in the world, it was impossible to make out any lion, mosaics, country houses or ancient art treasures on the photo, however hard Poldi gazed at it from every angle. Rather, it seemed that the exposed sheet inside the folder was a document of some kind with an illustration beneath it. The text of the document was illegible, pixelated mush, and Poldi surmised that the three-colour illustration was a structural drawing or diagram. Or something quite else.

"Hell's bells," she said in a disappointed growl as she pinned up the photo. Then, because she didn't want to seem ungrateful to the mechanics of chance, she added, "*Namaste,* camera."

Because everything in the world, my Auntie Poldi felt convinced, possessed a soul. To her there were no inanimate objects, only mute ones, so it was better to treat them with respect. If you did, they could sometimes prove remarkably generous.

Vague threats had never deterred my Auntie Poldi from anything, so she showed up at Russo's tree nursery the very next day and spoke to his workers again. When was the last time they'd seen Valentino, what was his relationship to the boss, and had they noticed anything unusual about the recent behaviour of either man? She had no more success than she'd had on the two previous occasions.

One of her interlocutors was Turi, the old man with the missing little finger. "Look, signora," he said unhappily, purging his Italian of as much Sicilian dialect as possible, "we aren't allowed to talk to you — the boss has expressly forbidden us to. We don't know anything anyway. Poor Valentino was a good lad, and that's the way we all want to remember him. So please, signora, leave us to do our work in peace and go home. It really would be the best thing for everyone."

Poldi was about to persist, needless to say, but before she could tackle poor Turi again she saw him stiffen with panic. Remarkably agile despite her bulk, she spun round and saw two dappled brown shadows streaking towards her. Not Oscar and Lady, the friendly mongrels, but two nightmares on four legs. Even before she could utter a cry, they sprang at her and knocked her over on her back amid the pruned olive trees. She caught a glimpse of her wig as it came adrift and flew up into the summer sky, then all she could see was a pair of vicious canines barking furiously in her face.

In shock, she simply stared at the German shepherds for one, two, three seconds. Then she emitted a full-throated yell that conveyed all the rage and fear within her.

"Get off me, you filthy brutes!"

This left the dogs quite cold. They continued to bark just as loudly and didn't retreat an inch, snapping at my aunt if she stirred but not biting her.

"Hans. Franz. Enough. Heel."

A crisp command in German, with a strong Italian accent. It's an odd thing, the

138

Italian predilection for ordering dogs around in German. I have no idea how it originated.

The dogs pricked up their ears and got off Poldi. This enabled my aunt to sit up and obey her immediate impulse: she groped for her wig in the dust and hurriedly replaced it just before Russo's shadow fell across her.

"We meet again, signora."

He sounded as dispassionate as a supermarket cashier, almost bored. Poldi tried to scramble to her feet but was defeated by her bad knee. Kneeling in front of Russo in a supremely humiliating way, she made another vain attempt to rise. At a sign from Russo, two members of his staff eventually set her back on her feet. Hans and Franz continued to growl at her viciously.

"I must have failed to express myself clearly enough yesterday," Russo began, once Poldi was standing in front of him, panting.

"Would you put on a show like this if the police were here?" she growled.

"Glad you reminded me. I must call the Carabinieri at once and report a case of trespass. It wouldn't surprise me if something has been damaged or stolen."

"If you think I'm going to piss my pants, you arrogant bastard, think again," she yelled at him in Bavarian.

"Have a nice day, signora."

Russo turned on his heel and clicked his tongue, whereupon the German shepherds sheered off and trotted back to the administration building. Poldi adjusted her wig, striving to convey dignity and composure. She was aware that she had made an enemy.

Fuck him, she said to herself.

Montana turned up that same afternoon.

"Would you care to tell me what you've been up to?"

He looked positively furious. Poldi thought it suited him better than his hangdog expression. Far more in keeping with his dark-blue suit and dark-blue shirt, aviator sunglasses and well-polished brogues. He didn't look creased and crumpled any more, but filled with indignation and *Italianità*. He seemed impervious even to the heat. "He's smartened himself up" was Poldi's first thought when she answered the door. Her second thought was adults only.

"I told you to keep out of it," he thundered. "Even here in Sicily, the police are responsible for murder inquiries. No one else."

Poldi treated him to a long, meaningful look. "Are you through?"

140

Montana drew a deep breath. "No, far from it."

"Then you'd better come in, you're standing right in the sun. Coffee?"

"I mean it, Donna Poldi," Montana insisted as he followed her into the house. "You're merely making trouble for me and hampering my inquiries."

"How?"

"Don't you understand? When Russo makes a complaint, he naturally goes to the very top. Colonnello Cucinotta of the Carabinieri is a good friend of his."

"But you're state police."

"That's just it. The colonnello naturally calls my chief at once and gives him hell: What's all this about some German woman conducting unofficial inquiries into the Candela case, not to mention harassing honest citizens and breaking the law? My boss and the colonnello detest each other and seize any opportunity to get a dig in. The chief was naturally incensed by this. He calls me, reads me the riot act and threatens to take me off the case unless I get things under control."

Poldi handed Montana a cup of coffee and proffered the whisky bottle. "Like a dash?"

"Dai," growled Montana.

Pleased by this imperative in the familiar

141

second-person singular — it meant "Go ahead" — Poldi topped up his cup and treated herself to a dash as well.

This time, Montana downed his espresso immediately.

"I get it," said Poldi. "You're scared of being taken off the case. Or even of being fired."

He gave a little bark of laughter. "Nonsense, I'm not scared. Nobody's going to take me off the case or fire me — I'd like to see them try. Nobody else wants the confounded case, but I don't want to look like the kind of fool who can be led by the nose, not in front of my colleagues."

Montana held out his coffee cup and Poldi promptly poured him another slug. "Ah, now I get it," she said. "You don't want to look bad."

This cupful, too, went straight down the hatch. "Precisely," he said.

For this is the worst thing that can happen to any Italian male, especially a Sicilian. Economic crises, volcanic eruptions, corrupt politicians, emigration, the Mafia, uncollected rubbish and overfishing of the Mediterranean — he can endure anything with fatalism and a *bella figura.* The main thing is never to present a *brutta figura,* a *figuraccia. Bella figura* is the Italian credo.

142

The basic equipment for this includes a well-groomed, unostentatiously fashionable appearance, a pair of good shoes and the right make of sunglasses. Above all, though, *bella figura* means always looking good, never foolish. For an Italian this is a must, not an option, and quite indispensable. It also means you don't embarrass your fellow men. Impatience is unacceptable and direct confrontations are taboo. You share restaurant bills with your friends, don't put your foot in it, never receive guests in a dirty or untidy home, ask no intimate questions, address anyone with a university degree as *dottore,* bring some dessert with you when invited to dinner and — even at the risk of rupturing your abdomen — finish everything on your plate. You put your faith in beauty and proportionality and try to make the world a better place. Sometimes you even succeed.

My Auntie Poldi and the commissario were standing close together, coffee cups in hand like little security barriers. Poldi didn't speak, just looked at Montana expectantly, and he got the message.

Which was that he first had to deliver.

"We've found various clues on Valentino's body. That's all I can tell you."

Poldi pulled a disapproving face.

"Soil on the soles of his shoes and traces of gorse pollen," Montana amplified. "But there's gorse all over Sicily. We're still checking where the soil came from."

"Not from the beach, in other words."

"We're working on it."

"What about the red sand?"

"It's not from around here, anyway, because it doesn't contain any volcanic particles."

"Can you hazard a guess?"

Montana shrugged his shoulders. "Sicily's a big island."

"What about the autopsy?"

He shook his head. "No signs of a struggle. Valentino was simply shot at point-blank range."

"And his mobile phone?"

Montana shook his head again.

Poldi thought for a moment, then nodded. "Okay. I promise not to bother Russo again."

"You must promise to stay out of the case altogether."

Poldi wouldn't go as far as that. "Come with me. I want to show you something."

She led Montana to the corkboard in her bedroom. Logically enough, she also combined this with a subtle innuendo conveyed by the discreet scent of roses with which she had previously perfumed her bed.

Montana, still holding his empty espresso cup like a protective talisman, groaned when he saw the collage of photographs, newspaper cuttings and woollen threads.

"This must stop, signora."

Poldi tapped the photos of Valentino and Russo, which were linked by a thick red thread. "I feel sure that Valentino had been doing some kind of dirty work for Russo. Among other things" — she ran her finger along a green thread leading to another photo — "the theft of a lion sculpture from Femminamorta. Valentino's conscience may have pricked him and he wanted out. That made him a risk, so he had to be eliminated."

"That's utterly implausible," Montana exclaimed nervously.

"Wait," cried Poldi, and she pointed to the pixelated photo of the transparent folder. "Yesterday I happened, purely by chance, to see Russo and Patanè putting their heads together in Taormina. They were poring over this. What do you think it is?"

Montana examined the photo, peevishly at first. Then he detached it from the big collection of items on the wall and looked at it more closely.

"Well?" Poldi said tensely.

145

He handed the photo back. "Part of a topographical map, I'd say."

Poldi would never have thought of that.

"Exactly," she cried. "And of what area?"

"How should I know? What's it supposed to prove, anyway? Do you have a copy?"

"Keep it," she said magnanimously.

Montana pocketed the print as if it were the business card of some irksome sales rep. "Listen to me: Italo Russo enjoys a spotless reputation. He's one of the biggest local employers and a generous patron of various social institutions and projects."

"A typical Mafioso" was all Poldi said. "And don't tell me the Mafia is an invention of the North Italian fascists."

With a sigh, Montana put his coffee cup down. "I must go. You've made me a promise."

"Don't worry, commissario. I take a keen interest in your *bella figura.*"

Poldi no longer found it hard to keep her promise after her encounter with the attack dogs. But she got no further with the case; she simply got stuck like an old lift and felt as if her brakes had locked at high speed. Not even Montana's suggestion got her any further. Riposto's public library contained dozens of volumes of maps of the surrounding area, but having combed them without success, she gave up. Especially as there was no certainty that the map in question showed part of the immediate vicinity.

In the hope that Montana would again show up at her house with some new suggestion or on some threadbare pretext, Poldi spent the ensuing days simply waiting. But he didn't come on Saturday, nor on Sunday, nor on Monday. Nor did he phone her. Instead, she received a call from Mimì Pastorella di Belfiore. Although he spoke German as before, my aunt didn't immediately recognize his sibilant whisper.

"But Donna Isolde, we had such a lively discussion about Hölderlin."

The penny dropped with an unpleasant clang.

"Er . . . Oh yes, of course."

"I feel we should pick up the thread of our joint passion once more and as soon as possible. Don't you?"

Poldi broke out in a sweat. "What did you have in mind?"

"How about dinner this evening, Donna Isolde?"

"Er, no, I'm awfully sorry, Signor Pastorella, but —"

"Mimì. Please call me Mimì, Donna Isolde."

"I'm awfully sorry, Mimì, but I've got a family engagement this evening."

"I quite understand. Then make it tomorrow night. There's something I'd like to show you."

"I'm afraid I won't be able to make it tomorrow night either, Mimì. The whole of next week is out, and the one after that is even busier — I'm completely booked up."

Mimì didn't speak. Unable to hear anything but his faint breathing, Poldi was afraid she might have given him a stroke.

"How about if I call you when it's convenient?" she asked in a bright, conversational tone.

"Please do that, Donna Poldina." His voice sounded even fainter and more feeble than before. "I shall await your call."

Poldi hung up in a lather. "My God, that's all I bloody well needed." Then, as if the phone were to blame for everything, she snarled at it: "Don't call me again. Don't put anyone through unless it's Montana, *capisci*?"

But zilch. No Montana. They were difficult days. Never had her thirst seemed greater, the heat more unbearable, life more complicated, the next step more arduous. But Poldi kept a grip on herself. She didn't touch a drop, even though it demanded titanic self-control.

She would have liked to sit on her roof terrace, gazing out over the sea and smoking like Etna, but her right knee was playing up again and made it agony for her to climb stairs. So she pinned a notice to her front door — SONO AL BAR — and plonked herself down outside the Bar Cocuzza, where she drank ice-cold almond milk and smoked one MS after another.

"*Namaste,* life," she sighed, gazing at the sea, and gave the sad signora a friendly nod. "The rest of the world can kiss my ass."

All she did apart from that was hanker for nightfall, for Montana, for a sign, an idea — for something. At least she wasn't waiting for death any more. That was a start.

6

Describes how Poldi crosses swords with an incorruptible public servant at Valentino's funeral and makes a discovery. On the following Sunday she goes mushroompicking and promptly makes two further discoveries. She then does something out of character and is reminded of Ruppertstrasse in Munich.

My Auntie Poldi did not see Montana again until Tuesday, at Valentino's funeral. Although she hadn't received an invitation, she was fortunate that Signora Anzalone from next door was always *au courant* where funerals were concerned.

The little cemetery was situated in a suburb of Acireale near the motorway, amid lemon orchards, expanses of wasteland and unofficial rubbish dumps. Isolated cypresses and palm trees reared their heads behind the drystone walls, which were plastered with old advertising posters. Poldi noticed as she drove through the little suburb of Aci Catena that they included a lot of advertisements for fortune tellers and palmists.

By the time she got to the cemetery car park, the mourners had already assembled in front of the gateway, which resembled a small, overly pretentious provincial railway station. Poldi found this somehow appropriate. Montana was not among the mourners, she was disappointed to note. Nor was Russo, but she did spot Valentino's parents. Standing beside the coffin with the *padre,* they were heatedly haranguing an elderly man who was stubbornly shaking his head. There was clearly a problem of some kind.

Poldi was once more wearing her black dress, plus a veil for camouflage. She had really meant to remain inconspicuously in the background, observing everything with forensic professionalism, but her curiosity was aroused by the dispute, which was becoming ever more heated and involved the noisy participation of more and more of the mourners. As far as she could gather when she had edged a little closer, it was about a missing *marca da bollo* on the burial permit.

The principle is both simple and effective. In Italy, the payment of administrative fees is certified by little official stamps or stickers affixed to the documents in question. These *marche da bollo* can be purchased in *tabacchi,* which, in addition to cigarettes, purvey lottery tickets, picture postcards, local bus tickets, newspapers, stationery, chewing gum, gossip and useful information about the neighbourhood.

The document which Valentino's father was brandishing in the old man's face was adorned with an administrative stamp of this kind. An insufficient one, however, because instead of the requisite twenty-three euros fifty cents only sixteen had been paid. And because of the missing seven euros fifty cents the cemetery janitor was refusing to allow the Candelas to enter. There was nothing to be done — he simply shook his head with adamantine obstinacy and invoked the regulations. Needless to say, someone had already set off for the nearest *tabacchi* to purchase the missing stamp, but he seemed to have gone missing, too.

Like the ambient temperature, the argument with the janitor quickly grew heated, and the more heated it became, the more adamantly the old man stood his ground — quite why remained his own dark secret. He barred admittance to the cemetery like the Spartans defending Thermopylae. It went without saying that my Auntie Poldi could not idly stand by.

"My good man," she told the janitor, "there must surely be some sensible way of resolving this issue."

The old man stared at her as if he was the nymph Galatea being wooed by Polyphemus the Cyclops, but he may simply have been thrown by her German accent.

"I'm sorry," he said testily, "I have to observe the regulations."

He tried to turn on his heel, but Poldi hung on to him. The mourners had in the meantime formed a circle around him anyway, so escape was almost impossible.

"Look, signore," Poldi went on, "I can understand your point of view. I come from Germany, where people would back you a hundred per cent. You're doing a great job here. No, seriously. Regulations are regulations, after all. The thing is, though, Germany is a cold country. Where burials are concerned, a day or two's delay doesn't matter there, whereas here in Sicily the sun beats down on us unmercifully, which is why Frederick II praised the Sicilians for being the inventors of humanitarianism. We in Germany can only dream of that. Look, we're all hot. I'm hot, you're hot, Valentino's poor parents are hot — and Valentino, who's waiting in his coffin to be laid to rest forever, is also hot. I dread to think what a high old time the putrefactive bacteria are having in his body right now. You don't really want to cross swords with us. You're only doing your job and we haven't paid the full fee. We're the problem that's spoiling your well-earned lunch break, and the last thing we want is to keep you from your *pranzo,* so help us not to be your problem any longer. Do we really want to go on bickering until we fry our brains and the sewage gas in Valentino's coffin explodes, or do we find a kind, humane, practical solution such as the Germans would envy?"

Silence reigned and everyone stared at Poldi. One or two people nodded, brows were mopped and cries of *"Ecco"* or *"Brava"* could be heard.

The janitor seemed puzzled by Poldi's rhetoric, but he eventually succumbed once more to whatever had been bugging him that day.

"No," he said. "You'll just have to wait until someone turns up with the missing stamp, and that's that."

This drew cries of indignation from the assembled mourners, but the old man, seemingly unmoved, elbowed the crowd brusquely aside. That was when Poldi blew her top. She hurriedly fished a fifty-euro note out of her handbag and grabbed the janitor's arm again. "Now listen to me," she snarled at him in Bavarian, thrusting the money into his hand. "I know exactly what you're after, you old fox. Here, take this and pipe down, all right?"

Bavarian and a bribe — it ought to have been a surefire combination, but it completely missed the target. The obdurate janitor uttered a cry of rage, flung the note to the ground, stamped on it and treated Poldi to a tirade in Sicilian. Hurt, offended, insulted, profoundly sullied and humiliated, he eventually turned his back on her and forged a path through the crowd. It was all over. Diplomatic relations were severed for good. Not even mass indignation and threats to storm the cemetery could change his mind. He simply locked the cemetery gate and disappeared into his lodge.

It was almost noon by now. The sky resembled polished steel; the air above the car park was shimmering. Poldi groaned beneath her veil and waited for the dam to burst — for a revolt to break out and the janitor to be lynched. Instead, the mourners were merely overcome by fatalistic resignation. Valentino's mother might have been turned to stone, the *padre* mopped his brow, the last indignant voices fell silent. Perhaps it was simply too hot. The Sicilian midday sun was reducing rage to fatalism. After a brief consultation it was decided to deposit the coffin and wreaths in the shade of a eucalyptus tree beside the cemetery gate and wait for the missing administrative sticker to arrive.

Poldi sensed that she had gone too far, that she might have made a mess of things. She was about to hurry after the old man when a strong hand caught her by the arm.

"Leave it, Signora Poldi."

Montana seemed to have materialized like magic, once more wearing his creased grey work suit and aviator sunglasses. Poldi was so taken aback by his sudden appearance and so electrified by his touch that she was briefly lost for words.

"I'll deal with this."

Poldi saw Montana speaking to the old man through the window of the lodge. The janitor kept shaking his head until Montana showed him his ID and asked him something. Then the old man visibly knuckled under and, with a look of bitter resignation, ended by opening the gate. Amid applause from the mourners, Montana spoke briefly to Valentino's parents and the *padre,* and Valentino could at last be carried to his final resting place.

"Like a knight in shining armour," said Poldi, when she had caught up with Montana in the graveyard.

He grinned at her and looked around to see if they could be overheard. Then, casually, he said, "We found some money in Valentino's room."

"How much money?"

"Nearly ten thousand euros. In a plastic bag behind his wardrobe."

Poldi stared at him in disbelief. "So you took my theft theory seriously."

"I'm thorough, that's all. His parents say they knew nothing about it. I'm inclined to believe them, because the money certainly wouldn't have been there any longer if they had."

"Ten thousand euros?"

"Mm."

"Maybe Valentino saved it."

"That's one way of putting it. All new, consecutively numbered notes in four batches, none of them containing less than two thousand euros."

Poldi resorted to her native tongue. "Well, I'll be buggered."

"Eh?"

"Hearty congratulations, my dear. And all because I went on at you like that. What do you say?"

No response.

She nudged him. "Well, go on, say it — say the magic word. *Dai.* It's not hard."

Montana sighed resignedly. "Thanks."

Poldi beamed. "You owe me one." She lowered her voice to a whisper. "And now you're going to look around to see if Valentino's employer turns up for his funeral."

"Or the person he owed that money to. Who knows?"

"Anyone here you suspect?"

Montana grinned at her again. "Was it true, that business about Frederick II and what he said about the Sicilians?"

Poldi made a dismissive gesture. "No, but I'm sure dear old Fred would have agreed with me."

"So you were lying."

"In a good cause. Besides, it wasn't a lie, strictly speaking, it was oratory."

"You lied to a public servant — you tried to bribe him. I could take that personally."

"Are you flirting with me, commissario?"

Montana looked at her through his sunglasses. He wasn't grinning any more. All at once, his face looked as hard and impenetrable as the midday sky.

"Don't do it again, Poldi. And never lie to me. Never."

Without waiting for her to reply, he strode off in search of a better view of the mourners. Poldi cursed herself for having interfered.

Valentino's last journey ended in a wall containing three tiers of burial niches. In the top row gaped a rectangular aperture which would be sealed with a stone slab as soon as Valentino's coffin had disappeared into it for good. The few wreaths included one from "Piante Russo" on behalf of the entire workforce. Poldi felt that the whole ceremony passed off far too cursorily and with insufficient solemnity, as though Valentino couldn't be walled up and forgotten quickly enough. Although she knew this wasn't the case, the thought suddenly depressed her. Piqued by Montana's harsh words, she began to weep and gave her tears free rein. She wept for Valentino, who had deserved something better than such a death and such a funeral. She wept for my Uncle Peppe and all the people in her life who had left her undeservedly and far too soon. And she also wept a little for herself.

Having recovered her composure and given her nose a good blow, she noticed a tall, red-haired man who hadn't caught her eye before. He added a small bunch of flowers to the other floral offerings, then hurriedly withdrew and made for the exit. He was sunburnt and wearing dark glasses. Not a Sicilian, Poldi surmised, and in his late forties. She would have liked to take a photograph of him, but felt it would be inappropriate. However, she saw that Montana was following him.

"Who's that?" she asked an aunt of Valentino's, who was standing beside her.

The woman shook her head. "Never seen him before."

Poldi thought for a moment, then followed Montana to the exit. When she emerged into the car park, the commissario was standing beside his car, lighting a cigarette.

"Who was that?"

"No idea," he grunted.

"Did you get his licence number?"

Montana shook his head. "He drove off in a taxi."

"A taxi?"

"Believe it or not, we've recently got taxis in Sicily. We may even get electric light before long." Looking irritable, he mashed out his unsmoked cigarette, said a curt goodbye, got into his car and left Poldi standing there.

"Idiot," Poldi called after him. Her heart felt as heavy as Etna.

■ ■ ■ ■

It didn't escape the aunts that Poldi was making no progress with the Valentino case and suffering from a recurrence of the blues. Accordingly, Aunt Teresa and Uncle Martino took her mushroom-picking the following Sunday. Their objective: *joie de vivre.* Their means to that end: beautiful natural surroundings, fresh air, physical exercise and — of course — mushrooms.

Aunt Teresa and Uncle Martino went mushroom-picking on Etna nearly every weekend and were normally accompanied by their ground-floor neighbours the Terra-novas, with whom they were linked not only by thirty years' acquaintanceship but also by fierce competition for the biggest and finest mushrooms.

According to Uncle Martino, nowhere in the world afforded a wider variety of edible mushrooms — or bigger ones, of course — than the infinitely fertile volcanic soil on the slopes of the Mongibello, or Etna, and the mushrooms stored in Aunt Teresa's chest freezer suggested that he was right. It was said that the Satan's mushroom, which is regarded as extremely poisonous elsewhere in the world, became excellent fare when grown in that soil. I never tried one, nor did my Auntie Poldi, because she didn't like eating mushrooms anyway, far less picking them. Poldi wasn't keen on the great outdoors in general, being more of an urbanite. The most she had ever done was drive out of Munich to bathe and sunbathe with Uncle Peppe beside the Staffelsee, which is as warm as the Mediterranean. Truth to tell, though, even in that sadly remote and closed chapter of her life she preferred to sit in a lakeside beer garden rather than lie on a towel on the sand.

She had nevertheless allowed herself to be talked into the excursion, especially as Montana still hadn't called and her depression was growing worse with each passing day like a grain of sand in an oyster shell. Except that the oyster shell was her heart and the pearl a build-up of memories, self-pity and melancholy.

Aunt Teresa knew this, and she also knew how to dislodge that kind of grain of sand. The mushrooms were merely tasty supernumeraries in a miniseries about the magic of life, and Aunt Teresa and Uncle Martino enacted it every day and weekend of their lives.

Like any private undertaking in Sicily, the playlet began with a delay of two hours or more. Sicilians can be as punctual as Prussians in the professional sphere, but personal arrangements are subject to an elastic expansion of the concept of time. It is as if those hours must be sacrificed to a demanding god who measures his subjects' lifetime by the extent to which they waste the lifetimes of others. Besides, every sensible Sicilian allows a margin of at least two hours where private assignations are concerned, but Poldi still hadn't reached that stage.

She sat waiting from eight that morning onwards as arranged, fragrantly scented, carefully attired and alcohol-free — not counting a little revivifying *prosecchino*. Since she was venturing out into the wilds, she wore a khaki linen ensemble in the colonial style: voluminous trousers, leopard-skin top and a matching jacket with a uniform collar and ubiquitous pockets, colour-coordinated strappy sandals and, by way of a feminine highlight, a big bunch of colourful ethnic-look necklaces. She was a white Masai, a kind of Bavarian Tania Blixen: she was ready for mushroom-picking.

By the time Martino and Teresa finally appeared at eleven, however, she was not only sick of the idea of mushroom-picking but had also calmed her nerves with two bottles of beer. Aunt Teresa spotted this at once.

"I thought you weren't drinking any more."

It was a reproach, not a question.

"And I thought you were picking me up at eight," Poldi countered defiantly. "What was the problem this time?"

Teresa sighed. "He was fetching the newspaper."

"For three hours?"

"Then he took the dog for a walk."

"But we're just about to take it for a walk."

"Then he couldn't find his reading glasses."

"You mean one of the hundred and twenty pairs scattered all over your house?"

"And then he had to take Marco to the airport."

Poldi was beginning to understand. "And on the way back I suppose he dropped in at the fish market and bought some swordfish."

"Figs," sighed Teresa. "There's no fish market on Sundays."

"My, that's lucky."

Martino had parked the Fiat at the end of the Via Baronessa. There Poldi saw herself confronted by the day's next challenge: Totti, a good-natured mutt named after AS Roma's legendary international footballer. A typical mongrel of the sort that roams slums and favelas all over the world, dozes beside dusty farm tracks and explores rubbish in backyards, Totti was yellow with a black muzzle, huge ears, huge paws and a heart of gold. He was cheerfully lounging on the back seat behind my uncle, but when he sighted Poldi he went mad with delight, barking and bouncing around the car in a frenzy.

"You can sit in front," said Aunt Teresa.

But Poldi couldn't bring herself to do that when a living creature was evincing such joy at her arrival on the scene. Submissively, she squeezed into the back beside Totti and allowed herself to be licked and rampaged around on until the dog calmed down and sat on her lap, exhausted by so much jubilation.

During the drive, Poldi kept seeing dilapidated houses in the midst of the countryside.

"Who do they all belong to?" she asked.

"The Bourbons," Uncle Martino told her, "or the pathetic relics of the Bourbon nobility. But don't be deceived; they still pull the strings behind the scenes, even though most of them have barely enough money to maintain their splendid mansions and country houses."

Poldi already knew this. Thinking of Valérie, she suddenly wondered if she might have been a little too trusting towards her new friend.

Meanwhile, Uncle Martino had the bit between his teeth and was recounting what Poldi had also known for ages: that whole gangs specialized in breaking into the usually derelict buildings and stripping out and selling valuable mosaics and frescoes, tiled floors and sculptures, so that sundry dentists, nightclub owners and German expatriates could install them in their tasteless seaside villas. Uncle Martino liked to talk himself into a rage about his topic *numero uno,* the contention that Sicily was going to rack and ruin, whether or not his listeners were familiar with the subject. Aunt Teresa eventually told Martino to shut up, and that he was giving her palpitations, whereupon — in conformity with the immutable scenario that had governed their forty-plus years of marriage — he retorted that he refused to be silenced, either by her or by corrupt politicians or the CIA or by Totti, who had joined in the debate and was barking furiously. Thereafter Martino launched straight into his topic *numero due:* the Mafia involvements of premiers Andreotti, Craxi, Berlusconi and Co. He continued in that vein until exhaustion reduced everyone to silence, which he broke with a contented *"Amore."*

And all was well.

Poldi surreptitiously swallowed two aspirin, stared out of the window and strove to ignore brother-in-law, sister-in-law and dog. A thought had flitted past her like a shooting star traversing the night sky; it had flared up and died, leaving only a fine striation on her memory. She suddenly realized that she had overlooked something, possibly something important, but she couldn't with the best will in the world recall what it was. She fished out her notebook and searched for some pointer hidden among the entries. But nothing. Nothing save the faint skid mark of a brief flash of inspiration that might never recur. This disturbed Poldi beyond measure — so much so that all she wanted to do was go home and concentrate.

But she could forget about that for the moment, because they had by now reached the target area for mushroom-picking.

Picking mushrooms on Etna is not hard, because one's only competitors are the Terranovas and a local peasant or two. The few Sicilians who feel tempted to venture into the oak woods on Etna find it sufficient to park in the shade somewhere beside the road, have a picnic, and leave the place strewn with litter. They never walk more than ten yards into the trees. Nor does my Uncle Martino. Why should he, when he has the car?

As usual, he simply turned off the road at some point and drove straight through the trees until the Fiat came to rest. Then they all got out. My Auntie Poldi, my Aunt Teresa, my uncle and Totti emerged into the cool, shady hush of the ancient oak trees, stretched their limbs, breathed deeply, and said "Ah" and *Che bello* the way one does when entering an old and almost pristine place. The oaks were widely spaced, their crowns well exposed to the sky, like a tribe of ancient beings convoked by a voice with something important to announce.

At this altitude the air was cool and vernal. Pleasant midday sunlight came flickering through the treetops to bathe the warm, springy forest floor, which deadened footsteps and lightened the heart. It was like a German forest transported by some kindly god to Sicily in August.

Totti promptly disappeared into the trees in search of rabbits or a flock of sheep to stampede.

"It rained up here yesterday," Martino announced. "I know a few places where there are bound to be some mushrooms."

Poldi felt less certain but decided to keep her trap shut. "What should I look for?" she asked.

Aunt Teresa thrust a basket into her hand. "Mushrooms."

Martino, Teresa and Poldi, each equipped with a basket, fanned out and combed the undergrowth. Poldi was instructed to pick anything that even remotely resembled a mushroom because her haul would be submitted to expert triage later on. After a quarter of an hour her brother- and sister-in-law were out of sight and earshot and she was feeling thoroughly fed up, especially as she was only wearing sandals. She had rejected sturdy shoes as an imposition ever since setting foot on Sicilian soil.

Sighing, she sat down beside a big oak tree, swigged from her hip flask and tried to concentrate on the lost idea — on the moment when it had so suddenly flashed through her mind and then faded. But in vain. Poldi stared up at the surrounding trees, which were rustling softly.

"That's right, whisper away. I'll remember what it was, never fear."

As though in response, the staccato rat-a-tat of a woodpecker rang out. The forest was laughing at her. That was fine with

Poldi, who had never had much time for self-pity. She laughed, too. "Bravo, birdie. Thanks, that'll do."

While communing with nature in this way, she noticed two young oak trees a few yards further on, standing close together with their branches seemingly entwined in an embrace. Keen to take a picture of this ligneous image of eternal love, she fished her little camera out of her bag. And that was when the lost thought came back to her: photograph.

"Photograph?" I queried when she told me about it later. "And?"

"And nothing. Just photograph."

"But you immediately knew which one."

"Hey, I'm no Stephen Hawking. Which reminds me: did I ever tell you how your Uncle Peppe and I met Stephen Hawking? It was such a nice evening — my, how we laughed."

"You're straying from the point, Poldi. Which one?"

"I didn't have a clue, but at least I was on the right track. So I turned on the camera's display right away and checked to see what I'd snapped in recent days. And then I found it."

"The photo?"

"Exactly."

"Which one, for God's sake?"

"The one of the traffic cop in Taormina, of course. It had etched itself into my subconscious, so to speak. Freud and all that."

She showed me the photo. I, too, could see it now.

"Wow," I exclaimed, electrified. "What then?"

"Why, then I found some mushrooms. That's because I was in a sudden state of heightened perception. I tell you, if a sack of rice had fallen over in China, I'd have heard the thud."

For as Poldi clasped her hands in gratitude and bowed and said "*Namaste,* forest," she noticed where she'd been sitting, namely, in the midst of the biggest mushroom population that had ever sprouted in the penumbra of an oak forest: colossal fungi with caps as big as Basque berets. It was pure beginner's luck.

Uncle Martino and Aunt Teresa were utterly confounded to find Poldi waiting for them beside the car with her basket overflowing, the more so since they themselves had failed to find a single mushroom. Nil. Zero. *Niente.*

"The Terranovas must have got here before us this morning," sighed Uncle Martino, despondently eyeing Poldi's haul. It was all of the finest A1 quality, and no mistake. "It's the only explanation. I know just where to look."

"*Amore,*" sighed Aunt Teresa.

"Pure beginner's luck," Poldi insisted, proffering her basket to the dejected couple. "Please. I've never liked mushrooms anyway."

But Teresa and Martino's mushroom-picking reputation precluded this. Brusquely rejecting Poldi's offer, they compelled her to keep the monster fungi and advised her to enjoy the forest giants tossed in butter with a nice bowl of pasta. Or to freeze them for future consumption.

The drive back resembled a baseline rally.

"At least take half of them."

"No, they're yours, you keep them."

"Just a few. Please."

"No, you found them, they're yours."

"I'm giving them to you."

"We can't accept them."

"Madonna, don't be so ridiculous."

"Oh, so you think we're being ridiculous."

Nothing worked — no protests, no appeals to reason, no "*Amore,*" no imprecations. Martino did take a photo of Poldi's basketful, intending to rub the Terranovas' noses in it, but she had to keep all the mushrooms herself, even though their smell alone made her feel nauseous and revived a few sinister childhood memories.

So what did she do with that unwanted plethora of brown-and-white fungus? Acting upon a sudden impulse, she gave it away to sad Signora Cocuzza. And lo, a miracle occurred: Signora Cocuzza not only failed to decline the mushrooms with thanks, she thanked Poldi with a smile that might have passed for benign. A small gift, those mushrooms, but — not, of course, that Poldi could have known this — it would soon be repaid three times over.

As soon as she was back home and alone at last, Poldi excitedly got out the photo album containing her collection of policemen and examined the picture of the handsome *Vigile* with a magnifying glass. There was no doubt about it: Valentino was visible in the background.

"Well, I'll be buggered." It defeated her how she could have overlooked Valentino all this time and — for that matter — why she hadn't spotted him that day in Taormina. The only explanation: at that moment, the handsome traffic cop's charisma must have bred a kind of tunnel vision, a focusing of perception on one single object such as only lionesses achieve when hunting in the Serengeti.

Valentino, by contrast, had clearly noticed Poldi, because he was looking straight into the camera. Unfortunately, the depth of field was insufficient to provide more details, but she felt sure that the boy was looking dismayed and caught out. Tense, too. This may have been due to his companion, for Valentino wasn't alone. He was sitting outside a café near the Porta Messina with a considerably older man. Red hair, sunburn, sunglasses, white polo shirt. Central European. That was all Poldi could make out, but she had no doubt that he was the man she'd seen at Valentino's funeral. "Mr. X," as she promptly christened him, seemed to have followed the direction of Valentino's gaze and was also looking in her direction. She tried to recall the actual moment. It had been on the Wednesday, two days after Valentino's disappearance, when she was already making inquiries about him. This shocked her, because she had overlooked him when she was already searching for him. And all because of the handsome policeman. Or perhaps, she thought dejectedly, because she couldn't wait to get home as soon as possible and wait for nightfall with an XL Martini glass in her hand. She recalled that her thoughts had revolved around a Martini as she hurried through the Porta Messina and along the street to the bus station from which shuttles left for the multi-storey. That was when she had spotted the *Vigile* in the midst of the turmoil with his whistle and white gloves, plucked the camera from her pocket and pressed the button. It had all been rather hectic, pure instinct, and instead of continuing to watch the handsome policeman's choreography a while longer, she had hurried on to the bus station. And all because of Signor Martini on ice, waiting for her at home.

Valentino and Mr. X were visible only through a gap between two cars. There was something lying on the small café table, but Poldi couldn't make out what it was. Even Samuele, whom she set to work on the digital original of the photo on Monday morning, failed to get anything more out of it.

The more she examined Valentino's face in the picture, the more certain Poldi became that he was looking thoroughly startled. And as for Mr. X's expression, he seemed to be staring at her like a hawk targeting a field mouse — seemed even to follow her with his gaze when she moved to and fro. The photograph mesmerized her;

she couldn't stop looking at it. She sat on the sofa until late that night, scanning every square millimetre of the print with a magnifying glass until her eyes were smarting, and she went off to bed with the disturbing suspicion that she might accidentally have photographed Valentino's murderer. Which meant that she herself might be in danger.

Poldi felt perturbed. She wondered if Mr. X had recognized her at the funeral. She'd worn a veil and stayed close to Valentino's family. On the other hand, she had made quite an exhibition of herself with the janitor. However, my aunt wasn't the type to get rattled easily — she'd coped with worse situations in Tanzania — and so she did what she always did when scared: she got mad. Thoroughly mad. And when she worked herself up into a rage, she tended to take the bull by the horns. Which meant, in this context, that she had to find Mr. X before he found her. But for that Poldi needed some help, so she swallowed her pride and texted Montana an invitation to a candlelit dinner — though she naturally omitted the word "candlelit."

I've got something for you. Dinner at nine?

She stared at the display on her mobile

for a good hour, waiting for an answer. Then:

OK

Although Poldi thought his response might have been a bit more enthusiastic, she planned the evening with meticulous care, feeling that she couldn't afford to make another mistake in this regard.

To invite the commissario to dinner and present him with the full broadside of her décolleté was naturally in the interests of her investigation, as was the off-the-shoulder red gown in which she welcomed him that evening.

"Because, listen," she told me later, "career-wise, the old rule of thumb is —"

"I know," I cut in. "When the chips are down, show plenty of cleavage."

"You simply display your assets, man or woman alike."

"What would you advise in my case?" I asked her. "I mean, always assuming I'm not completely beyond hope?"

Poldi submitted my appearance to critical appraisal. "You're developing a little tummy. You could use a bit of exercise. Abs and pecs never do any harm in moderation. Shorts are a no-no except on the beach, men's legs being what they are. But why wear your nice hair so short? Let it grow, so a woman can imagine running her fingers through your wealth of dark curls, know what I mean? Apart from that, you've got nice forearms and strong hands like your father and Peppe. You can afford to display everything from the elbows down."

That was a start, at least.

Montana needed no such tuition. I mean, he was an Italian — he knew which look to adopt for which occasion. He showed up punctually in a smart black ensemble: slip-ons without socks, Asiatic linen chinos and, worn over his waistband, a tailored shirt only marginally tight over the beginnings of a tummy but revealing a muscular chest. Collar open, naturally, and sleeves neatly rolled up to the elbows, giving Poldi an unobstructed view of his thoracic hair and silky skin. His olive complexion, dark beard and moustache made him look like Odysseus paying a quick visit to Circe. Or so Poldi thought, and it was all she could do not to hurl herself at him and gobble him up on the doorstep. Instead, she just leant forward a trifle and presented her left cheek for the obligatory mwah-mwah between friends.

To her disappointment, Montana did not

take her up on this offer but merely held out a small, gift-wrapped package done up with gold ribbon. "Some gelato for dessert," he said. "From Cipriani."

"How kind," Poldi said sourly.

"Oh, and this . . ." He was holding a bouquet of white roses and olive sprigs. It was as if he had seen into the depths of my aunt's soul, for it must be explained that a bouquet of olive sprigs and white roses from the gardens of Nymphenburg Palace was what Poldi had been holding in her hand when she plighted her troth with Uncle Peppe at the register office in Ruppertstrasse. That horticultural link between Bavaria and Sicily had remained her favourite form of floral decoration ever since. It reminded her of Peppe, of love and pleasure and life itself, and it cheered her when days were dark.

"How ever did you know?" she whispered in awe as she took the bouquet from him.

"Boh," said Montana, a trifle embarrassed, and the evening took its course.

7

Tells of falling between two stools and the three phases of seduction. Montana discloses some personal details and briefly succumbs to jealousy and passion. Poldi finds solace in familiar arms, goes looking for Mr. X and is once more overtaken by her past in Taormina.

The commissario had accepted her invitation with reluctance and slight uneasiness, Poldi told me at the beginning of September.

"Not because of me, of course," she explained, "but because of the food. He's a Sicilian to his fingertips. German beer is one thing, but German cuisine? Heaven forbid."

To Montana's great relief, Poldi dispensed with Bavarian delicacies such as white veal sausage, dumplings, cabbage, etc., and served up a Sicilian classic instead. This was *pasta alla Norma,* for which she used Aunt Teresa's bottled tomato sauce, fried aubergines from Signora Anzalone's garden, and *ricotta salata* brought by Uncle Martino from Noto — for Noto, it must be stressed, is the only legitimate source of *ricotta salata.* The pasta was accompanied by a nice Nerello Mascalese from the slopes of Etna and followed by Montana's gelato, so all the makings of a perfect evening were present.

Filled with optimism by her bouquet, Poldi did not pull out all the stops right away. The night was still young, after all, and it would fall into three phases.

Phase one: confidence-building measures.

Phase two: exchanges of information.

Phase three: the best part, including further exchanges.

"Would you mind opening the wine, Vito?"

Poldi got another chance to admire Montana's shapely forearms as he wielded the corkscrew. He poured two glasses while she continued to stir the *sugo.*

"What shall we drink to?" she asked.

"To the truth."

"To the truth."

They clinked glasses. Poldi only sipped her wine because — to repeat — the night was still young. Montana followed suit, then watched her at the stove.

"A decent drop, that."

"Thanks. I'm sure you know your wines."

"So-so. You have a nice house."

"Please make yourself at home. Won't you sit down? You may smoke if you wish."

"I'd sooner watch you cooking, if you don't mind."

Montana was clearly in no hurry to learn what sort of information Poldi had for him. Phase one couldn't have been going better.

"I don't mind in the least, my dear Vito, but you must entertain me a little in return."

He shrugged his shoulders. "Entertain you how?"

"Tell me a bit about yourself — and we drank to the truth, don't forget."

Montana sighed. "Well, go on, ask away."

"Are you married?"

A superfluous, purely introductory question.

"Divorced four years ago. My ex-wife lives in Milan; she's a lawyer. We have two children, Marta and Diego. The girl's a medical student in Rome, the boy is studying mechanical engineering in Milan."

Poldi made a mental note of the children's names.

"Then you're all on your own here in Sicily."

He sighed. "It's complicated."

"Oh, sure. That's that, then." Poldi laughed her husky laugh and added the *penne rigate* to the pot, because *pasta alla Norma* is always made with *penne.* "What brought you to Sicily?"

The commissario sighed again, but this time it was a sigh that came from deep inside and was accompanied by a recurrence of his morose expression. "I was transferred here for disciplinary reasons."

Poldi turned towards him in surprise, but she had no need to press him further; he merely gave another shrug and went on speaking.

"I came from here originally — from Giarre, to be precise — but I went straight to police college in Milan after completing my national service. Sicilians have a hard time in Milan, if only because of the dialect. They're regarded as Africans, village idiots, thieves, cheats, scroungers. I stuck at it, though. I learnt to speak proper Italian and got rid of my dialect. But listen, I've no wish to bore you with my life story —"

"My dear Vito, believe me, you'll soon know if you're boring me. Right now you can carry the pasta to the table and light the candles."

She thrust the dish into his hand and watched him light the candles. He did this with the undivided attention he bestowed on every activity, and Poldi promptly pictured what else his hands could doubtless do with the same undivided attention. She had to pull herself together once more to remain entirely in the here and now.

"Excellent," was Montana's enthusiastic comment on his first mouthful.

"But woe betide you if you say 'Just like my mamma's.'"

He grinned. "My mother was probably the only Sicilian woman who couldn't cook. As for my wife, well . . ."

"Are your parents still alive?"

Montana cleared his throat. "Let's change the subject."

Poldi guessed that she had touched a big scar, one of many. This pleased her, but she temporarily left it at that and raised her glass again.

"To Sicily and the Sicilians."

Montana shook his head. "No, to Sicily without the Sicilians."

Poldi gazed at him all the time while drinking, and the commissario never even blinked in embarrassment.

"I'd had a pretty good career in the state police," he went on. "During the eighties I spent some time with a special anti-Mafia unit in Rome. Then I went back to homicide in Milan."

"That sounds excellent. So what happened?"

"There was a murder in the red-light district, and I leant rather too heavily on a politician, a senator from a very long-established dynasty of North Italian industrialists with links to the Roman Curia. Bingo. Five years from retirement I suddenly became the Sicilian scoundrel again. I was denounced, defamed, denigrated and harassed until I became completely ostracized at work."

"Did they have any solid evidence against you?"

Montana put his fingertips together in the age-old Italian gesture of impotence. "Oh, you know. After so many years in the force there were bound to be a few things; it was quite inevitable. A little favour here, a less than kosher deal there — the little compromises without which no detective can find his way through a morass of lies, corruption and secrecy. I'm not trying to gloss over anything — of course I occasionally got my hands dirty — but I usually got my perp in the end."

Poldi thought of her father, Georg Oberreiter, who had never made a mistake or got his hands dirty in forty-plus years' service,

185

but he had very seldom spoken about his work, and it suddenly occurred to her that she knew very little about him.

"I quite understand."

"No, I doubt if you do. I'm not trying to justify myself, but my problem with the aforesaid senator was that I don't take bribes. Well, when you're isolated, everything happens very fast. He pulled a few strings, did the signor senator, and before I knew it I'd been transferred to Sicily, to Acireale, and neutralized in the arsehole of the world. Know what that meant?"

Poldi shook her head.

"It was the maximum sentence. They could have retired me early, but no, they transferred me. It wasn't just that they sentenced me to the provincial claustrophobia I'd been happy to escape from four decades earlier; it was worse than that. I'm the foreigner again. The outsider from the north. The Sicilian who thought he was too good for Sicily and came unstuck. Neither one thing nor the other. The reject. The loser. Someone to be distrusted. Someone fighting a losing battle. My colleagues cold-shoulder me. I can't expect any assistance in the Valentino case, and I'm making very little progress. Whenever I interview witnesses I come up against a wall of silence. It

186

doesn't surprise me much — I'm Sicilian, I know the score — but it gets on my nerves. It makes me mad; it drives me insane."

Montana told Poldi all this without a moment's hesitation, valiantly endeavouring to look into her eyes and not at her cleavage.

Poldi cleared away the plates and brought the gelato. Pistachio and chocolate. Innocent though that sounds, it is a typically Sicilian confection as baroque and magnificent as the whole of Sicily's cuisine. A cuisine like the whole island, a superabundance of aromas, marvels, sensations. A spectacular odyssey for the palate, even in a dish as commonplace as *pasta alla Norma,* in which the sweetness of the tomato sauce blends with the salty ricotta and the slightly bitter note of the grilled aubergines. Sweet, salt, bitter, piquant — Sicilian cuisine is all-embracing and pleasurably involves all the senses in a single dish. A gelato must also be like this. Sweet as a whispered promise, the pistachio ice cream salty as sea air, the chocolate ice cream faintly bitter and a little tart like a lover's goodbye the next morning.

Perfect for my Auntie Poldi, in other words, and while she allowed a concentrated dose of Sicily to dissolve on her tongue, she conceived of Montana, too, as a baroque dessert of that kind. Sweet, salty and bitter, cool and melting.

"And then a German woman meddles in my inquiries and makes me look stupid," he went on. "I'm almost tempted to chuck the case and let those idiots in the Carabinieri bust a gut instead, but I don't give up easily — that's my trouble."

Poldi nodded sympathetically. She was growing steadily fonder of Montana in a way she'd believed was no longer possible. And although I can report only what my aunt told me, of course, I feel sure her emotions were ablaze. I can picture them sitting there together, my Auntie Poldi and Vito Montana, in the house at No. 29 Via Baronessa, stirring their melting pistachio and chocolate gelato and sipping the rest of the wine just to avoid having to say any more, because the ice cream was melting away and they didn't know where the evening would lead, so it might be better if it led nowhere. Or so I imagine.

"I know what you mean, Vito," Poldi said at length in a husky voice, laying her hand on his arm. "I know something about falling between two stools."

Montana produced his cigarettes. "May I?"

"But of course, Vito."

Poldi watched him light a cigarette with his usual air of concentration, saw him inhale the first few lungfuls of smoke in silence and look at her searchingly. She realized that he still regarded her as part of his case. It was high time to introduce phase two.

"Have you managed to establish the identity of the red-haired man at the funeral?"

Montana shook his head. "The taxi driver was no great help. The man flagged him down outside the cathedral in Acireale and had himself driven back there. He clearly didn't speak much, but the cabby is sure he was a foreigner — an American, he suspects, because he tipped him so generously."

"And I suspect Valentino's family didn't have a clue who he was or what he was doing at the funeral. Although he did bring some flowers with him."

Montana nodded. "However, there is some news from the lab."

Poldi sat up, galvanized. "Really?"

"Those idiots in Messina took a hell of a time, ostensibly because half the staff are on leave, but Valentino was obviously drugged before his death."

"No."

Montana remained quite calm. "The evidence isn't a hundred per cent, but the lab in Messina found traces of flunitraze-pam in Valentino's urine. That's a strong sedative."

"Knockout drops," Poldi said in hushed tones.

"Also available as tablets, which are known as roofies or flunies. They work very quickly and last for up to seven hours."

"So the murderer drugged Valentino first and then shot him?"

Montana stubbed out his cigarette. She noticed that he never smoked more than half.

"Well, Poldi, what have you got for me?"

Poldi was well prepared. She reached into the drawer beneath the table, pulled out the photograph and put it down in front of him.

Montana stared at the print without touching it. "When was this taken?" All at once, his voice sounded as brittle as splinter-ing slates.

"The Wednesday before Valentino died."

"And you never said a word to me about it all this time?"

"Good God, Vito, it wasn't until yesterday that I noticed the two of them were in the photo."

He gave her a puzzled look. "But you took

the damned thing."

She rolled her eyes. "My God, I snapped the *Vigile*. I didn't notice that Valentino and Mr. X were there until last night."

"The *Vigile*? Why him?"

"Oh, Vito, it's a long story, and certainly no grounds for jealousy. So what do you say?"

The commissario said nothing. He picked up the photo at last, though only with his fingertips, and studied it closely.

"It's the truth, Vito," Poldi insisted. "I didn't notice the two of them at the time. But look at the startled expression on their faces. What if I accidentally photographed Valentino's murderer?"

Montana looked up at her. "What then?"

"Then I could be in danger."

"Is that why you invited me here tonight?"

Salty, bitter, sharp — his tone of voice suddenly combined them all, and Poldi thoroughly disliked that fact.

"I could offer myself as bait." It was supposed to sound jocular, but it didn't. It sounded despairing.

Montana thought for a moment. Then he rose and pocketed the photo.

"Thanks for dinner. I'll call you."

That put paid to phase three. The commissario hurried to the door before Poldi could even get to her feet. She tottered after him with legs like mozzarella and got there just in time. "Vito, wait. This is ridiculous."

He looked at her. "Ridiculous, you say?"

"No. Yes. I mean —"

She got no further, for Montana, halfway out into the street, which smelt of jasmine and cat's piss, suddenly bent forward, drew my Auntie Poldi to him and kissed her. He kissed her as desperately and greedily as a drowning man and as gently as summer rain. Or so Poldi felt. It was a lingering kiss, and she didn't hesitate to respond with all her might. She could smell him, feel his breath, feel his hands around her neck and on her hips, feel his chest against hers — and more.

There it was. Poldi found it undeniably sweet, and for the first time in ages she felt complete again, entirely herself and alive. When she tried to pull him back into the house, however, he gently released himself.

"Goodnight," he said in a low, hoarse voice.

And went.

My Auntie Poldi was beside herself.

"Perhaps he was just . . . well, shy," I hazarded when she told me about it on my next visit.

"Shy? Montana? Are you mad?"

"Or perhaps he simply wasn't that far along."

"What the hell does that mean?"

"Relationship-wise, I mean. He wouldn't be the first. Perhaps it was all happening too fast for him. I mean, perhaps he felt you'd somehow, well —"

"Felt I'd somehow what?"

"Well, rushed him. Emotionally, I mean."

She stared at me with her mouth open.

"You know why you haven't got a girl-friend, don't you? Because you don't know the first thing about a woman's emotions. *Rushed* him? What bullshit. *He* pounced on *me.* He was overwhelmed by his own passion. I felt it, that fire, that magma rising in his volcano; I'm an expert on these things. The frigid way he simply cleared off, that was thoroughly calculated. He was jealous on account of the *Vigile*'s photo."

"Passionate and calculated?" I was bold enough to ask. "How do you reconcile the two?"

"Why, yin and yang, id and superego, get it? Heart and brain. The man is a detective chief inspector, and a detective chief inspector is the supreme alpha male, a perfect synthesis of emotion and reason."

"If you say so."

193

"No need to say 'If you say so' in that oh-so-clever way. I know precisely what I'm talking about. You can't imagine how furious I was. Fancy leaving me standing in the doorway, the heartless block of ice. I'd have taken him on a magic carpet ride that night, introduced him to a host of erotic marvels and adventures."

This was rather too much information for me. I gave a sheepish cough.

"And now you're embarrassed, aren't you? That's just why you're getting so constipated with that novel of yours: because you always look away when it hurts. You're scared of emotion."

"Yes, well, it's getting late. Goodnight, Poldi."

"Stay where you are and look at me. What do you see?"

I sighed.

"Go on, what do you see?"

"You, Poldi."

"No, *under* the surface."

I looked at my Auntie Poldi in her ethnic caftan, with her wig slightly askew and her make-up reminiscent of an Egyptian pop singers. She was holding a nearly empty glass of whisky in her hand but had stopped drinking.

"Disappointment?"

She shook her head. "Deeper."

"Pain," I said. "Love. Longing."

"And the reason?"

I drew a deep breath. "In second place: Montana."

She knit her brow. "Aha. And in first place?"

"Sicily. The pain of feeling that Sicily doesn't return your love as enthusiastically as you thought it would. And the hankering to finally feel at home here. That's what *I* know something about."

Poldi drained her glass and continued to look at me intently. Her expression conveyed that I wasn't, after all, a totally forlorn hope. Or so I told myself.

"Sleep well."

Then, mustering her strength, she heaved herself off the sofa and tottered bedroom-wards.

My Auntie Poldi was definitely feeling hurt, and no wonder, especially as Montana failed to call her the next day. The other aunts, filled with Latin solidarity, were unstinting in their condemnation of the commissario's foul play. Their unanimous opinion: there must be another woman in Montana's life. He wasn't worth it, of course, not after toying with Poldi's emotions like that, but if she were to bring herself to give him another chance despite this, she would be bound to succeed in the long run. That was a copper-bottomed certainty.

"*Forza* Poldi," cried Aunt Luisa. "What other woman could hold a candle to you?"

"A younger one?" Poldi croaked darkly.

"Nonsense," cried Caterina. "You've got good skin, a firm backside, and you're fun."

"I'm old and fat."

"You're an armful of a woman in her prime."

Poldi cast her eyes up at the ceiling.

Aunt Teresa summoned Uncle Martino. "*Amore,* tell Poldi what she is."

"The loveliest of all Isoldes."

"Bravo. There you have it."

But Poldi didn't find genuine consolation until she flung herself into the arms of Signor Bacardi. They did it together sour, on the rocks, with Coke and with tonic. Sweet and sour, salty and bitter. Even on the way downhill she made Sicily another defiant declaration of love, but alcohol is a perfidious plank in the ocean of self-pity. "It keeps you afloat for a while, saves you from drowning and infects you with optimism, but then it drags you down — glug-glug-glug — into the depths." Poldi knew what she was talking about.

So what saved her from the nadir of self-pity? Love? *Joie de vivre?* Wrong. Her hunting instinct. Her forensic urge. The photograph of Valentino with Mr. X.

Hung-over, thirsty, devoid of appetite and ill-tempered, the first thing she did on the morning after her fall from grace was check her messages. Still no word from Montana, just worried messages from Valérie and the aunts.

Montana didn't call for the next few days either, but Poldi had her pride. She was now eager to solve this murder, if only to show him up and make him look foolish — make him look one big *figuraccia*.

Pale and still a bit under the weather, she showed the photo on her mobile around town. To Bussacca at the *tabacchi,* to the sad signora, to the neighbours, but nobody seemed to recognize the red-haired man.

"There was this police psychologist on Channel Five's *Faces of Crime,*" Signora Anzalone volunteered in her habitually conspiratorial whisper. "He said murderers always return to the scene of the crime; they can't help themselves. They're driven there by their feelings of guilt, their curiosity and arrogance."

Spot on, thought Poldi, puzzled that the same idea hadn't occurred to her long ago.

She thought it improbable that Mr. X would show up on the beach at Praiola, however. It was likelier, especially as he didn't seem to avoid crowds of people, that she would bump into him in Taormina. He might even live there. Poldi promptly called Teresa, because she naturally knew that proper surveillance, whether of a person or a thing, is always maintained by two people. Two pairs of eyes see better than one, and one member of the team can always take a break. Besides, it can become a terribly boring business, and experience had taught Poldi that boredom and hard liquor go hand in hand.

"Keep watch on the whole of Taormina? How do you propose to do that?"

"Mainly the Corso, but other hotspots as well."

"Around the clock?"

"Of course not. I'll split us up into three shifts of four hours. That makes twelve. We can't manage more."

"How about recruiting Martino?"

"This kind of surveillance wouldn't suit someone who can't sit still for ten minutes at a time. Besides —"

"Yes, I know. But how will *you* stick it for twelve hours?"

"My time's my own."

"But Luisa's isn't; she has to work."

"Only half-days. She can take over the evening shift. She might even meet someone."

"Stop it. You know how jealous Franco gets. And who'll look after Caterina's dogs and collect little Carmela from nursery school?"

"Martino?"

"You must be joking."

Poldi could hear her sister-in-law breathing heavily as she ran the whole idea through her mind again.

"Perfect. If we solve the case, the Terranovas will eat their plastic flowers with envy."

It was unnecessary to ask the other two sisters, because, as I've already mentioned, Aunt Teresa called the shots and all the aunts were fans of police procedurals.

Picturesquely situated overlooking the sea, Taormina is one of Sicily's favourite tourist haunts. Goethe visited there, as did Oscar Wilde and Thomas Mann, followed by film stars like Greta Garbo, Marlene Dietrich and Elizabeth Taylor. In the middle of the town is a Roman amphitheatre — misleadingly called the Teatro Greco — at which top-class film festivals, concerts and ballets take place during the summer. Mind you, there is always a risk that some international star will be upstaged by a volcanic eruption, for a gap in the middle of the stage affords a splendid view of Etna. In the nineteenth century a German photographer named Wilhelm von Gloeden, who landed up in Taormina because of lung disease, photographed local youths striking lascivious poses in front of ancient columns, well made-up and naked save for a loincloth or a laurel wreath. Prints of those photographs can be bought on every street corner in Taormina, and they helped to establish the liberal reputation of the town, which is still a favourite domicile of the gay community.

Poldi and Caterina, who had taken over the early shift, seated themselves outside the Mocambo Bar the very next morning. Not too conspicuously far forward and not too far back, sometimes in the shade, sometimes wearing sunglasses, with a good view of the piazza and the Corso. Still a little tense for the first hour, Poldi drank one coffee after another in her determination not to miss a single man who walked past. After an hour she was worn out and had a cramp in her neck. It surprised her to note that Caterina, on the other hand, was sitting there quite relaxed in her stylish sunglasses, legs elegantly crossed. She turned her head smoothly and serenely to and fro like a radar dish, seemingly uninterested, yet no one escaped her attention.

"Two o'clock. The one with the rucksack."

"Too short."

"Eleven o'clock. Just coming out of that shop."

"Too young . . . Hey, how do you manage it?"

Caterina shrugged. "Just pretend we're teenagers again. Remember how we used to check out the boys without them noticing?"

"Except that I always wanted them to notice."

"Just relax, Poldi."

Easier said than done. Poldi did get the hang of it after a while, though. She melted into her surroundings and imitated Caterina's radar sweep. The only trouble was, Mr. X failed to surface amid the never-ending stream of faces that flowed down the Corso under the two aunts' gaze. German families in clamdiggers, scruffy young backpackers in flip-flops, hand-holding English gays, American youngsters with coffees to go, boisterous children romping around the piazza, chic Spanish ladies with strident voices, good-humoured, sunburnt Dutchmen, old men chatting in groups, pallid priests carrying briefcases, locals in a hurry and leisurely businessmen — as though propelled by strange tidal forces, this ever-murmuring, shuffling stream flowed back and forth between Porta Messina and Porta Catania, meandered into side streets, eddied sluggishly around street painters' easels and debouched into the Piazza Duomo, where photos were taken, sandwiches munched and the view enjoyed. And all of this monitored and commented on by Poldi and the other aunts.

In the meantime, Poldi's mobile beeped almost hourly with text messages from Montana: *Call me. Where are you? Can we talk? Please call.* The sort of messages that rent her heart and made the position unmistakably clear: that it was over before it had begun.

With a bitter taste in her mouth, Poldi deleted all these messages and blocked Montana's number. She felt a little better after that.

Caterina was relieved around noon by Teresa, and Luisa took on the evening shift late in the afternoon. Poldi and her cheerful assistants changed cafés frequently so as not to be too conspicuous. They drifted across the Corso with the crowds, consumed an ice cream here, a panino, orange juice, iced tea, coffee or pastry there. Anything but alcohol — not even a little *prosecchino* or a tiny limoncello as a sundowner. It was a genuine struggle, but Poldi remained steadfast. No alcohol and finding Mr. X was her plan.

Except that Mr. X didn't cooperate.

Poldi knew, of course, that the success of a stake-out depends on two factors: patience and stamina. One has to emulate the gecko, which crouches on a rock, rigid and motionless, awaiting the moment when it can unexpectedly pounce on its prey.

She did spot the *Vigile* again, but he had long ceased to interest her. On the contrary, she now found him far less attractive, positively conceited, affected and stupidlooking. Not to be compared with Montana — worlds apart, in fact.

Ah yes, Montana. Whenever she thought of him, a little ache detached itself from her heart like scree breaking adrift from a mountainside and sliding into the valley with a lingering sigh.

"Forget about him," said Aunt Luisa. "Look around you. This place is teeming with hundreds of good-looking men in their prime."

Poldi made a dismissive gesture. "They're all gay."

"Not from the looks they're giving us."

"Giving you, you mean."

"You really think so?"

"You're hot," Poldi said earnestly. "As an inconspicuous assistant on a stake-out, you're almost useless."

Luisa beamed. "Franco would blow a gasket if he heard that. Have you any idea how long I've been wanting to do something like this? I mean, go out and about again, mix with people, chew the fat, have a little adventure, maybe indulge in a harmless flirtation." She grasped Poldi's hand and squeezed it. "I'm so glad you're here."

But one swallow doesn't make a summer, and even the most diligent stake-out failed to come up with Mr. X. After three days of shift work in Taormina the aunts were running out of steam and even Poldi was feeling rather jaded.

A mass of thoughts whirled through her head when she came home late at night and sank down exhausted on the sofa. Thoughts of a certain policeman, of Valentino, of Luisa's words, of the topographical map, of Mr. X, of Valérie and Russo, even of her parents. Sentimental thoughts of opportunities missed, precious time squandered and botched goodbyes. It was in this state of mind that she received a letter from Tanzania, which she burned, unopened, in the ashtray. And then, out of the blue next evening, Montana appeared in the Corso Umberto.

Poldi had just paid the bill and left her usual generous tip, so she was temporarily distracted. That's the thing about stakeouts: something always happens just when you aren't looking. When she did look up he was standing beside her table in his creased grey work suit. His grumpy face lit by the setting sun, he might have been magicked there by some genie with a taste for bad jokes. He shook hands with Aunt Luisa and introduced himself. It was all Luisa could do not to beam at him, because that would have been bad form without Poldi's all-clear.

"I'll leave you two alone together," she managed to say without grinning, and hurriedly withdrew, though not without giving the commissario an appraising glance.

Montana sat down on the vacant chair. No kiss, no word of greeting.

"What are you doing here, Poldi?"

"I could ask you the same thing. How did you find me?"

Montana shrugged. "Mobile phone tracking."

Poldi was speechless for a second. "You mean I'm still under suspicion?"

"Why don't you answer your phone? Why didn't you respond to my texts?"

She looked at him. "Because we've nothing to discuss, Vito. And, my dear, because I've been busy."

Montana looked even more downcast than before. "What are you doing here, Poldi?"

"Just sitting. It isn't against the law, is it?"

"All day long?"

"No, just at this moment."

Montana shook his head. "We had an agreement, Poldi."

"Yes, thanks for the reminder, and goodbye," she growled in German.

"What?"

"Our agreement concerned Russo, and I've kept it. Have you discovered the identity of Mr. X?"

He shook his head. "Have you?"

Poldi rose from her chair with a sigh. "It's getting late; I must go home." And because she couldn't resist, seeing him so downcast, she gave him a little pat on the head. "So long, Vito Between-Two-Stools."

"I'll call you," said Montana, and Poldi actually managed a smile.

"Whenever it's convenient."

She left the café without once looking round and collected Aunt Luisa, who had been loitering in front of a shop window.

"My, he's sexy," Luisa whispered.

"I don't want to talk about him."

Luisa nodded. "Of course not. He is sexy, though."

"Luisa."

"I was only saying."

Poldi pulled herself together. She went to the multi-storey with Luisa, paid for her ticket in the machine, found her Alfa, sat behind the wheel, and only then wept a little. Only a little, because she didn't really have much time for self-pity, but there are occasions when one just can't help it. Not even my Auntie Poldi could, so she shed a tear or two, and Luisa held her hand the whole time and kept saying, "There, there, Poldi."

Mr. X didn't show up the following day either, but that evening Poldi was overtaken by her past in the shape of an old acquaintance: black leather suit, shades, rings on every finger. He was on his own. No one had recognized him, no one was hassling him for an autograph; he simply walked down the Corso, spotted my Auntie Poldi, and sat down at her and Luisa's table.

"Why, Ringo," Poldi cried, profoundly touched, and threw her arms around him.

"Just a minute," I interrupted suspiciously

207

when she described the scene in detail.

"Ringo who?"

"Why, Ringo Starr, of course."

"You don't mean *the* Ringo Starr?"

"I was surprised myself that he recognized me after all those years, but he homed in on me as if it was only yesterday when Peppe and I had a meal with him and his Barbara. Such a nice couple, those two."

I stared at her. "I don't believe you."

"Don't, then."

"What did Ringo Starr want?"

"Nothing. A bit of a chat, that's all. How was I, and how was Peppe doing — he didn't know that Peppe wasn't with us any more, you see. We'd completely lost touch. Oh yes, and he wanted to know what I was doing in Sicily. He promptly started to flirt with Luisa, and he invited us to his open-air concert at the Teatro Greco the following night. Backstage, of course."

"Of course."

"And then he said we'd be welcome to visit his house in Surrey any time we got sick of our Mediterranean paradise, the winters there were so splendidly dank and dreary. "Wonderful, darling," I told him, "we'll give it some thought." And what do you think I did then?"

"You showed him the photo of Mr. X."

"*Cento punti.* And just imagine, Ringo recognized him."

8

Tells of Inspector Chance and how Poldi discovers the identity of Mr. X with his help. She has to swallow her pride several times in quick succession, and she isn't the only one. She gets a lecture on aerodynamics, is able to hold Montana's hand and eat a dumpling, and eventually has every reason to feel satisfied.

One of the most successful investigators in the whole history of crime since Oedipus, Poldi knew, is Inspector Chance. No case has ever been solved without him, and he's always needed at some stage. Poldi liked to picture Inspector Chance as an ill-shaven slob whose mother still does his washing. Trainers, old jeans, scruffy hoodie, nerd glasses, never really grown up. An unreliable colleague with no particular ambition except in regard to his work-life balance. He does the minimum of work in his office at the far end of some corridor, where the air smells of cleaning fluids and stale coffee — a cubbyhole where junk and old files are stored and he's sometimes simply forgotten. That's all right with Inspector Chance, just as long as no one bugs him and he can work at half-speed ahead. He seldom shows his face at departmental meetings or operational briefings, on the firing range or in the field. He prefers to be warm and cosy. No stress — if he's hassled, he just clams up. If prevailed on to process a file at the start of a case, for instance, Inspector Chance can be relied on to send the investigation down the tubes. Inspector Chance has a problem with authority. He's moody and has a mordant sense of humour. An only child, Poldi surmised. No wonder Inspector Chance isn't popular with his colleagues, who tirelessly compile facts and leads and toil away in order to render him redundant. Given his lax work ethic, he should have been kicked out long ago, public servant or no. Ironically enough, however, Inspector Chance can point to some notable successes. Completely belying his puny appearance, he can pounce with unexpected speed and precision, unravel knotty problems, collate leads and shine a light on hidden mysteries. He is needed, and he knows it.

On the other hand, he never complains if colleagues deck themselves with his laurels — he's quite relaxed about it. He usually profits from their meticulous spadework, after all, so he expects no thanks. A little *namaste* at most, and Poldi made sure to give him one.

Namaste, Inspector Chance. *Namaste,* Ringo.

Ringo had already spent a week in Taormina for the concert and a video shoot. In keeping with his status, he was staying at the Timeo, the best hotel in town, and it was in the lobby of that luxury establishment that he had seen Mr. X deep in conversation with someone. Ringo had recognized that someone as a person to be avoided, after being buttonholed and bullied into accepting his business card the day before. That was why Ringo remembered Mr. X. And because he had heedlessly pocketed the business card and forgotten it instead of throwing it away, he was able to give it to my Auntie Poldi. The business card was that of Corrado Patanè.

"Well, well, well," I exclaimed when she told me. I was impressed.

"That surprised you, didn't it? Yes, but you only win the lottery if you buy a ticket."

"So you hurried over to the Timeo and

made inquiries, of course."

"It was the logical thing to do, but I might have known they wouldn't give me any information about a guest, the smart-arses. They wouldn't even tell me if Mr. X *was* a guest."

"They'd probably have told Montana, though."

"Yes, I thought of that, naturally."

"So what stopped you?"

Her pride, of course. My aunt was determined to solve this case on her own and then rub Montana's nose in it. To hell with him.

But Poldi also knew that she mustn't push her luck too far. Inspector Chance was capricious, and he liked to knock off early sometimes. Her persevering stake-out had rewarded her with a lead — *namaste,* Inspector Chance, *namaste,* Ringo — but how to proceed further?

She could, of course, seek out Patanè and ask him point-blank about Mr. X. The surprise effect might even elicit an honest answer, but it was likelier that Patanè would flatly deny having seen or even met him, let alone known him personally. After all, the sole weapon in Poldi's armoury was an old acquaintance's recollection of a fleeting encounter several days ago. And besides,

Ringo was no spring chicken and his memory might not be entirely reliable on account of his widely publicized — though decades-old — prior history in regard to the consumption of mind-expanding substances. Fundamentally, therefore, Mr. X was still a phantom.

And possibly Valentino's murderer.

And consequently a potential danger to Poldi.

She could, of course, run the risk of entering the lion's den alone and wait for Mr. X at the Timeo, but my aunt had never been one to let pride and vanity stand in her way when the chips were down. The solving of this case was her top priority, even if she had to swallow her pride. And Poldi knew a thing or two about swallowing one's pride.

With a sigh, she unblocked Montana's number in her mobile phone and sent him a text:

Can u come to the Timeo? It's important.

Pling-plong-pling. The reply came back at once.

Now?

Poldi:

214

Please.

Then she sent Aunt Luisa home and waited for Montana. Less than an hour later, from a comfortable sofa right at the back of the lobby, she saw him enter the luxury hotel and look around for her. She savoured the sight for a moment before she waved to him, feeling a familiar tension permeate her body as she did so; the sort of tightening of the skin that's a prelude to sunburn, a presentiment of the special pain for which one yearns on lonely nights.

"Tell me," she said once he had sat down beside her, "have you made a vow or something?"

"Meaning what?"

"Well, to go on wearing that awful grey suit on duty until it hangs off your body in rags and tatters."

Montana's face creased in a sour smile.

"Is that why you sent for me?"

"No." Squaring her shoulders, Poldi gave him a succinct account of her investigation to date. Montana didn't interrupt her once, just knit his brow briefly at the mention of Ringo. Then, without a word, he rose and went over to the reception desk. Poldi saw him show his ID to the snotty youth with gelled hair behind the counter, saw the snotty youth raise his hands defensively, saw Montana add something to which the snotty youth clearly took great exception, saw a manager summoned and his fingers speed over a keyboard, whereupon, quite magically and unbureaucratically, a printout slid out of the printer and was discreetly handed to the commissario, with a look of indignation.

Montana signalled to Poldi that he would be busy for a little while longer and put in a call on his mobile, pacing up and down the lobby as he did so. Poldi found that she enjoyed watching him pace up and down, even in that eternally crumpled suit. After a while, he closed his mobile and came over to her.

"There's good news and bad news. The good news is, we know who the man is: a Dr. Frank Tannenberger. Lives in Munich."

Munich, of all places. Poldi heaved a sigh of surprise.

"He flew back the day before yesterday," Montana added.

"And the bad news?"

Montana looked harassed. "It's a crock of shit. The man is a senior official in the" — he glanced at the printout — "Bayerische Staatskanzlei." He almost dislocated his tongue pronouncing the words. "What the hell's that?"

"A kind of department of the Bavarian state government."

"What do you mean, "state"? I thought Bavaria was a German province."

"Are you crazy? We're a Freistaat, a *free* state. We can go independent any time we choose and do our own thing. Federally speaking and in spaghetti-Western terms, the Bavarian Free State is a loaded Colt pointed at the heart of Germany."

"I see. Anyway, this Dr. Tannenberger visits Taormina regularly on official business and always stays at the Timeo. A regular guest at government expense, it seems."

"So where's the crock of shit?"

"Don't you understand? If I want to question him I'll have to put in an official request for travel expenses. Have you any idea of the paperwork that would entail? It could take weeks. And all because of some vague hint from an ex-Beatle and a German woman who came briefly under suspicion and has been obstructing my inquiries ever since. Madonna, they'll bust a gut laughing at the prefecture. Besides, the man's a government official — I'd be stirring up a hornet's nest again, and me with my prior history with that senator? Thanks a lot."

Poldi looked at him. "The man may have

murdered Valentino."

Montana drew a deep breath. "I'll have a word with the German authorities tomorrow, then they can question this Dr. Tannenberger."

Poldi shook her head disapprovingly. "What if you simply fly to Munich and ask Dr. Tannenberger a few questions?"

"Unannounced, you mean? What if he isn't there at all?"

"Have you got the Internet on your smartphone?"

"Er, yes. Why?"

"Give it here."

Poldi took Montana's phone from him and keyed "Dr. Frank Tannenberger Bayerische Staatskanzlei" into the search box of his browser.

"Got him," she exclaimed. "Our Dr. Tannenberger, aka Mr. X, heads the department for EU relations at the Bayerische Staatskanzlei. If the head of department flies regularly to Sicily in person, it must be in connection with some major project. He's bound to have to report to some committee or other, so he wouldn't jet off elsewhere right away. No, believe me, he'll be sitting in his office overlooking the Hofgarten, good as gold."

Montana shook his head firmly. "It's no

use anyway. An Italian policeman can't go nosing around in Germany, least of all when a German government official is involved."

"But as a private individual? What's to stop you?"

"That's a crazy idea. Nothing I discovered could be used in court. On the contrary, if this man Tannenberger claimed I'd threatened him, the whole case could go down the tubes and me with it. It'd be a crock of shit."

"You're repeating yourself, Vito. So what *are* you going to do?"

Montana clasped his hands together impotently to indicate that they were tied by forces beyond his control. "I can only go through proper channels."

Poldi thought for a moment. "Well," she said eventually, getting to her feet, "you're probably right. We'll just have to wait and see."

"Where are you going?"

"Home. It's getting late."

"I thought we might have a drink together."

It wasn't that Poldi hadn't had the same idea, but she had certain reasons for staying sober on two levels. Besides, she was in a hurry all of a sudden.

"Another time. I'm really tired, and I've

got a headache coming on."

"Shall I drive you?"

"Don't worry, I left my car down in the Lumbi car park."

She leant forward and kissed Montana lightly on both cheeks. "See you."

He caught her by the arm, though, and eyed her suspiciously. "Poldi?"

"Vito?"

"What are you up to?"

"Nothing. Look, I really am tired. Would you let go of me, please?"

Poldi called Luisa from her car as soon as she passed the autostrada toll booth.

"For tomorrow morning?" Luisa, who worked for a travel agent, was taken aback. "Do you know what time it is?"

"Please could you try, Luisa?"

"But what about your —"

"No good. I'll have to manage on my own."

Aunt Luisa wasn't the type to refuse a favour, no matter what the time was.

"I'll call you back right away. Drive carefully."

By the time Poldi reached Torre Archirafi, Luisa had managed to make the reservations online — not for peanuts, it must be added. Poldi gulped in dismay when Luisa told her the cost of the flights. Her small pension was just enough to cover her everyday living expenses, and she had really hoped to reserve her meagre savings for urgent house repairs and other emergencies. On the other hand, she told herself, this was a kind of emergency in itself. Never mind: she would simply be unable to afford another pair of strappy sandals this summer. The case took priority.

The flight left at ten. Catania Airport, which had long been awake, smelt of kerosene, coffee and *cornetti* and was humming a melody of wanderlust and homecoming. Extended families thronged the arrivals hall, waiting to welcome relations from Germany and Belgium, England and Denmark. As soon as the automatic doors opened even a crack, someone always tried to squeeze through and help Alfio and Alessia get their baggage off the carousel. Young German students patiently queuing up in front of the check-in desks shook their heads as they were barged aside by grey-haired Sicilians with monstrous suitcases big enough to emigrate with. At the security barrier, a symbol of the Italian crisis: raised voices, gesticulating hands, everything brought to a standstill. Somebody — not Uncle Martino for once — had been found to have a shrink-wrapped octopus in his hand luggage, as a gift for his nearest and dearest in Mannheim, and was loudly protesting at having to leave it behind. My Auntie Poldi groaned.

Have I already told you that my Auntie Poldi was scared stiff of flying? Well, she was. She mistrusted the laws of aerodynamics, the complex technology and, above all, the young men in the cockpit and their unctuous, oh-so-reassuring in-flight announcements. She was afraid of the way airliners lurched and wobbled, of the dull roar of the engines, of air pockets and landing procedures. She detested travelling through the air cooped up at 500 mph and an altitude of five miles, with nothing but a bit of aluminium between you and a free fall. Or death by asphyxia. Twenty years earlier, Poldi and my Uncle Peppe had almost succumbed to the latter on a flight from Munich to Catania in a friend's small private jet, which lost cabin pressure over the Alps. They spent a quarter of an hour gasping and panting for their lives in atmospheric pressure similar to that prevailing on the summit of Annapurna. Since then, Poldi had been as averse to flying as Satan to holy water. Sometimes, however, even Satan gets splashed, and sometimes even Poldi had to bite the bullet. She normally backed up her willpower with tranquillizers, but they were precluded this time by her need to keep a clear head. Her only remaining hope was that a friendly fellow passenger would take pity on her and hold her hand. That was what Poldi and my Uncle Peppe had done at 25,000 feet: held each other's hand. The whole time. One's fear of death may not be entirely dispelled by holding someone's hand, even a total stranger's, but it helps.

As befitted the occasion, Poldi was wearing a muted dark-blue jumpsuit with pumps and a military blazer. For one thing, she had a penchant for uniforms, and, for another, intended to look a trifle intimidating. Her huge sunglasses were suggestive of a former film star hoping that someone will recognize her and whisper her name behind her back. She was feeling rather agitated. Because of her impending flight, of course, but also because of her forthcoming encounter with Valentino's putative murderer and because of Munich. She wondered if it might be an omen that she was returning to her old stamping ground after only three months, alone and empty-handed, just as she had returned from Tanzania, distraught, with a void in her heart and her bank account. Talking of omens: when she turned away from the check-in counter, boarding card in hand, Montana was standing in front of her. She stared at him as if he were the archangel Michael, for even without a fiery sword Montana presented an impressive appearance that morning. He, too, was wearing dark blue, together with a white shirt and a tie, black brogues and his usual aviator sunglasses. He looked like a cop escorting a prosecution witness to the trial of the century: grim-faced and ready for anything. In other words, sexy as hell. Or so my Auntie Poldi thought.

"My," she exclaimed.

"Did you seriously imagine I'd let you loose on a witness in my case?"

"But how did you know I was —"

Montana took my flummoxed aunt by the arm and towed her out of the queue in front of the check-in desk. "From your face and the way you said we'd just have to wait and see."

Poldi liked that.

"But what about going through proper channels and travel expenses and all that palaver?"

"Proper channels be damned. I've already been transferred once for disciplinary reasons."

Poldi liked that, too. She also liked the

thought that she would be able to hold Montana's hand during the flight.

"*Forza* Montana," she cried in delight, but Montana wasn't in the mood for levity.

"I'm tempted to arrest you here and now and have you taken home, but sadly I can't stop you from flying to Munich. So listen, here's the deal: *I,* and only I, will interview Tannenberger. You will do a bit of interpreting and otherwise keep your trap shut."

Poldi looked at him like a schoolmistress confronted by a pupil who has asked for the heating to be turned off in February. "Nonsense," she said, shaking her head, and strode briskly to the security gate. "Coming, Vito?"

The first thing Poldi did on board was ensure she could sit beside Montana and hold his hand.

"I'm scared of flying," she explained. "For the next three hours, you're going to make sure I don't flip."

Which is precisely what he did. He held her moist hand tightly throughout the flight and explained every aeronautical sign of life.

"That's the engines starting up . . . We're being backed out onto the runway . . . When it shakes we're taking off . . . The runway is long enough . . . That's the landing gear being retracted . . . Now the pilot's retracting

225

the slats and flaps . . . Look, there's Etna. And there's Torre . . . We've now reached cruising height, that's why he's throttling back . . . There aren't any air pockets . . . No, the wing isn't broken, those are the ailerons."

"How do you know all these things?"

"I have a pilot's licence."

Poldi stared at him. From her expression, he might just have disclosed he was 007.

"You . . . have . . . a . . . pilot's . . . licence?"

"Sure. I'd be glad to take you up with me sometime."

"You can forget that right away, Signor Mystery Man."

She shook her head in amazement. "A pilot's licence."

And apropos of secrets, Montana said suddenly, "About the other night —"

"I don't want to know," Poldi broke in. "You said it was complicated, so let's leave it at that."

"Are you feeling hurt?"

"No. Why? We're both adults."

"Aren't you curious?"

"Me? Not in the least."

"Lie to me once more and I'll let go of your hand."

Poldi liked that, too. That he could be

amusing. That he had a way of flattering without fawning over her. Not that she had anything against a bit of fawning in small doses.

"Shut up and explain about air pockets again, will you?"

From the airport in Munich they took the S-Bahn to the Hauptbahnhof and then the U-Bahn to Odeonsplatz, time enough for Poldi to recover from the flight and return to stress level green. It was a warm day with a colouring-book sky of blue dotted with white.

Montana was amazed at all the people in pavement cafés and beer gardens.

"How do you Germans run your economy if no one here works?"

"How do you like Munich?"

"Mm. How long did you live here?"

"Nearly all my life. Two lifetimes or three. I stopped counting after a while."

"Like a cat, eh? Later on, will you show me where you used to live?"

"No."

But Poldi was nonetheless pleased by Montana's interest in Munich. Not just as a venue for the Oktoberfest or a fashionable shopping paradise, but as the former mid-point of her life. It made her feel rather proud and put her in a conciliatory frame of mind. The city hadn't expelled her, after all; it had merely become too small for her. She decided to explain that to Montana sometime, if he was still interested, and perhaps she would steel herself again to board a plane and show him her favourite places. A nice idea, come to think of it.

The next moment they were standing in front of the impressive building that housed the Bavarian State Chancellery.

"Is this it?"

"In all its glory, yes."

"Let's try our luck, then." Montana strode resolutely towards the main entrance, but Poldi held him back. "Not so fast. Do we have a phone number for the man?"

Montana handed her the printout from the Timeo.

Poldi dialled the number given on the hotel registration form.

"Yes?" said an impatient voice after the third ring.

"Herr Tannenberger?"

"Who is this?"

The irritable tone of someone under pressure.

"My name is Oberreiter. I've just come from Sicily. I missed you at the Timeo, unfortunately."

"Where did you get my number? What's

this about, anyway?"

"It's about Valentino. You know; you were at his funeral. A few issues have arisen in connection with his death, and I'd like to resolve them with you."

Silence at the other end of the line. Then, "What sort of issues?"

"I'd sooner discuss them with you in person, and it would be helpful if you could manage it right away, before you fly off to Panama or Cuba."

"That's impossible. I don't have the time."

"Outside the main entrance in five minutes, all right? Because if you don't come, I'll have to speak to the police at once."

The man at the other end of the line cleared his throat.

"Where are you now?"

"Where I said: just outside. Practical, no?"

"Is he coming?" Montana asked when Poldi rang off.

"Five minutes."

"What did you say?"

She gave him a broad smile. "Abracadabra."

The red-haired man appeared less than five minutes later. Poldi recognized him at once and gave him a wave like one colleague meeting another for lunch. Tannenberger, wearing a dark business suit, appeared taller to Poldi than he had at the funeral. He stopped short when he saw Montana, but Poldi hurried over to him before he could dive back into the building.

"Hello there, Dr. Tannenberger," she said cheerfully. "Glad you could manage it. I'm Frau Oberreiter — I just had the pleasure of speaking to you on the phone — and this is Commissario Montana of the state police in Acireale. He's the senior investigating officer in the Valentino Candela case."

"I didn't think the police would be present."

"They aren't. Commissario Montana is here in an entirely private capacity. If he wasn't, your department would have been notified by now, so it's up to you."

Tannenberger reluctantly shook Montana's hand but remained tense, as though ready to run at any time. He wasn't wearing a ring, Poldi noted, but his wrist was adorned with a showy Officine Panerai. Hardly a typical civil servant's wristwatch at a measly ten thousand euros.

Tannenberger turned to Poldi. "And who exactly are you?"

"A sort of interpreter for Commissario Montana, let's say."

"What does 'sort of' mean?"

"She was a friend of Valentino's," Montana said in English, determined to get at least one word in.

"Why, I couldn't have put it better myself," Poldi exclaimed. "I snapped you together shortly before his death, do you remember? At the café in Taormina."

Tannenberger looked back at the State Chancellery like someone watching an ocean liner about to sail off at full speed without him. Then he glanced at his Panerai. "I can spare half an hour. Let's go into the Hofgarten."

He didn't utter another word until they had found a vacant park bench in the shade of an old chestnut tree, but he kicked off at once before Montana had a chance to ask him a single question, and Poldi translated.

"Let me make one thing clear from the start: I did not kill Valentino. I was here in Munich on the day of his death, as you can easily check. I even have witnesses for the relevant time. All I would ask is that you proceed discreetly. I'm in a permanent relationship, you see." Having waited for Poldi to translate this statement, he turned to her and went on before Montana could step in. "I remember you taking that photo. It was on my last evening with Valentino — I had to return here the following morning.

231

Valentino was rather dismayed when he caught sight of you. He wanted to run after you, but I stopped him."

Tannenberger paused for a moment, as though drained of strength by this revelation, and waited for Poldi to translate again. "You can't imagine how shocked I am by Valentino's death. I feel as if my heart has been ripped out, but I can't afford to grieve for him openly."

He trembled suddenly, but pulled himself together at once. Poldi guessed what was coming.

"I first met Valentino about six months ago, on my first official trip to Taormina. He was carrying drinks around at a reception — one of his part-time jobs. It was love at first sight. For me, at least. I never really fathomed his feelings."

Tannenberger paused again and looked at Montana. "What do you want to know?"

"Who killed him?"

"I don't know. I didn't learn of his death until I returned to Sicily. That was the day before his funeral."

"Who told you?"

"Signor Patanè."

"What's your relationship with Signor Patanè?"

"He wants to tender for the construction

232

of an international cultural centre in Taormina under the auspices of the European Union, to be co-financed by the Bavarian Free State."

"And what was the relationship between Patanè and Valentino?"

"Valentino worked for him occasionally, as far as I could gather. It was he that introduced us, anyway. An extremely unpleasant, tiresome individual. He has no chance of getting the contract, but he keeps pestering me with invitations and offers to sell me houses or construction sites in prime locations — on so-called special terms. But that sort of thing doesn't work with me."

"In what capacity did Valentino work for Patanè?"

"I don't know. Valentino had numerous jobs. He was no fool. He wanted to come to Germany and make a life for himself here."

Yes, Poldi remembered that. She remembered her German lessons with Valentino, his ambition, his optimism.

"Did that alarm you?" she asked. "I mean, because of your permanent relationship?"

"I wanted nothing more, and that's the truth. I was crazy about Valentino. I would have squared it with my partner."

"But you didn't."

Tannenberger didn't reply.

Montana nodded when Poldi had translated for him. He seemed convinced.

"The last time you met," he resumed, "did Valentino strike you as different in any way?"

"Yes, he seemed nervous somehow, but he flatly refused to tell me what was wrong. Only that he had to settle a few things before he could come to Germany."

"What sort of things?"

"I don't have the faintest idea."

"Did he mention old mosaics?" Poldi asked. "Or lions?"

"Lions?"

"Yes, you know, stone figures guarding the entrances to old country houses."

Tannenberger shook his head. "Not that I recall."

"Did you get the impression that he might be involved in something? Something illegal, I mean?"

"Yes, in a way. As I said, he wouldn't talk about it."

"But?"

"Well, he once said something along those lines. That he'd discovered something, and that someone would pay him a lot of money to keep quiet about it."

"You don't say. What had he discovered? Who was going to pay him a lot of money?"

"He wouldn't tell me. He merely said I wasn't to worry."

"And didn't you?"

"My God, what do you think? I was in love with Valentino. Of course I was worried, but what could I do?"

"You could have gone to the police when you heard about his death," said Montana.

Tannenberger said nothing. His mobile beeped. He glanced at the display and killed the call.

"I must go. Any more questions?"

"It's possible I may yet have to question you officially," said Montana. "Or request my German colleagues to do so. If anything else occurs to you in the next few days" — he handed Tannenberger his card — "no matter what, maybe a chance remark of Valentino's, a triviality, anything at all, please call me."

"Or me," Poldi put in, "and I'll pass it on to the commissario. You now have my number in your call records. Isolde Oberreiter."

"All clear." Tannenberger pocketed Montana's card, rose to his feet and hurriedly shook hands with Poldi and Montana. He obviously couldn't wait to return to his secure habitat, the State Chancellery.

But then Poldi thought of something else.

"One more thing," she called after Tannenberger. "Do you still have Valentino's mobile number?"

"Yes, of course, but I didn't manage to reach him on either of his numbers after our last meeting."

"If you'd be kind enough to give me them . . ."

Five minutes later the unfortunate Herr Tannenberger was back in his office. Poldi and Montana were still sitting on the park bench, and it was still a fine day — even finer, perhaps, than it had been a few minutes earlier. While Poldi was preening herself on her investigatory success, Montana was calling a colleague at police headquarters in Acireale.

"Gaetano, I want you to trace and check on a mobile phone for me. Got something to write with?" He dictated the second number on the slip of paper in his hand. "Repeat that. Good. I need the works. Present location, most recent calls, text messages, all the radio cells from the day before Valentino Candela's murder up to today . . . In Munich, but I'll be back tonight . . . Don't ask stupid questions, just do as I say . . . Damn it, Tano, then get a decision. This is the second mobile, the one we've been looking for all this time . . . I'll explain

236

it all to you tomorrow . . . And Tano, don't mess around, this is important, okay?"

He rang off and grinned at Poldi. "Our little trip may have paid off after all."

"No, Vito, what you really meant to say was 'I'm so glad you came with me, Poldi. Many thanks. If it weren't for you I wouldn't have made such progress.' "

Montana lit a cigarette, blew some smoke rings into the summer sky and then looked at her.

"Well, what shall we do with what's left of the day?"

Although this wasn't exactly the answer Poldi had wanted to hear, she did detect a certain promising subtext. This, together with her little triumph and the Bavarian blue-and-white of the beautiful sky, raised her spirits and whetted her appetite for roast pork and life.

"What do you feel like, sweet or salty?" she asked.

"Both."

If that wasn't an innuendo, she didn't know what was.

Some roast pork plus a dumpling and two beers later, however, they had to head back to the airport. Gaetano didn't call, but Montana seemed unworried. To Poldi's delight he made a far more relaxed, almost light-hearted impression, recounted amusing anecdotes about his police work, and questioned her about her various Munich lives. And although Poldi didn't find his interest in her past the least bit feigned, she realized that he was drawing a veil of charm and gaiety over himself; a pleasant tissue of allusive levity, delicate but impenetrable. He never once made physical contact with her, not even fleetingly or as if by accident. He kept her at arm's length and swathed himself in a shadow as dark and deep as a lake at night and too intimidating to penetrate with a word. Or a kiss, thought Poldi, and that depressed her once more.

On board the plane, though, Montana immediately did his chivalrous duty again. He held my aunt's hand and lectured her on the physics of flight, meteorology and landing procedures.

When they landed at Catania shortly before nine, Poldi felt as if she'd been away for an age. Stranger still, she felt pleased to be home again.

Home.

A keyword.

"Need a lift?" Montana asked as they emerged from the airport building like two helpless tourists whose luggage hadn't accompanied them.

"I've got my own car here."

"In that case —"

"Well —"

"I'm parked over there."

"I see."

"It was a nice day."

Poldi could hardly endure his chilly courtesy. "Will you keep me informed about those mobiles?"

"Of course. I'll call you."

Bacio on the left cheek, *bacio* on the right. Montana wanted to be off, that couldn't have been more obvious. Poldi watched him hurry over to the multi-storey — no, not hurry, scoot. Then she found her Alfa in the other car park and drove back to Torre. She was tired and couldn't wait to get home; she wanted a beer. Or two. What a day, what a wonderful, bloody awful day. As if that wasn't enough, she lost her way twice after exiting the airport and missed the bypass. She had to drive all the way through Catania, which was gridlocked, and take the long, winding Provinciale instead.

When she turned into the Via Baronessa at last and was fishing the key out of her bag, she saw someone standing outside her front door.

"You again," she said when she had joined

him. Montana appeared to be trembling. It was as if a struggle were raging somewhere inside him — threatening to tear him limb from limb.

"Thank you for coming today," he blurted out. "Thank you for —"

That was as far as he got, because Poldi had had enough. Almost beside herself with passion and thirst and melancholy and the aftereffects of her fear of flying, she cupped Montana's head between her hands and kissed him fiercely, hungry for life and fulfilment in the here and now. She was relieved to feel that Montana neither recoiled nor hesitated. A tremor ran through his body. The next moment she tasted his smoky tongue in her mouth, felt his big hands on her breasts and, somewhat lower down, that thing to which no adjective does justice: his huge, pent-up, feverish, titanic *Sicilianità*. Breathing heavily, she unlocked the door, pulled him inside, undressed him on the spot and led him into her bedroom. And there at last, or so I imagine, amid sighs, moans and breathless little cries of pleasure, the argosy of their passion finally departed under full sail. I imagine that together, propelled by the telluric currents in their emotionally charged if less than youthful bodies, they embarked that night on an erotic odyssey, discovered mysterious continents and cloud-swathed mountains, Amazonian rivers, chasms, caverns, volcanoes and savannas, traversed storm-lashed oceans, cruised before the trade wind, dropped anchor in sandy bays, reached the edge of the world and sailed back again. Or so I imagine, anyway. The only thing they certainly didn't do that night was sleep.

9

Describes the author's problems with synthetic fibres and some spicy details of a night of passion. Poldi plans an undercover operation for which she seeks an agent provocateur. Rearrangements are made in the Via Baronessa, Aunt Caterina delivers an address on interior decoration, Totti displays strength of character, and Patanè gets a shock. Poldi conceals a discovery from Montana and declines to discuss their future relationship. And these are not the only items of bad news.

As agreed with my aunt, I returned to Torre in the middle of September to continue work on my family epic — or, alternatively, to founder on it like a shipwrecked sailor grounding his lifeboat on a storm-tossed reef. I hadn't got very far with it to date, being still on the first chapter. My great-grandfather Barnaba had just been trampled by a donkey, whereupon he had a vision in which the Devil commanded him to emigrate to Munich and build up a flourishing wholesale fruit business there. The year was 1919, a historical juncture I was anxious to dramatically resurrect with the aid of meticulous research and amazingly detailed descriptions of contemporary life. Unfortunately, network coverage in Torre was still extremely poor. How, I wondered, did people write novels in the old days without Google and Wikipedia? At all events, various things had to happen in my family saga before Barnaba could emigrate to Bavaria without a single word of German. He had first to elope with his beloved, the incredibly beautiful and mysterious Eleonora, carry her off in his rowing boat, get her pregnant, and marry her. In that order. Eleonora's parents still had to die an atrocious death because of the indispensable "backstory wound." The sky needed to rain frogs and Barnaba still had to become enslaved by the preternaturally beautiful Cyclops Ilaria. This was a magical, fantastical element I was determined to incorporate because nearly a century later Ilaria's great-granddaughter would seduce Barnaba's good-looking and jazz-loving but otherwise rather colourless great-grandson, so that the said protagonist and hero could enter a mythical, parallel universe. Something along those lines.

Having arrived in Torre with a handful of loose storylines, I nervously pulled them apart, spread them out in front of me, sorted them in accordance with their colour and length — and utterly failed to see how I could plait them into a viable narrative. I couldn't even tease them out properly, because they were composed of synthetic fibre. No wonder I yearned in desperation for the evening, when my Auntie Poldi would at last break out the whisky, bring me up to date with the Valentino case, and treat me to some spicy details of her relationship with Montana. She herself did little more than sip her drink.

On my last evening in Torre she spoke of her night of passion with Montana.

"You're welcome to spare me the details," I groaned.

"My, how inhibited you are," she exclaimed. "I won't spare you a single damn thing. There's no need to squirm like that; I'm telling you all this in your capacity as an author, not my nephew. It's like you're a doctor, really, or a priest. Understand?" She tweaked her wig straight. "That Vito, he knew exactly what to do with his hands.

Gentle, they were — they caressed me into a state of ecstasy, then squeezed me till I screamed. With sheer delight, I mean. He was no stranger to the female body, I could tell. No matter where he touched me, the place seemed to burn, and his hands weren't the only talented things about him. I always say that detective inspectors are superlative specimens of humanity, sexually as well. My God, I had an animal in my bed that night, a wild beast, a mythological force of nature. Mark you, the same applied to me. I knew which buttons to press. We were insatiable, and he — I must gratefully acknowledge this — had heaps of stamina for a man of his age. That's down to the healthy Mediterranean fare — you notice it at once. Half an hour's rest, one little kiss from the fairy sorceress, and his *pesciolino* at once turned back into a magnificent swordfish. My, what a splendid sight he was, lying stretched out in front of me like a stranded Odysseus. Naked and defenceless — apart, of course, from that lover's harpoon, which —"

"That's enough now, Poldi. I'm being serious."

A searching gaze. "Because I'm getting on a bit, or because I'm your aunt?"

"Because . . . you're digressing. Please let's get back to the case."

"How am I digressing?"

There was one point that did interest me, though.

"Tell me, did you keep your wig on the whole time?"

"What sort of daft question is that?"

"Did you or didn't you?"

"Who's digressing now? All right, do you want to hear how the case developed, or don't you?"

I visualize Poldi and Montana as atoms in a particle accelerator of fate. First they race round and round in predetermined orbits, faster and faster, and then . . . *Crash*. Big Bang. Black hole. The God particle. Dimensional displacement.

Perhaps a strange silence reigned over Torre Archirafi the morning after that memorable night, as if some umpteenth dimension had become stuck — as if that nocturnal eruption of lust and libido in the Via Baronessa had convulsed the whole town and exhausted it.

I doubt if they spoke much that morning, Montana and my Auntie Poldi. Perhaps it was merely the embarrassment of a naked confrontation in daylight, but there may still have been something unspoken and ominous between them. Montana showered, got dressed and drank his coffee. Then he had to go to the prefecture to find Valentino's mobile.

When Poldi was alone again in her house, which suddenly seemed much quieter than usual, she could hear a murmurous roar. It wasn't just the sea, it was her blood. She could hear it coursing through her veins, feel her heart pumping life and pleasure through her body, tirelessly and ubiquitously. She could hear children playing outside her door. The road sweeper's Vespa went puttering along the Via Baronessa. Signora Anzalone slammed her front door. Tired but happy, Poldi continued to sit on the sofa for a while, listening to the life outside and within. She could still smell Montana, still feel him inside her and all over her skin. An agreeable sensation.

And while savouring that agreeable sensation all on her own, Poldi debated how to proceed with her case. For even after last night she still regarded the case as *hers.* A case she was duty-bound to solve. And would.

She could naturally have waited for the results of Montana's examination of Valentino's mobile phone, but she didn't want to; she wanted to be one step ahead of him. Besides, she felt there must have been some reason why fate had played Corrado Pata-nè's business card into her hand. A building contractor; to Poldi it seemed obvious that he must have been Valentino's employer. All she had to do was prove it, but how? By means of an undercover operation, for example: the simulated purchase of a mosaic floor. Or a lion guardant.

Poldi naturally realized that she could not, after her last rather abortive encounter with him, simply call Patanè and ask him to quote on Sicilianizing her home. She would have to proceed more cleverly, set up the sting with skill, gain the man's trust. The only question was —

At that moment, breathless with curiosity, Aunt Teresa called to hear how her trip to Munich had gone — "Munich" being a cheeky euphemism.

"No, I don't believe it," she cried delight-edly when Poldi told her about her night with Montana. "I want to hear every last detail."

"Drop in this afternoon, all of you," Poldi told her, "but I warn you: you'll be green with envy." Then the light bulb came on in her head. "Make sure Caterina comes, won't you?"

My Aunt Caterina, the middle one of my father's three sisters, is in a league of her own. She's the shortest of the three, but no one would ever overlook her. She doesn't have to raise her voice, wear high heels or attract attention by dressing smartly. She's more the practical type. What makes her so noteworthy is her deportment. My Aunt Caterina has a stainless-steel backbone. She looks like a film star with Uncle Bernardo in an old snapshot from the seventies. Ramrod straight in a red cocktail dress, legs nonchalantly crossed, she gazes steadily into the lens with a faint smile as if asking the beholder a question to which she expects an answer. She is still a beauty, but Bernardo's death, coupled with the advancing years, responsibility for the family firm and solicitude for her children and grandchildren, has left its mark on her. Not on her attitude, though. What she wants, she gets. Always. Her beloved Bernardo, for example, was a simple, taciturn cabinet-maker whose request to marry his daughter my grandfather had scornfully rejected. Aunt Caterina married Bernardo regardless and joined him in establishing Mancuso Mobili, a small furniture factory. Its products are elegant, expensive and sometimes rather too grand for Sicilian tastes, but they have sold successfully for many years, overseas as well. My cousin Ciro has run the business since Uncle Bernardo's death, but he never takes a major commercial decision without consulting Aunt Caterina. She was Poldi's ideal agent provocateur.

"Not on your life" was Caterina's response when Poldi outlined her plan that afternoon.

Poldi and the three aunts were sitting over a non-alcoholic Crodino in the shady courtyard, an ideal place in which to celebrate Poldi's erotic successes. Uncle Martino had consequently been forced to remain at home on this occasion.

"Wait till you've heard the full details, won't you?"

"You've no need to go on, Poldi. I won't do it. It's dangerous, it's against the law and it won't work. I don't want to hear another word. *Basta.*"

Poldi sighed and threw up her hands.

"Then I'll do it," Luisa cried enthusiastically. This earned her a stern look from Caterina and Teresa. My Aunt Luisa had been the baby of the family, and her sisters always regarded her as such.

"Why on earth shouldn't I?"

"Because you're too easily hoodwinked," Poldi said drily, and the other two aunts nodded. "How many stray cats and dogs have you taken in over the years, just because they gazed at you in a heart-rending way?"

"Eight," Aunt Luisa said meekly. "No, ten counting Max and Luna."

Teresa and Caterina rolled their eyes.

"I'm sorry," Poldi said like the fat, ugly chief in a crime series, "but you'd be easy meat on a mission like this. You're too easy to see through."

"Me? Since when?"

"Since always," sighed Teresa.

Silence descended on the courtyard. The aunts sipped their Crodini. Teresa glanced at Caterina.

"You're not serious," said Caterina.

Yes, she was.

"I can't do it because of my heart," said Teresa.

Caterina sighed. She took another sip, then said, "All right, Poldi, tell me again."

"There's virtually no risk," Poldi resumed promptly. "You call Patanè and introduce yourself, say you got his number from Dr. Tannenberger and that you'd like your house prettified with some old tiles and antique features."

"*My* house?"

"Well, mine, of course. Patanè doesn't know I live here. If he takes the bait, arrange to meet him here, see what he's got to offer and ask him to quote you. Say you'd like a nice old lion sculpture, too. If he quotes you a price, haggle a bit or he'll smell a rat."

"And then?"

"Then nothing. We just wait. If Patanè can deliver the goods and Valérie's other lion goes missing, he'll have as good as convicted himself. Vito will do the rest. *Click* go the handcuffs."

"But I'll be incriminating myself as well."

"How? You'll ask Patanè where his treasures come from and he'll naturally have an explanation ready. He'll assure you everything's above board. That puts you in the clear."

"You reckon so?"

"Of course."

"And where will you be all this time?"

"At the Bar Cocuzza. If you need help, I'll be here in a flash."

Caterina looked unconvinced.

"We'll all wait in the bar," Aunt Teresa put in. "Martino as well, and Totti will remain in the house with you."

"Is that supposed to reassure me?"

"I'd do it," Aunt Luisa volunteered again.

Poldi ignored her and concentrated on Caterina alone. "That's the best plan I could think of," she said.

"It's absolutely crazy. Hare-brained."

Poldi nodded. "Utterly insane, I know."

"So when do I call him?"

Poldi produced a phone like lightning and handed it to Caterina, together with Patanè's business card. "Right away would be best."

With her sisters and her sister-in-law looking on, Caterina took the phone, squared her shoulders, drew a deep breath and dialled the number. Poldi could hear the ringtone, then an irritable *"Pronto?"*

"Good afternoon, this is Caterina Mancuso of Mancuso Mobili. Is that Signor Patanè? . . . Good. Signor Patanè, I got your number from a dear friend and associate, Dr. Tannenberger of Munich . . . Yes, the very same. He strongly recommended you to me. If anyone can assist you in this matter, he said, Corrado Patanè is the man. He intimated — in the strictest confidence, of course — that you've been short-listed for the cultural centre in Taormina."

Poldi signalled to Caterina to tone it down a bit, but Caterina ignored her and pressed on regardless.

"Mancuso Mobili has recently acquired a house in Torre Archirafi, Number Twenty-nine Via Baronessa. Our intention is to use it as a showroom in the future, but it'll need

253

revamping first. I envisage converting it into a miniature palazzo with antique paving and some baroque decorative features, the aim being to present our furniture collection in a stylish manner. Would you be interested?"

The answer was clearly yes. Although Poldi couldn't catch what Patanè was saying, his voice oozed with obsequious greed.

"Fine," said Aunt Caterina, very calm and composed. "In that case, shall we say eleven tomorrow morning?"

"You did it?" Poldi asked incredulously when Caterina rang off.

"Don't tell me you're surprised."

Poldi smiled at Caterina and raised her glass. "No, actually I'm not. You were great. We've got him by the balls now. Cheers."

At eleven the next morning, Poldi, Teresa, Luisa and Martino were seated in the Bar Cocuzza, soothing their nerves with coffee, *cornetti* and granitas, staring at Poldi's mobile phone on the table, and evaluating Caterina's text messages from the Via Baronessa.

Not here yet.

Still not here.

254

Where is he?

Doorbell.

"Operation Trapdoor" was under way. Poldi had prudently unscrewed the doorbell nameplate and slipped it into her handbag. She had also readied her house in other respects for Patanè's visit by stowing all her clothes in the wardrobes and putting away any telltale letters, documents and photos. Above all, she had taken down the corkboard in her bedroom and eliminated every pointer to the true owner of No. 29 Via Baronessa. Nothing could really go wrong.

Not really.

Midday came, then one, and the suspense mounted. Poldi checked her mobile every other minute, but Caterina gave no further sign of life. Poldi's phone did beep once, but it was Montana.

I've got something. When can we meet?

Poldi texted back at once:

Drop in this evening.

Montana's response:

I could make it right away.

Poldi thought for a moment. Then:

But I couldn't.

That sounded more brusque than she intended, but my aunt was rather worried about Caterina at that stage and wanted to keep the line open. Half past one came, and she couldn't stand it any longer. She was on the point of going back to the house when Caterina called at last, an alarming under-tone in her voice.

"He's gone; you can come."

"Are you all right, Caterina?"

"Just come."

They paid and left in a hurry. At the front door they were jumped up at and licked by a good-humoured Totti. Caterina, too, seemed wholly unscathed. Poldi looked around suspiciously for traces of a struggle, but there was nothing to be seen.

"So how did it go?"

"He took the bait," Caterina reported. "But then something odd happened."

One thing at a time, though, because this is a bit like Chinese whispers. I got the story from Poldi, who got it from Caterina.

It seems that Patanè turned up three quarters of an hour late, trailing an aura of BO and stale tobacco smoke.

Caterina nonetheless welcomed him politely without betraying her instant repugnance, ushered him inside, offered him a coffee and some water, and permitted him to look around the ground floor, which he did with the mistrustful curiosity of a cat at the vet's.

"How did Totti react?" asked Uncle Martino.

"He was a dead loss," said Caterina. "He even licked Patanè's hand, then retired into the shade and didn't show his face again."

So much for Totti's watchdog qualities. Uncle Martino was extremely satisfied with the results of Totti's test, however, because he hated watchdogs. It should be mentioned that Uncle Martino is a convinced and incorrigible philanthropist, pacifist and Slow Foodist. But I'm digressing again.

According to Caterina, Patanè's mistrust was as slow to evaporate as a dense autumn mist dispersed by the November sun. He wanted to know how long Caterina had owned the house, and Caterina, as arranged, sold him the story that Mancuso Mobili had recently acquired it from a deranged German woman who'd found the Sicilian climate too much for her and hightailed it back to Germany — hence the decor, all of which would soon be ripped out. Patanè swallowed this myth, but he didn't really thaw until Caterina had detailed Mancuso Mobili's imaginary expansion plans and made several references to her associate and good friend Dr. Tannenberger. Then, with a flourish worthy of a stage magician, he opened a portfolio of photographs of mosaics, stone figures, plasterwork and whole staircases, all of which Patanè could supply and all, of course, entirely legally acquired. The pieces allegedly came from dilapidated country mansions and palazzi — absolute ruins which would sadly have to be demolished in the near future. It was his dearest wish to preserve at least a modicum of the magnificent Sicilian craftsmanship of the late eighteenth and nineteenth centuries and transplant it to places where it would live on. It was, he said, a form of organ donation by brain-dead old buildings.

Everything had its price, of course. Patanè had no wish to disguise this, but nor did he wish to talk actual figures — for the moment. He suggested that Caterina examine the portfolio at her leisure while he made a little tour of the house in order to absorb its atmosphere and ignite the vital spark of inspiration. Because (to quote him verbatim) "the house must speak to me and whisper what it needs."

While Patanè roamed the house like a sniffer dog in customs, Aunt Caterina had time to study all the photographs closely and even photograph them with her mobile phone. There was no gate lion, though. Caterina heard Patanè climb the stairs to the roof terrace. But he came back down in a hurry. She just had time to put her mobile away. Looking suddenly nervous, almost alarmed, Patanè grabbed the portfolio, said a hasty goodbye and left the house as if his coat-tails were on fire.

"Peculiar, wasn't it?" Aunt Caterina concluded. "Then I called you straight away."

"Didn't he say anything else?" Poldi insisted.

Caterina shook her head. "He said he'd forgotten he had an urgent appointment with the dentist and would be in touch, that's all. Then he was off."

Poldi looked at the stairs that led to the roof terrace. It was some time since she'd been up there because of her knee. "Besides, it's *your* domain now," she had magnanimously informed me on my last visit. "I must respect your privacy. I'd sooner sit out on the esplanade."

But now she was curious as to what could have given Patanè such a toothache.

"Let's take a look," she said, and went toiling up the stairs with Teresa, Caterina, Luisa, Martino and Totti in her wake.

And discovered the gate lion.

Poldi gave me quite a telling-off later — why on earth had I never said anything about it? — but somehow I'd never associated the lion on the roof with the lion missing from Femminamorta. I swear it. I had simply never registered the thing. When I first spent a week at Torre in August, just after Poldi moved in, I was far too preoccupied with my novel — in other words, with ruminating, head-scratching and nail-chewing. Besides, I seldom visited the terrace because it was too hot up there during the day and I preferred to listen to Poldi in the evenings. In any case, I mistook the lion behind the head of the stairs for an ornament that had always been part of the house, especially as it was firmly cemented to the terrace wall.

"But not up there," Poldi cried in bewilderment when she was giving me an earful. "Good God, it must have struck you that that was a totally daft location for a gate lion. For one thing there's no gate, and for another no one can see it there."

What could I say? She was right. I shrugged sheepishly.

"Know something?" Poldi sighed. "Before you write another line, shut your eyes and ears and switch off all your other senses and let a bit of life blow in." On which note, she poured me another whisky.

So, firmly cemented to the terrace wall and partly obscured by the head of the stairs, Femminamorta's missing lion guardant contemplated Poldi rather sullenly and with a hint of reproach. Unlike me, she recognized it at once.

How had it got there?

There was only one explanation: Valentino.

Now Poldi came to think of it, she had left Valentino alone in the house on the morning of his last day's work for her, his job being to repair the leaky roof. She also remembered the half-full sack of cement he'd brought.

"That's when he must have cemented the lion into place. I remember him mixing the stuff."

"So why didn't he say anything?" asked Aunt Teresa.

In Poldi's opinion, there was only one plausible explanation for that as well.

"Why, because he wanted to hide the thing up here. He knew I could hardly make it up the stairs, and I hadn't met Valérie at that stage. Besides, he certainly didn't know he was going to be killed soon afterwards. I suspect he only intended to park it here for a short time."

"Why?" asked Aunt Teresa.

"Why, in order to sell it, of course."

Poldi's belief that Valentino had stolen the lion was now set as firmly as the cement. The only question was, on whose behalf had he stolen it?

"That's obvious," said Aunt Caterina. "Patanè."

But Poldi felt suddenly doubtful, given that the stone lion hadn't featured in Patanè's catalogue. This aroused a suspicion she kept to herself.

"What are we going to do with it?" asked Aunt Luisa.

"Nothing whatever," said Poldi. "It's staying where it is for the time being. Not a word to anyone."

"What about Montana?"

Good question.

Poldi decided not to tell Montana about the lion either, at least for the moment. This went against the grain, because she always liked to be honest with the men she slept with. On the other hand, the lion's discovery might well have put her a step ahead of him. And besides, what difference would a day or two make? She did, however, intend to inform Valérie the next day. She felt she'd been rather neglecting her friend lately, and Valérie would be bound to welcome the lion's return.

That evening, as arranged, the commissario appeared in the Via Baronessa, sans gelato but this time with red roses. He obviously hadn't come straight off duty, because he smelt of shower gel and had exchanged his grey suit for black chinos and a black polo shirt. Poldi wasn't too keen on that kind of leisure look, but she overlooked it in the case of Italians, especially when they wore black. Having trimmed the roses and put them in a vase, she towed Montana into the bedroom and undressed him.

"Hungry?" she asked a few pleasurable sighs later, when they were sharing a cigarette in bed.

Montana shook his head. "Don't bother."

"Of course you're hungry. I'll make us something."

"No, really not. I . . ." He cleared his throat.

Poldi caught on. "You've got to go?"

"Afraid so. Got a call from headquarters earlier."

"I see. But there's always time for a bit of rumpy-pumpy, eh?"

"Please don't be sour."

"Who's sour? Duty's duty and sex is sex."

Montana sighed and sat up in bed.

"I get it," said Poldi. "Now I'm sounding like your wife."

"Ex-wife. Poldi, listen, I —"

"No talk of relationships, for God's sake," said Poldi. "Everything's fine, Vito, honestly. Did you find Valentino's mobile?"

"Afraid not," said Montana, relieved to change the subject. "It's probably somewhere on the seabed, but we have the connection details. Valentino was on the move quite a lot just before his death. We can trace his route roughly with the aid of the radio cells his mobile was logged into."

"And where was it logged into last?"

"Here. The radio cell around Torre."

"Praiola beach, in other words?"

"I suspect so."

"But that wasn't the crime scene?"

"Exactly."

"So the murderer came across Valentino's mobile there and destroyed it or threw it into the sea."

"I assume so."

Poldi cogitated.

"Who did Valentino speak to on the phone before his death?"

"I'm not at liberty to tell you that, Poldi."

Poldi looked at him. "Oh, Vito."

"Okay, okay, but I have to be professional . . . Not to Russo, anyway, nor to Tannenberger. I had the latter's alibi checked, by the way. He really was in Munich."

"So Valentino spoke to Patanè."

But Montana shook his head again. "No."

Poldi was quite surprised.

"No? Who was it, then?"

Montana hesitated, and when Poldi saw the look on his face, the sudden, bitter taste in her mouth was like the aftermath of a monumental binge.

"Vito?"

Montana sighed and straightened his shoulders. "Your friend Valérie Belfiore."

10

Tells of the poison of mistrust, of old bat-teries, sugared almonds, kitsch, love and the magic inherent in lists. Poldi tries to discover who called Valentino from Valé-rie's phone and receives a surprising invitation. She suffers a disappointment at the old mineral water bottling plant, how-ever, and abandons herself to melancholy and wine. She also observes all kinds of things, interprets gestures and feels pes-simistic.

I picture Valentino's mobile phone lying somewhere on the seabed in the wide, warm Gulf of Catania. I see it bobbing to and fro in a gentle current, pawed by inquisitive octopuses that mistake it for a species of crab to be cracked open. I picture the mobile acquiring a build-up of algae and little sea snails in the course of time — even, perhaps, becoming encrusted with coral. I visualize it in the distant future as part of a wonderful coral reef. But little would remain by then of its plastic and electronics. Those, I imagine, would all have dissolved in the seawater, together with any fingerprints and traces of DNA, all the information in its memory, all the selfies, snapshots, GPS co-ordinates and text messages. All of them would have dissolved and dispersed into briny infinity, the homeopathic *ne plus ultra*. I picture the truth itself dissolving, slowly but irresistibly.

I also picture Poldi, who couldn't sleep that night for various reasons, all of them connected with the truth.

Valentino's truth, Montana's truth, Valérie's truth. The truth, Poldi imagined, was like a button holding an expensive dress together at one particular point. It was stupid not to undo it. Enough to drive one crazy. Insufferable. Intolerable. Plain unacceptable. Or so Poldi felt.

That was why she drove to Femminamorta the next day with a heart like stone and numerous questions on the tip of her tongue. She couldn't simply ask Valérie about the phone call, because Montana oughtn't to have told her about it, so she would have to proceed more subtly. And, to be honest, my Auntie Poldi wasn't the soul of subtlety.

At the gate with the solitary lion she was stopped by a young man sporting a smart suit and gelled hair.

"I'm sorry, signora, you can't drive in at present."

"Why not?"

"They're shooting a film."

This was something altogether new. Having been in the trade, though, Poldi didn't argue.

"But I can go in if I leave the car here, can I?"

"Of course, signora."

Parked sideways-on in the inner courtyard of the old country house was a brand-new Lamborghini Aventador. As glaringly orange as an overripe mandarin at sunset, it was a squat, sleek, 700-horsepower nightmare whose manufacturer employed the adjective "merciless" to advertise it.

"Which tells you all you need to know about the drivers of such monstrosities," Poldi told me later. "Peppe had a friend like that named Toni. I know there's no comparison, but Toni owned a white Porsche. Special, wickedly expensive mother-of-pearl paintwork — sperm white, we always called it. Peppe was a bit envious until Toni let him drive the thing. And what did Peppe do? He crashed it on the A92 between Garching and Mintraching — but then, Peppe smashed up nearly every car anyone lent him. Understandably, that put paid to their friendship. Anyway, Toni always wore white trousers. White was his colour, and I always used to say, "White Porsche and white pants equal no brains and a limp dick." I didn't need to study psychology; one look was enough, and where Lamborghini drivers are concerned, my maxim applies in spades. On the other hand, this one was only rented."

Valérie was nowhere to be seen. A young woman in a strapless wedding gown was lolling on the rented Lamborghini while two young men took stills and videoed her. Italians get married with a vengeance, and staging weddings has become an entire branch of industry in itself. One absolute essential is grandiose photographic and video documentation. For this purpose, bride and bridegroom are carted off to picturesque locations where they have to pose for hours, walk up and down a beach, gaze into each other's eyes, exchange a kiss, and then pace the beach again. Sports cars or powerful motorbikes are standard props, and wedding photography is a recession-proof profession for which no cripplingly long apprenticeship is necessary.

The photographer circled the Lamborghini like a hyena hovering around a pride of lions at their picnic, panned and swooped with his camera till Poldi became dizzy just watching him, and told the young woman to follow his every movement and keep looking into the lens. Not an easy task. The young woman was no photographic model; Poldi could tell that from the desperate way she tried to reproduce the erotic poses struck by pin-ups on car calendars. She was a real-life bride wearing far too much cream silk, lace and tulle. The gown seemed to flow from her upper body and melt on the Lamborghini's orange paintwork like vanilla ice cream. Her legs were completely hidden, so she looked like a mermaid whom some fortunate fisherman had hauled out of the Gulf of Catania and was now putting on public display.

The fortunate fisherman himself was standing a little to one side with a handful of friends and relations, his expression a mixture of pride and embarrassment.

Then came his turn. He had to join his bride on the bonnet and look cool, which was something he signally failed to do. The bridal pair seemed more irritated than amused by the palaver going on around them.

"Mon Dieu."

Poldi heard Valérie's voice coming from the garden, then her laugh.

"Hearty congratulations, all the best and lots of children," Poldi called to the bridal pair before disappearing behind the house, where she found Valérie chatting with Russo and Mimì Pastorella. Russo, who was wearing a pale-blue suit with a flower in the buttonhole, clearly belonged to the wedding party. Despite the heat, Mimì had donned a dark, ancient three-piece which some tailor seemed to have moulded out of a solid bale of cloth a century earlier. Hölderlin had curled up at his master's feet, stumpy tail twitching occasionally, and was chewing a small plastic lion. All in all, not a sight to gladden my aunt's heart. She would rather have spoken with Valérie alone. Conversation ceased as soon as the trio caught sight of her.

"Donna Isolde!" Mimì cried out delightedly.

"Poldi. *Mon Dieu,* I was just talking about you."

With a sigh, Poldi subsided onto a plastic chair. "In what connection?"

Valérie offered her some coffee. "Mimì

271

and Signor Russo were asking after you, but — *mon Dieu* — what could I tell them? I haven't heard from you for days."

"Well, here I am again."

Mimì promptly seized the opportunity to grasp her hand and quote some Hölderlin in his habitual whisper. The Dobermann at his feet pricked its ears.

Poldi made no comment, either on the quotation or its sequel, a kiss on the hand. She turned to Russo. "Who's getting married?"

"My eldest daughter."

"Oh?" Poldi had genuinely thought Russo younger than he was. "I mean, how wonderful. You must be very proud."

Russo's smile was noncommittal. "The man's an idiot. A dentist from Florence, and like all Tuscans he hates us Sicilians. But what the hell: Stella loves him."

"There's going to be a big party tonight," said Valérie, turning to Poldi. "Would you like to come?"

"No thanks, not if it's a family occasion."

Valérie gave Russo a meaningful look.

"It isn't as family as all that," he said. "I'd be delighted if you could make it, Signora Poldi. You're warmly invited."

"I shall keep a place beside me free for you, Donna Isolde," whispered Mimì.

"God Almighty," Poldi exclaimed when she told me about the episode a month later. "I was in a real bind. If I refused, Russo would be offended. Why? Because — get this — you can decline any invitation except a wedding invitation. But if I accepted, I'd be landed with Mimì the whole evening. Plus Hölderlin. And anyway, how was I to get through a wedding party sober? On the other hand, I told myself, this might be my one chance to penetrate the inner circle of the organization, if you know what I mean."

"It would also," Russo added, "be a good opportunity to bury the memory of our unpleasant former encounters once and for all."

"In that case," Poldi said graciously, "I'd love to come."

Having received a signal that the photographer was finished, Russo took his leave of Valérie with a friendly kiss on both cheeks.

Poldi waited for Mimì to leave, too, but it didn't even seem to cross his mind. Unwilling to depart without settling the matter of the phone call, she broached the subject with her usual subtlety.

"Tell me, Valérie, where were *you* the evening before Valentino was murdered?"

Mimì, who was patting Hölderlin, did not

273

appear to be listening.

Valérie didn't even blink. She merely gave a little sigh. "Your boyfriend the commissario asked me the same question yesterday."

"He isn't my boyfriend."

"*Mon Dieu,* Poldi, what is all this? I didn't call Valentino — I already told the commissario that."

"It's true, Donna Isolde," Mimì chimed in. "I was here the whole time."

"It was the day after the dinner at Mimì's," Valérie added. "I wanted to invite you over, but I couldn't get hold of you."

"Yes, I was a bit below par that day," muttered Poldi, remembering her fall from grace after the ghastly Hölderlin evening. "Who else was with you?"

"Russo dropped in with Patanè in tow to make me an offer."

"What sort of offer?"

Valérie exchanged a glance with Mimì. "He's after the house and grounds, of course. He offered me a million."

"You don't say."

Valérie laughed and made a dismissive gesture. "He could offer me ten million and I wouldn't sell. The two of them soon left. I told the commissario all this as well. *Mon Dieu,* Poldi, you don't seriously think *I* murdered Valentino."

Now it was Poldi's turn to sigh. "Who knows? Perhaps you were jealous of Herr Tannenberger."

"Who's that, and why should I have been jealous of him?"

"Or Valentino tried to sell your lion back to you, and you didn't want to pay."

"Aha. So I naturally took my lupara, shot him in cold blood and dragged him down to the beach. All by myself, and all because of a stone figure. *Mon Dieu.*"

Mimì said nothing, just continued to fondle his Dobermann and contemplate Poldi's perplexity. He might have been looking at a cute but bedraggled mongrel puppy he couldn't help. Or wouldn't.

Poldi knew from Montana that it had only been a short phone call, barely two minutes. She also knew Valérie's phone, which she was forever misplacing somewhere in the house, an antiquated model with big keys and an asthmatic battery that kept running out. This didn't worry Valérie, because she generally used her mobile for making calls. Poldi had persuaded Montana to disclose that Valérie's mobile number had not appeared in Valentino's list of calls.

It was quite possible, therefore, that someone in the house had spoken with

Valentino unobserved, especially as the doors were usually left unlocked. Even when they weren't, most people knew there was a spare key beneath the little plaster Madonna in the votive niche beside the front door. Valérie wasn't afraid of burglars. She had once told Poldi that Femminamorta was a place charged with positive energy. My aunt, who knew a thing or two about positive energy, had needed no convincing of that.

"All the same," she told me several weeks later, when explaining her train of thought, "I couldn't help wondering why anyone else would have used Valérie's phone. Explanation A: he or she didn't want to use their own mobile because they already planned to kill Valentino. Explanation B: he or she doesn't own a mobile. Are you with me?"

"You bet," I said. "So that ruled Valérie out."

"Whoa. Positive energy or not, once suspicion has you by the scruff of the neck, you don't shake it off so easily. An investigator must never exclude the possibility of an Explanation C; that's just the tricky part."

My aunt suspected that she'd been thoroughly bamboozled, and bitter personal experience had taught her a thing or two about that as well. On the other hand, she had no wish to lose a friend. She never wanted to lose anyone she'd taken to her heart.

"Do you remember where the telephone was that afternoon?"

"I know it was lying on the chest of drawers in the passage when I went to bed that night. But the battery was flat again."

"You remember that, do you?"

Valérie shrugged her shoulders. "It's always flat."

After a moment's thought, Poldi made two decisions. First, not to let mistrust poison their friendship, and second, not to be bamboozled any more.

"Will you still take me with you to the wedding party?"

"Why even ask?"

"I mean, because I suspected you just now."

"But it's your job."

"My job?"

"*Mon Dieu,* Poldi, you're a detective now. You can't rule anyone out. It's hard on your friends, but you're faithfully obeying the call of justice. How does that sound?"

Poldi hadn't looked at it like that before.

"Lousy. But you're right."

Anyone who heaves a pensive sigh at the idea of a Sicilian wedding and pictures

Dolce & Gabbana models of all ages seated over pasta and wine at a long table in an olive grove, happily singing and playing mandolins while the newlyweds dance a passionate tarantella, has never attended any such function. Poldi hadn't either, so the reality hit her like a punch in the solar plexus. A Sicilian wedding takes the following form: umpteen guests assemble in a *sala di ricevimento,* usually some barn of a multifunctional building with a tiled floor, where they sit on plastic chairs and eat immoderately for hours on end. That's the prime essential. For drink there'll be one bottle of wine per table, and that's enough because, as already mentioned, Sicilians don't drink much. They make up for that by eating, and that they do without a break. Meanwhile, the young newlyweds sit by themselves at a table of their own with a view of the whole wretched proceedings, which are over by eleven-thirty at the latest. Music? Only from the band, if any. Dancing? No way. High jinks? Forget it. A Sicilian wedding is about as amusing as detention. Its sole object is to impress the friends of the bridal pair's parents and, more especially, their business associates, by filling them to the gunwales with food.

Only when they can't say "phew" any

more is that mission accomplished. The *bella figura* principle applies here, too. The last thing anyone wants is to look like they're hard up, like business is bad and the future anything but rosy, even if the general economic situation says otherwise. One gauge of the parents' prosperity is the *bomboniera* presented to each guest by the bridal pair: little china, glass or even silver containers produced in a wide range of prices by an industry of its own and filled with white sugared almonds, these being the traditional talismans at Italian weddings. From a sober, Protestant point of view, of course, they're the worst kind of superfluous kitsch. One must, however, adopt an oriental mode of thought, for the *bomboniera,* like the bride, is a sweet thing robed in splendour. And that's the whole point: what the bridal pair are sharing with all their guests is something wholly useless and, depending on one's point of view, tasteless but nonetheless sweet: love.

Poldi understood this, of course, but it did nothing to lift her spirits that night as she opened and shut the lid of her expensive silver *bomboniera* and watched Russo jovially nudge dignitaries in the ribs, crack jokes, dispense kisses and simultaneously keep an eye on some three hundred wedding guests. His ex-wife and her new husband were the only people he seemed to ignore to the best of his ability, and they repaid him in kind.

Recalling the Uncle Martino rule of thumb — physical stature — for gauging whether or not a man belonged to the Mafia, Poldi surmised that all the male guests under five foot three in height were members of Russo's organization: contract killers, extortioners, consiglieri, bone-breakers, protection racketeers, purveyors of bribes, lion stealers, drug couriers, money launderers and crooked attorneys. She imagined that Russo was murmuring instructions, whispering warnings and delivering verdicts. Anyone who wasn't an insider at least knew the score and looked the other way, sealing his lips and shutting his ears — or so Poldi imagined. She wasn't frightened. It gave her a kind of grim satisfaction to be sitting there as the only steadfast champion of justice.

"And," she confessed to me later, "I must admit it gave me a certain kick."

Poldi caught Russo's eye from time to time, and she realized that the father of the bride was keeping her under observation. Either her or Valérie, who was sitting beside her, chatting to Mimì and Carmela about family matters.

Russo had had the interior of Torre Archi-rafi's derelict mineral water bottling plant decorated for the occasion and transformed into an artificial olive grove with trees from his nursery. That could have been quite atmospheric, had the olive trees not been standing in black plastic tubs, had plastic furniture not been enlisted yet again, and if Russo had staged the whole thing in the open air or at least dispensed with neon lighting. No wonder Poldi was once more beset by melancholy memories to such an extent that she did, after all, drink a glass or two of wine. She didn't have to drive.

"I couldn't stop thinking of the time I got married to your Uncle Peppe," Poldi told me when I was back with her again. "We didn't invite the family, just our hundred best friends, and we partied in the big covered market at the stall belonging to Giovanni, Peppe's special buddy. It was in the early eighties, and — not that this'll mean anything to you — we used to listen to Prince and the Police, so Prince and Sting were played as a matter of course. The Spider Murphy Gang played 'Skandal im Sperrbezirk,' but also 'Roxanne' and 'Purple Rain.' And everyone got drunk and smoked pot and laughed and sang and danced and screwed in the loo till noon the next day. And the next night we started all over again. That's a proper wedding for you. It's simply a question of showing respect for love."

That was why Poldi had given the bridal pair a special present, which she handed them between the first and second main courses: Oshun, the Bantu fertility goddess, an ebony figurine with short legs, a swollen belly, little coloured chains around its neck and huge breasts proffered to the beholder in both hands. Not tourist trash but a genuine antique, at least two hundred years old. The young couple, who had no idea who the woman in the wig and red dress was, thanked her politely and deposited her bizarre gift discreetly beneath the table, where they forgot it at the end of the evening. I'm not superstitious, but I like to imagine that a young cleaner found the figure later and took it home with her, and that she was soon afterwards blessed with a happy marriage, several healthy children and lifelong prosperity.

But to revert to the wedding party, where the second main course was being served: *sarde a beccafico,* baked sardine rolls stuffed with a paste made of breadcrumbs, olive oil, pecorino, parsley and pine kernels. They're delicious and look small and innocuous. Most people would bust a gut after three, but the wedding guests shovelled mountains of them onto their plates. The general mood couldn't have been better.

Except in Patanè's case. He was sitting morosely with his equally morose-looking wife at one of the outermost tables — in other words, not in pole position, socially speaking. Poldi saw him make repeated attempts to attract Russo's attention, but his host stubbornly ignored them.

Back at the table, Poldi picked at her food without appetite, poured herself some more wine to help Mimì's commentaries on Hölderlin bounce off her, and devoted herself to sinister theories about the ties between Russo, Valérie and Patanè. In order to sort out her ideas she felt in her handbag for a ballpoint. She was momentarily puzzled to find the bag on her left-hand side instead of the right, but she'd already had a glass or two. Taking a paper napkin, she made a list of everyone currently under suspicion.

RUSSO
PATANÈ
TANNENBERGER
VALÉRIE
~~HÖLDERLIN~~ MIMÌ

"You've got to make lists in life," Poldi advised me some weeks later. "Lists are magical — that's because they develop a life of their own. Once you start one, it insists on being continued ad infinitum. You may cross out an item from time to time, but you're never finished. A list is never complete, remember. One thing leads to another, and — bingo — it contains items you'd never thought of before. And all because you started to write them down. That's also the secret of writing in general: making a start, getting words down on paper. Just because it's suddenly there in black and white on a sheet of paper, the written word develops genuine momentum. I tell you, lists are the mechanics of the subconscious. Lists of names, for example. One name on its own doesn't make a list, obviously. Nor do two names. Three names? Still not enough. Four names qualify, but they look half-hearted. Only when there are five names, or preferably six, can you call them a list. Mind you, a list mustn't be too long or it becomes ineffective, like central heating with all the windows open in January. Remember that."

So saying — open brackets — my Auntie

Poldi summarized the reciprocal relationship between information and entropy. Close brackets.

She stared at the six names on the paper napkin, which seemed to stare back at her like reflections in a Venetian mirror. She could cross out Tannenberger right away, but the other five could all have been responsible for the phone call to Valentino, and they were all there that night. Poldi even spotted old Turi at one of the tables on the periphery. He was wearing an ancient suit far too big for him and single-mindedly devouring one sardine roll after another. Poldi was about to get up and keep him company for a bit when Valérie nudged her and pointed to the list. "You don't believe me, do you? You still think I had something to do with Valentino's death."

"You have to admit it's strange the last call he received was made from your phone."

Poldi made to refill her glass, but Valérie took the bottle from her and tapped the paper napkin. "You really think one of us is Valentino's murderer?"

Poldi crumpled up the napkin and stuffed it in her handbag. "Are you having an affair with Russo?"

"What?" Valérie exclaimed in bewilderment. "*Mon Dieu,* what gives you that idea?"

"Well, the way he keeps looking at you. And those kisses this morning. And the cosy way you were sitting together. A hostile relationship looks different somehow."

Valérie stared at Poldi. "I'm going home; I've got a headache," she said, snatching up her handbag. "Have fun."

"Valérie."

But there was nothing to be done. Valérie left the makeshift banqueting hall without saying goodbye to anyone. Poldi wondered whether to run after her and apologize, but she suddenly felt old and fat, overheated and rather sleepy. How many glasses had she drunk? She hadn't kept count, but it couldn't have been all that many, given the lack of liquid reinforcements.

"Bugger it," she muttered to herself. Scanning the nearest tables for a full bottle of wine, she saw that Patanè had at last managed to have a word with Russo. From his gestures, he was pleading his innocence of something. Russo, looking annoyed, said something in reply, whereupon they both left the hall. It went without saying that Poldi had to go after them. She wasn't there just for fun, after all. Somewhat unsteady on her pins, she rose and followed the two men.

It was already getting dark when Poldi emerged into the open, somewhat bemused by wine and melancholy. In order to shake off her slight feeling of dizziness, she began by drawing a deep breath. The evening hummed her a serenade of laughter, raised voices and blatting mopeds. Redolent of diesel fumes, tobacco smoke and the sea, it bathed dilapidated house fronts in the picturesque glow of sodium lights. A fine night, perfect for embarking on a new life or ending an old one. Outside the old bottling plant, enveloped in neon lighting and swarms of mosquitoes, young friends of the bridal pair were fooling around and smoking. A little to one side, discreetly sited in shadow, stood a platoon of Portaloos with a small queue in front of them, and parked immediately behind them were the vans of the catering services. Russo and Patanè were nowhere to be seen.

In an unobtrusive and wholly professional manner, Poldi sauntered around the factory and eventually spotted Russo and Patanè in an ill-lit gap between two parked cars. They were gesticulating fiercely and appeared to be arguing. Cautiously crouching to the extent her knee permitted, my aunt stole closer — right up to an SUV, which concealed her better than the Fiat Cinquecento beside it. Although she could distinctly hear the two men's voices from there, she couldn't understand a word. Russo and Patanè were arguing in Sicilian, and that, it should be pointed out, has as much in common with Italian as Swiss German with Frisian. The gulf between Italian regional dialects is far greater than in most countries, and Sicilian is more than a dialect. It is a guttural, almost Arabic-sounding mélange, the phonetic heritage of all the races that have ever occupied the island. Significantly enough, Sicilian has no future tense. On the other hand, Sicilians often use the complicated *passato remoto* in everyday speech. This tense, which elsewhere occurs only in literature and does not exist in German, describes events that lie very far back in time and are consummated and irrevocable — really, truly, officially in the past. That's that, it's over and done with. *Basta.* Sicilians would, for instance, use the *passato remoto* after their siesta, when referring to the lunch they ate earlier in the day. The message is unmistakable: we live in the here and now, and only in the here and now.

Be that as it may, Poldi couldn't understand a word. The men's body language, on the other hand, was crystal clear: Russo was pissed off with Patanè, who appeared to be

288

furiously justifying himself. Russo grabbed Patanè by the collar and snarled at him. All Poldi could hear was "Afaculitishpacofalacha," but she guessed it must be a curse or the threat of violence. Sure enough, when Patanè tried to free himself, Russo shoved him hard in the chest, then punched him in the face. Poldi instinctively ducked down behind the car, so she didn't see if Patanè returned the blow. She merely heard the two men panting, followed by hurried footsteps on the other side of the SUV. Then something flew through the air and landed beside her. Red and white in colour, it lay there unmoving. It didn't shrink, didn't grow, just lay there. Poldi stared at the thing, trying to work out what it could be.

Then the solution dawned on her: it was a bloodstained handkerchief. No doubt about it. Poldi obviously couldn't allow such a DNA-carrier to slip through her fingers. She fished out one of the little self-seal plastic bags she'd been carrying around in her handbag since Valentino's death, meaning to secure the handkerchief. Alas, it was too far away. Miles away. At the other end of the world. Poldi tried to stand up, but for some reason she could no longer do so; she didn't have the strength. It didn't matter, though. Necessity being the mother of invention, she simply crawled towards the handkerchief on all fours and swam through an ocean of darkness and dizziness until she could at last take hold of the bundle of viscose and bag it. Done, finished, relax.

Poldi gasped, overcome by nausea, and vomited. Cursing Russo's lousy wine, she tried to stand up — really tried — but failed because the world had decided to rotate ever faster. She heard a voice coming from somewhere and saw some shoes just in front of her eyes. Good, well-polished, men's black shoes. And they were the last thing she saw. Fade to black.

Historico-Cultural Intermezzo

When Almighty God had created the world and everything in it, He had a tiny little bit of every continent left over. He was satisfied with Himself and His work, so He casually kneaded the bits together into a lump and slapped it down on His new world, and — bingo — there was Sicily.

At that the angels came hurrying up. "Wow," they whispered, rustling their wings uneasily. "What a beautiful thing you've created, O Lord. An absolute paradise — only the best bits from all the continents."

"So?" the Almighty said proudly. "It's wonderful."

"Yes," whispered the angels, "but the other parts of the world will be green with envy. There'll be a row, a regular hullabaloo. Not a good start."

The Almighty took their point. "Oh dear," He said, "what shall I do?"

"You need to even things up a bit,"

whispered the angels.
So He created the Sicilians.

— Popular Sicilian joke, as
told by my Auntie Poldi

11

Describes a misunderstanding, the after-effects of knockout drops, and sundry discoveries. Poldi fails to find her key, expels an uninvited visitor with the aid of a muzzle-loader, and makes discovery number one. She gets personal protection and accompanies the aunts to the lido. There she makes discovery number two, conducts a serious private conversation, and soon afterwards makes discovery number three.

Poldi got to her feet with an effort and saw Death standing in front of her. He was looking embarrassed and rather at a loss.

"Well, well," she said calmly. "So it's time, is it?"

Death put on his reading glasses and glanced at the list on his clipboard. "One moment; not so fast. You aren't on today's list. Something" — he cleared his throat nervously — "something must have gone wrong."

"You can say that again," Poldi grumbled, smoothing her dress down. "I always thought my end would be more dignified. Look at my dress. Do you know what that cost? Oh well, never mind, let's make the best of it."

She looked across at the bottling plant. The young people outside the entrance, the wedding guests lining up outside the Portaloos, the stray cats — they all seemed frozen in mid-movement. Even the glow from the street lights looked harsh and ossified.

"Just as a matter of interest, is this eternal damnation, or am I in Purgatory?"

"Weren't you listening?" Death snapped. "I just said something's gone wrong. It isn't your turn yet."

"Meaning what?"

"Meaning you aren't on the list," Death repeated more meekly. "I'm sorry."

"Hell's bells and buckets of blood," Poldi thundered. "Bugger the list. I'm dead and that's that."

"No, Poldi, you aren't."

"So where the hell am I, then? What is this?"

Death gave an embarrassed cough. "A, er . . . near-death experience?"

Poldi grabbed Death by the scruff of the neck and shook him a little. He was quite lightly built.

"Let go of me," Death wailed, brandishing his clipboard. "Please. I can put you down on the list any time, if you're really so keen."

Poldi released him. "Okay, then, let's do it. Where do I sign?"

But Death lowered his clipboard again, looking positively dejected. "No, can't be done. Listen, Poldi, it doesn't work like that. Those knockout drops in your wine weren't supposed to kill you. Though —"

"Though they nearly did, is that what you mean?"

Death became all formal again. "I'm not authorized to disclose information on the subject of destiny."

Poldi got the message. "So it's a balls-up of the first order."

"That's one way of putting it," Death conceded. He sounded genuinely apologetic. "I'm really sorry. Well . . . I'll be seeing you." He turned to go.

"Hang on," called Poldi. Death was looking rather exhausted, she saw, and no wonder. If you've been on the go since the beginning of time, you're bound to reach burnout sooner or later.

"What is it?"

"When *am* I for the chop? I mean, just for interest's sake."

"You really want to know?"

"Come on, we've been having such a nice chat."

Death hesitated. "Very well, Poldi, since it's you," he eventually said with a sigh. He consulted his clipboard again.

Although Poldi couldn't make out any of the names, she saw that they were listed in quite small print and neatly arranged in date order. Death ran his ballpoint down the list name by name and sheet after sheet.

And then . . .

"Ah, there you are. Officially certified, rubber-stamped and signed. Your date of death is the —"

Unfortunately, that was when Poldi woke up.

It's hard to say in retrospect who put the knockout drops in my aunt's glass, just as the whole course of the evening remained hidden behind a sort of blackout curtain. Poldi was able to reconstruct only parts of it later on, and we can't tell whether everything happened just the way she thought, whether certain conversations actually took place, whether her recollections are accurate, and whether she really overheard

Russo and Patanè arguing. The one tangible clue was a bloodstained handkerchief in a zipper bag and her final memory of a pair of men's black shoes.

Groaning, cursing and afflicted with the thickest of thick heads, Poldi recovered consciousness on the ground beside the SUV. She was still a little dizzy, she was thirsty, she had a metallic taste in her mouth, and the veil of oblivion was lifting only slowly. But she was alive. She did feel rather miffed at failing to learn her sell-by date, but there were more important issues to be addressed at present. Like what had actually happened.

She could remember nothing at this stage, only those black shoes and the fact that Death had said something about knockout drops, but that sufficed her for the moment.

Still groaning, she staggered to her feet like Polyphemus blinded by Odysseus, drew several deep breaths while waiting for the drumbeats in her head to subside a little, and looked around. It was still dark. She could make out the old bottling plant, but it wasn't illuminated any more. Everything was steeped in gloom. No one to be seen. The party was over.

And nobody missed me, let alone came looking for me, Poldi thought bitterly. She peered at her watch. Just after half past three. How long had she been lying on the ground? No idea. All she knew was that she could have simply died there, for all anyone would have cared. Balls to the lot of them.

Still rather wobbly on her legs, Poldi straightened her dress, retrieved her handbag from the ground and looked up at the night sky. The stars twinkled at her, and the moon seemed to perform a coquettish little hop before it dipped below the horizon.

"*Namaste,* life," Poldi said softly, somehow glad not to have been on tonight's list after all, and set off for home. Cautiously, step by step, stomach churning with rage and assailed by waves of nausea, she tottered home along the esplanade, steadying herself against the walls of the buildings that lined the waterfront. She felt she was in a totally unfamiliar place. She passed no one, no lights were on in the houses, and the dark sea was lethargically slapping the rocky shore. The whole town seemed to be guiltily avoiding her eye. It merely flickered its street lights in a nervous way and pretended to be asleep.

"If that's your attitude," muttered Poldi, "you can kiss my ass."

On reaching No. 29 Via Baronessa, she felt in her handbag for the key and found the self-seal bag containing the bloodstained handkerchief. She stared at the small plastic envelope, trying to remember where she'd got it from. She failed, and she also failed to find her key, even when she emptied out her handbag on the doorstep. The key was gone.

Just then, Poldi heard noises. They were definitely not in her head. Crisp, rhythmical blows, not loud but coming from not far away, they were interspersed with scratching and scraping sounds. The noises trickled down on my aunt from above like crumbling plaster, mingled with the sound of shuffling feet and heavy breathing. They were coming from the roof terrace, no doubt about it.

Poldi wondered what to do. Shout for help till the whole street was awake? Tiptoe away and call the police? No, because her stomach was still churning with rage, and besides, she knew from a reliable source that she wasn't scheduled to die yet. Whoever it was that had invaded *her* house with *her* key was going to get an earful.

Gingerly, she tried the front door. It was locked, but that didn't matter because Poldi, who often forgot her key, had taken the precaution of sticking a spare one to the back of her letter box. She lifted the little metal box off its mount as quietly as possible, detached the spare key and silently let herself in.

Without turning a light on, Poldi tiptoed into the living room and over to the wall on which hung the antique firearms Montana had eyed so suspiciously. She took down an eighteenth-century infantry musket dating from the War of the Bavarian Succession, a plain, unadorned muzzle-loader from the Fortschauer Armatur factory, 19 mm calibre, with a walnut stock and a long barrel. Its numerous dents and signs of use indicated that the weapon had probably mangled the intestines of several Prussian fusiliers, shattered their limbs and perforated their skulls. Poldi's father had taken an enthusiastic interest in that particular aspect of Bavarian history, and although Poldi had never really shared his passion, she had kept his small collection of firearms as a memento of him. The guns had long been deactivated, because the barrels were welded up and plugged with steel, but they still had their bayonets.

Despite the darkness and despite her headache and nausea, Poldi managed to fix the bayonet on the barrel. The musket, which now weighed heavy in her hands, seemed to awake from a long dream and whisper to her about the atrocities it yearned to commit once more. And who could blame it, it whispered. After all, killing was the only thing it had ever been taught to do.

But Poldi had no intention of allowing the musket to indulge in any shenanigans. She merely wanted to make a bit of an impression. And so, with the muzzle-loader at the ready and her stomach still churning with rage, she crept step by step up the stairs to the roof, whence the staccato noises were coming. By now, she had guessed what was going on up there. Anxious to exploit the surprise effect, she paused on the last step, drew several deep breaths, counted up to three, and then burst out onto the roof.

"Freezehandsuporifiredownonyourknees-andbequickaboutit!"

All of it in German, of course, to enhance the effect still further.

The figure, which had been attacking the cemented gate lion with a cold chisel, uttered a startled cry and spun round. It was dressed in black, together with gloves and a face mask such as bikers wear beneath their helmets.

Poldi gripped the musket even tighter and aimed the bayonet at the intruder. "Don't move. Down on your knees or I'll run you through."

Again in German, or rather, Bavarian,

because excitement had robbed Poldi of her fluency in Italian and she felt it would be counterproductive, under the circumstances, to stammer.

But the intruder didn't move. Rightly so, really, because "Freeze" and "Down on your knees" were rather self-contradictory and no one threatened with a musket wants to do the wrong thing.

For safety's sake, Poldi repeated everything in Italian. "Down on your knees, I said. Hands above your head. Move!" Anyone who has watched TV police procedurals for several decades will have items in their vocabulary suitable for such occasions. However, the man with the chisel still seemed unimpressed.

"Drop that chisel. Take off your mask." In order to underline her demand, Poldi lunged at the intruder as if about to skewer him with her bayonet. "Haaa."

That did the trick at last. The intruder dropped the chisel and raised his hands, but before Poldi could say more, he turned and climbed over the parapet. Or rather, he rolled over the low wall, because he didn't appear to be very athletic.

"Freeze or I fire!" Poldi shouted at the top of her voice.

But the intruder had already landed with

a thud on the terrace of Dottore Branciforti's next-door house and gone sprawling. Poldi heard a smothered cry. Leaning over the wall, she saw the intruder scramble to his feet with a groan, hobble across the terrace and start to climb down a creeper on the far side.

"I'll fire," yelled Poldi. "I'll fire on three. One . . . two . . . three . . . Bang. Bang. Bang."

"Did you really shout 'Bang'?" I asked Poldi on my next visit, when she was giving me as detailed a description of the incident as her memory of it allowed.

"Of course. Why, what else was I to do? At that moment the gun and I were, to all intents and purposes, a single entity. My basest human instincts had been aroused. Higher brain function on standby, nothing but the spinal cord in action, know what I mean? What was it Chekhov said? If a gun appears in the first act, it's got to go off in the fourth at the latest. Make a note of that; it was good advice given to a young writer. Of course the gun wanted to go off, and it did. Lucky that old musket was deactivated, or I'd have shot the man down in cold blood. That's because something had been triggered — inside me, I mean. Something atavistic and elemental. In other words —"

"The hunting instinct. I get it."

"Exactly. No need to roll your eyes like that, I was *in extremis.* I know a thing or two about extreme situations."

I nodded — always the best policy with Poldi in such circumstances.

"Would you really have pulled the trigger if the gun had been activated?"

An awkward question, I know, but somehow I didn't want to let Poldi get away with her big talk so easily.

"You're trying to trip me up, aren't you? The fact is, the fellow winced when I shouted 'Bang,' which proves *he* thought I was capable of shooting him."

"He got away from you, though."

"Yes, temporarily. Only temporarily. The truth is, I'd pegged him long ago."

I naturally wanted her to elaborate, but she yawned and said she was going to bed. Whether or not she was also a trifle stung by my scepticism, she deferred the sequel to her nocturnal adventure until the following evening.

I spent the whole of the next day working doggedly on my novel. I tried to conceive of it as a kind of weapon with which I had only to become a single entity for it to fire. But my novel behaved like a musket with the barrel welded up. It wanted, it genuinely wanted to go off, to hit hearts and shred nerves, penetrate skin, flesh and bone, I could sense it, but all that ever emerged in the end was an ineffectual "bang." I did, however, include in the first chapter a muzzleloader with which my great-grandfather Barnaba, beside himself with fury, plans to shoot the white donkey that had kicked him not long before. Barnaba swears that he will stalk the white donkey to the ends of the earth. Still limping, he corners it in the *macchia* of Acireale and takes aim. The donkey fixes him with its trusting, unsuspecting gaze. And then comes the transformation. Barnaba repeatedly hesitates, takes aim once more, hesitates yet again, and hasn't the heart to pull the trigger. In the end, he breaks down and begs the donkey to forgive him. A very emotional and affecting scene between man and beast, with a powerful pay-off of the kind I'd learnt at the writers' workshop. Just as a weeping Barnaba is about to hurl the musket into the crater of Etna like Frodo jettisoning the Ring, he notices something engraved on the barrel, but all he can decipher is the name of a city: M-u-n-i-c-h.

To that extent, my musket had gone off after all. Thanks, Chekhov. By that evening

I suspected I would have to delete the whole load of rubbish the next day, but first, exhausted by my fragile day's work, I flopped down on the sofa in the living room, where Poldi was already sipping a leisurely gin and tonic.

"Where did I get to?"

"To 'Bang.' "

"Oh yes, that was it." She seemed to be thinking — or concentrating, like a pianist about to play.

I was on the point of giving her a nudge when she started afresh.

"By that time, of course, the racket had woken half the town, but the intruder was long gone." She fell silent again.

"And then?"

"Why, then I called Montana."

Montana, cradling the musket like a vet holding an anaesthetized alligator, ran his thumb experimentally over the blade of the bayonet. "You might have killed him with this, Poldi."

"Why sound so accusing? I had to defend myself."

It was already getting light outside. A new day was seeping into the town, sweeping shadows from the streets, sharpening silhouettes and raising new questions. Looking east from the roof terrace, one could already make out the skyline beyond which the sun would soon arc out of the sea like a golden bubble rising from the depths. Down in the Via Baronessa, voices were fluttering like startled pigeons.

My Auntie Poldi guessed that the whole of Torre Archirafi already knew what had happened. Seated in a basketwork chair, she drank one espresso after another as she watched Montana's colleagues from forensics attacking the lion with brushes loaded with colophony. The lion stoically submitted to this treatment, sullenly hugging its coat of arms and defiantly crouching on the terrace wall as if determined never to abandon that position. The intruder had knocked off half its hind paws and half its tail in his attempt to detach it from the wall. How sad, thought Poldi, filled with compassion for the gallant beast.

Adhering to the inside of her arm was a plaster where the doctor on call had taken a blood sample. She was utterly exhausted, longing for sleep and oblivion. And for a beer.

Montana propped the musket against the parapet and sat down beside her. "Did you really shout 'Bang'?"

"I blurted it out in the heat of battle, so to speak."

She eyed Montana closely to see if he was grinning. He wasn't at all.

"And you didn't recognize him?"

"He was wearing a mask."

"What about his movements, his voice?"

She shook her head. "He wasn't particularly athletic, that's for sure."

"Anyone you suspect?"

"Well, putting two and two together, he's probably the person who slipped me the knockout drops."

Montana nodded. "What else can you remember?"

"Nothing. Almost nothing. Black shoes."

Montana held out the bag containing the bloodstained handkerchief, which she had previously given him. "Whose is this? When and why did you bag it?"

"I told you, Vito, I don't remember. I don't have the faintest idea."

"What's the very last thing you remember?"

Poldi sighed. "I'd like to get some shut-eye now, Vito. I didn't have a very good night, you know."

"You were extremely lucky, Poldi. If you hadn't been sick, you'd have been out for far longer."

"For good, you mean?"

Montana cleared his throat, and Poldi

could see he was genuinely concerned. That pleased her.

"We'll see what the lab says."

"Perhaps it was the same stuff you found in Valentino."

"Not that that would prove anything."

"Oh, Vito."

The forensics team were packing up their equipment.

Montana got to his feet. "Assistente Rizzoli will stay with you today, just in case."

"Can't *you* stay?"

Having briefly checked to see if his colleagues were watching, Montana grasped her hand. "I'm going to find the bastard. We'll be seeing each other again very soon."

Poldi felt like crying; not only because of her physical condition, but because it was always the same: whenever anyone had told her "See you soon," he or she had really meant "Goodbye forever." To Poldi, that sentence belonged in the shredder, like "There's a lot to be said for it," or "I'm really going to leave it at one beer tonight." She had a whole list of such self-deluding headlines. "See you soon" was in fourth place. First place went to the unbeatable "I really have changed."

But she pulled herself together and even managed to smile.

"Go get him, tiger."

Aunt Teresa, who turned up an hour later, shooed Poldi into bed and joined Assistente Rizzoli, a chubby-cheeked young police sergeant, in keeping watch while she slept. Poldi slept all that day and all the following night. The aunts took turns, and Assistente La Rosa relieved Assistente Rizzoli, who relieved Assistente La Rosa. Uncle Martino brought reinforcements in the shape of Totti, and Totti lay down outside Poldi's bedroom door and refused to budge. Poldi was unaware of all this. She never knew that Montana had paid a flying visit and dashed off again, or that Valérie had also looked in, dismayed by the night's events and the condition of her lion.

"They'll soon catch him, of course," said Aunt Caterina.

But Valérie brushed this aside. "There's absolutely no hurry. I'm just worried about Poldi. Do you think she's still in danger as long as the lion is here?"

Good question.

The aunts, who naturally feared the worst, decided to have a serious talk with Poldi.

But she didn't emerge from her bedroom until the next day, after almost thirty hours' sleep, reasonably refreshed, showered, made-up and looking like a resurrected saint in her white caftan.

"Some scrambled eggs and a big pot of coffee would be just the job."

She got them, followed by the serious talking-to.

"You must give up this investigation," Aunt Teresa told her. "It's becoming too dangerous."

Poldi looked at each of her sisters-in-law in turn, then at Uncle Martino, Assistente Rizzoli and Totti.

"Is that what you all think?"

The aunts nodded, Uncle Martino nodded, and Totti looked concerned. Assistente Rizzoli gestured defensively and abstained.

Good lad, thought Poldi. She continued to drink coffee and listen to the sounds spilling into the courtyard from the street.

"The case may soon be solved," she said at length.

"That makes it all the more unnecessary for you to go on investigating. Montana will soon catch Valentino's murderer," said Aunt Caterina.

Assistente Rizzoli backed her up. "Sure thing."

"Has Montana called?" asked Poldi.

"He looked in briefly and asked after you."

"I see. So he asked after me. Hasn't he arrested anyone yet?"

"Poldi." Teresa's tone became a mite sharper. "You're off the case."

"Says who?"

The aunts just looked at Poldi. Uncle Martino and Rizzoli kept out of it. Totti continued to look worried.

Poldi had never been the type to welcome interference in her life. On the contrary, as soon as she scented even the slightest attempt to manipulate her, she turned stubborn. She addressed herself to the dog. "What do *you* say, Totti?" They conducted a brief dialogue without words, then Poldi sighed and sat back in her chair. "What day is it today?"

"Sunday."

"Sunday again already. My, how time flies. Life simply trickles through one's fingers."

"You're off the case, Poldi," Teresa repeated softly.

Poldi waved this away. "Of course. I may be tired of life, but I'm not stupid. If anyone ends my mortal existence before it's time, it'll be me and nobody else." She drew a deep breath as if that said it all, relishing the aunts' surprise at her unresisting acquiescence. "So what shall we do with the rest of Sunday?"

"Let's go to the lido," Aunt Luisa cried eagerly.

It should be explained that my Aunt Luisa had scaled the Olympus of Catanian high society some years ago by becoming a member of the exclusive Lido Galatea, a sort of fashionable beach club without a beach, because the entire lido was concreted out into the sea on volcanic rock and was little more than a big swimming pool with a shack beside it.

As a rule, a lido is a private section of beach where loungers, sun umbrellas and cabins can be rented. It usually boasts a small restaurant, or at least a snack bar, and, of course, toilets and showers. Usually inexpensive, these amenities certainly make for more comfort than lying on a towel on the sand. In addition to comfort, however, a lido provides a definite boost to one's *bella figura.* Most Italians consequently have a favourite lido on their favourite beach and are as steadfastly loyal to it as they are to their local football club. In this connection, my Auntie Poldi once told me the following joke. Two shipwrecked Sicilians are rescued after years on a desert island. The captain of the rescue ship is amazed to see that the pair have installed three lidos on their island. "Why three?" he asks in bewilderment. "Well," replies Carmelo, "one for me, one for Massimo, and one we don't patronize."

Any regular patron of a lido usually rents a changing cabin for the whole season from Easter to the end of October. No form of membership is necessary unless the lido is a particularly smart one with all the trimmings. A lido designed for certain people who prefer to remain among their own kind and are happy to pay for the privilege. One that possesses a privacy wall, a supervised car park and security in general, together with childcare and handsome young lifeguards in briefs and polo shirts adorned with badges, miniature umbrellas in the drinks and Wi-Fi. A lido that is turbocharged in respect of *bella figura*. One like the Lido Galatea, named after the nymph that turned the head of Polyphemus the Cyclops. Appropriate somehow, given that heads are always turning to look at someone in the Lido Galatea, which is noted for its abundance of nymphs accompanied by Cyclopes of mature years. By dint of perseverance and a lucky break, Aunt Luisa had acquired membership and shared a cabin there with her friend Ilaria. And the best part of being a member was that one could bring guests.

In the best of spirits, Aunt Luisa showed

her membership card at the entrance and watched with satisfaction as Poldi, Teresa and Caterina were each handed a guest card.

"If you'd like a drink, Poldi — a lemonade or a granita, I mean — I'll give you my card and they'll put it on the tab. It's very practical."

"Aha."

Poldi surveyed the establishment with a jaundiced eye. She had no objection to sunning herself a little, paddling in the sea with Prosecco in hand and having a good time, but she harboured a fundamental aversion to any kind of smart set. For Luisa's sake she refrained from passing any remarks about plutocratic Cyclopes and their nymphs, made herself comfortable on a lounger in the sun, and marinaded herself in coconut oil. When in Rome, she told herself.

But a leopard can't change its spots. The sun's rays gradually restored Poldi's vitality, and the more desperately she strove to recall what had happened before her blackout, the more dangerously her level of melancholy rose like the juice in a battery on charge. From the sun-lounger upon which she was sucking orangeade through a straw, Poldi sneered at all the oiled flesh, tasteless designer bikinis, men in tanga briefs and noisy children staring at their brand-new smartphones and texting each other or experimenting unsupervised with their fathers' spear guns. Meanwhile, the fathers stood around in groups in the tepid water, pleasurably scratching their hairy chests and pontificating about the stock market, their mothers' cooking or their nymphs' physical assets. When Poldi's melancholy level passed the critical threshold, her patience snapped and she succumbed to a little attack of socialism.

"Just look at those big shots," she growled to the aunts, who had no idea what was going on. "They're criminals, I tell you, all of them. What's more, they think they can buy back their youth with the proceeds of their exploitation, the filthy neo-cons. They worship the god of profit — they'd unscrupulously sacrifice all the achievements of the Enlightenment to it, plus the rainforests, personal privacy and the future of Africa. Constitutional democracy and the United Nations — those are the bugbears of oligarchs and Mafiosi. All they're interested in is consecrating the global market and bending the entire world to their will. They aim to dominate humanity, and we all play along. We happily dance the rumba of decadence and consumerism."

That said it all.

Luisa stared at Poldi in bewilderment. "Eh? What?"

"Come on, you know what I mean."

As pleased and appeased as a bull terrier that has just torn its master's favourite sweater to shreds, Poldi was about to cool off in the water a little when she caught sight of Russo beneath a sun umbrella. Despite its exclusivity the Lido Galatea is a pretty big place, and on Sundays, when several hundred people are crowded together there, it is easy to overlook the odd acquaintance.

On his own from the look of it, Russo was making phone calls and nodding genially in all directions. The sight of him so infuriated Poldi that the curtain of oblivion lifted a little after all, affording her a brief glimpse of her memories' *mise en scène.* She saw Russo and Patanè quarrelling between the parked cars, which proves what a liberating effect misanthropy can have on one's mnemonic capacity. Determined to disinter her buried memories by means of a clarifying interview with Russo, Poldi heaved herself off the lounger and headed for him. On the way there, however, she made a further discovery: Russo had ended his latest phone call and was nodding to someone on his left. The latter, who was also lying on a lounger, raised his hand and they exchanged a few friendly words. Two men paying each other due respect — always a pleasant sight; but it knocked Poldi sideways.

Because the other man was Montana.

Montana with a woman all of twenty years younger. Tanned, athletic figure, black bikini, mane of hair. She looked self-assured and happy, like a thirty-something who has already ridden out some of life's storms and emerged with a few cuts and bruises but is still successful, still beautiful. A woman who gets what she wants, who may well be smart, even amusing. In other words, not a welcome sight from Poldi's point of view.

Stretched out on a lounger beside Montana, the woman was showing off what she had — not a great deal, in my aunt's opinion — and laughing heartily whenever he said something. She rested her hand on his upper thigh and gave him periodic little kisses — the kind that dispelled any hope she might simply be his sister or a good friend of long standing.

Poldi felt sick.

The two turtle doves didn't notice her until she was standing over them.

"Hello, Vito."

Montana stared at her in dismay but was so startled he remained glued to his lounger.

"Poldi. What are you doing here?"

"I could ask you the same thing, but don't worry, I'm not staying. Would you care to introduce your friend?"

The woman didn't even remove her sunglasses. "This is Alessia. Alessia, Poldi."

"Good afternoon." Alessia drawled the words so they sounded like a question, and didn't shake hands. The situation seemed to be dawning on her.

"I won't disturb you," said Poldi, a marvel of poise and self-control. "Have a nice day."

But before she could go about in a dignified manner and sail off close-hauled, Montana sprang to his feet and caught her by the arm. "Let me explain, Poldi."

"What for, Vito? You don't owe me any explanation. We're adults, after all."

"I've been wanting to talk to you about Alessia for ages."

"That would have been most amusing, I'm sure," Poldi said with an effort. "Over a pleasant dinner for three, is that what you mean? You'd better let go of me or I'll make a regular stinker of a scene. Then you'd really have some explaining to do to Alessia and your nice Sunday would be ruined. On the other hand, it already is, so what the hell."

Montana released her arm and gazed at her earnestly. "I'll call you. But give me a little time, okay?"

"I need a little time" — another self-deceptive phrase. Number three on Poldi's list. Her one wish was to get away, go somewhere where she could weep and drink in peace. And preferably, so she thought at that moment, simply drop out of the world and evaporate.

"You'd better not call me, Vito," she said harshly. "If you want to discuss the situation with anyone, simply ask your pal Russo."

"Listen, Poldi, I —"

But no, my aunt wasn't listening any more. She hurried back to Luisa, Caterina and Teresa, who had been watching the unpleasant encounter at a distance. Poldi had no need to explain much. Aunt Luisa handed over her caftan without a word, Teresa stuffed all their things into the beach bag, and Caterina steered Poldi out of the lido. It wasn't until they were all in the car that the other three couldn't restrain themselves any longer and asked for details. Poldi wasn't in the mood for talking, however, or even for weeping; she wasn't in the mood for anything except going home.

"Tell me something. What's the Italian for 'disciplinary complaint'?"

"*Denuncia disciplinare.* Why?"

"Oh, just asking."

But the aunts weren't stupid.

"What are you planning to do, Poldi?"

"Oh, shed a few tears, pull the covers over my head and call down curses on the dirty dog. Tomorrow is another day."

The aunts already suspected that Poldi was on the brink of another breakdown, and that Project *Joie de Vivre* was in the balance, so they impressed on Assistente Rizzoli, who was waiting in Via Baronessa like a stray cat, that she mustn't be allowed to drink.

A mission doomed to fail from the outset, of course, because Poldi had devised a plan on the drive home. Scarcely had the reluctant aunts left her alone with Rizzoli when she sent Montana a rather unfriendly text message embodying the term *denuncia disciplinare.*

The young policeman's mobile phone rang soon afterwards. He listened, said "Hm" and "But —" and "Yessir," then hung up, looking puzzled.

"I'm afraid I have to go, signora. Commissario Montana's orders."

"No problem," Poldi said happily. "I can manage."

Rizzoli hesitated. "Your sisters-in-law said you —"

"Don't worry about me, I can look after myself. Thanks for everything, and have a nice Sunday."

When she was alone at last, Poldi drove quickly to the HiperSimply to get in some supplies for the next few days. The party could begin.

But it didn't. It simply couldn't achieve lift-off; just gave a little jerk and then got stuck like an antiquated lift. Poldi climbed to the roof terrace with a stiff gin and tonic, flopped down in the basketwork chair, and raised her glass to the mutilated gate lion.

"Here's to you, my friend."

The ice cubes tinkled their serenade of coolness and refreshment, the scent of juniper hummed its promise of farewell and oblivion, the tonic promised tears and bitterness, the sun went down behind Etna, and the sea was as heartrendingly blue as Poldi planned to be before long. Another shitty day was drawing to a close. High time to round the bend into life's finishing straight, thought my aunt.

But human beings are allied to nature by special ties, and free will can sometimes be a capricious companion. Whether it was the light, the beauty of a summer evening, the balmy air, the murmur of the sea or the sound of Signora Anzalone laughing next door, Poldi couldn't get a drop down. She wanted to. She really wanted to. She was thirsty, she had a plan, and she had plenty of supplies.

But she kept raising the glass and putting it down. She watched the ice cubes leave a shimmering trail as they melted. She prepared once more to take at least a sip. "Drink-me-drink-me-drink-me," begged the gin and tonic. "Bottoms-up-bottoms-up." But she still couldn't do it. She tipped the drink into the gutter and tried some straight tonic for once. And it worked — it tasted of disappointment and slaked the worst of her thirst — but as soon as she added even a dash of gin, the strange embargo reimposed itself. She tried whisky, rum, grappa. Same result. Worse still, although she longed with every fibre of her being to get well and truly drunk, she felt sick if she so much as caught a whiff of alcohol. An entirely new development. Her body was poking fun at her, the lion fixing her with its sullen gaze.

"I get it," Poldi said grumpily. "Your Lordship objects. May I ask why?"

The lion said nothing.

"I see. But this won't get us anywhere, my friend."

The lion said nothing.

"Afraid I've got to contradict you. I'm absolutely done with the case — don't want anything more to do with it. Montana will solve it. Or not. Then they'll all raise a glass to success — Vito, his friend Russo and the lovely Alessia. I couldn't care less, because it's all the same to me. I'm off the case for good."

She paused to give the lion a chance to reply.

The lion said nothing.

"Yes, says the know-all who's been hiding up here all the time. I know I made Valentino a promise, but I can't go on, *capisci*? I'm through. I'm an old bag with a screw loose, talking to a stone lion even when she's sober."

The lion still said nothing.

"You find that funny, do you? Well, it's all over. That's that. I'm off the case, and tomorrow, my friend — tomorrow my gin and tonic will taste good once more, you'll see."

On that note she terminated the conversation and made her way downstairs, intending to go to bed.

I don't know if my Auntie Poldi wept that

night or the next; she didn't tell me. Sometimes, though, sorrow simply lies too deep, clinging to one like a difficult child and blocking all the exits. *Rien ne va plus.* I picture Poldi listening for ages to "Gloria" with the volume turned up full. *"Chiesa di campagna, Gloria. Acqua nel deserto, Gloria."* I picture her smoking far too much, clattering bottles together, calling down obscene curses on Montana, the Sicilians and life in general, and eventually falling into an exhausted sleep on the sofa.

When she woke the next morning with a headache from too many cigarettes and a surfeit of disappointment, and when she left the house to get some fresh *cornetti* from the Bar Cocuzza, there was a cat lying outside her front door with its throat cut.

12

Tells of cats, a lion and a phoenix. Poldi writes an epitaph, compiles a new list and finds an egg. On receiving a veritable revelation, she knows where to go and is expected there. She mobilizes Aunt Teresa and Uncle Martino and is forced to accept that nobody gets any answers unless they ask questions. She also learns that Sicily boasts many places with odd names, and that — with a bit of luck — nice surprises can be found there.

I had a rather embarrassing experience on my most recent visit to Torre Archirafi. I had slept badly and emerged from my lair in the attic earlier than usual, meaning to make myself some coffee in the kitchen and accelerate my progress with Chapter One. Poldi was already standing at the stove, stark naked except for her wig and waiting for the espresso pot to emit its final hiss. I don't have a problem with naked bodies, ageing naked bodies included, really I don't. When it's your own aunt, though, you feel strangely self-conscious. I did anyway, I admit. I stammered an apology and hurriedly retreated up the stairs.

"Hey, what's the matter?" Poldi called after me.

"Oh, nothing. I can wait till you're dressed."

"Am I embarrassing you?"

"No, no, everything's fine. I just thought of a phrase — I must get it down on paper."

"My, how inhibited you are. Come back, I'll put something on."

When I returned after waiting a minute for safety's sake, she had donned a colourful sarong that barely covered her and was down in the courtyard, pouring two cups of coffee. "One question, just for interest's sake" was her greeting. "Are you always such a shrinking violet when it comes to the female form, or is it my age?"

"Neither one nor the other," I essayed bravely. "But in your case I make an exception."

"Bravo, Mr. Author. Still half asleep and sharp as a knife already."

I joined her at the table and took the coffee she handed me. "Listen, Poldi, it's nothing to do with your age, honestly it's not, but you're my aunt. I couldn't help feeling a bit —"

"Inhibited, as I said."

"Call it what you like. I'm not going to apologize for feeling embarrassed."

"In summer we always used to go around naked in the old days, not only at home but beside the Isar and in the Englischer Garten."

"Good for you."

"My, what a sensitive soul you are. Are there any — you know, *passages* in your novel? I mean . . ." She looked at me expectantly.

"Yes, I know what you mean, and yes, of course there'll be some sex scenes, but all very artistic and tasteful."

She cast her eyes heavenwards. "Then give them to me to titivate when you get there. They need to be really *juicy,* know what I mean? Anyone who pays good money for your novel is entitled to some *meat.*"

I left it at that and drank my coffee, but I did have one question for her. During those few moments in the kitchen when Poldi had confronted me in such a state of undress, I had caught a glimpse of something on her left breast — something roughly the size of a beer mat, so not exactly small.

"Tell me, Poldi, what's that tattoo on your bosom?"

"Ah, so you noticed that, did you?"

Without ado, she undid the sarong from around her neck and let it fall. On your own head be it, I told myself, and forced myself to examine her tattoo with the professionalism of an art critic. It must once have been very colourful, but time and regular sunbathing had robbed the colours of nearly all their luminosity.

At first sight it looked to me like a cave drawing that a Stone Age shaman had daubed on the wall of a pitch-dark cave. Black streaks seemingly applied with raw charcoal looked as if they had risen to the surface from untold depths. These framed various coloured planes which ran into each other and merged like dabs of watercolour. I made out a species of fantasy bird with a short, parrot-like beak and a long, curly tail. The strange creature seemed to be crowing and spreading its wings in readiness to flutter into the air at any time. It looked as if it was straining and stretching as if loyalty to my aunt were all that was keeping it in its habitual place over her left breast. The longer I studied this tattoo, the more obvious it became that it was the work of a true master, not a botch-up perpetrated by a kifstoned amateur. The thing on Poldi's breast was definitely art.

"Wow" was all I said.

"Isn't it just," Poldi said proudly. "That's a phoenix rising from the ashes. I had it done by an anchorite monk at Pattaya in 1975. Everyone went to him. There wasn't much to do in Pattaya in those days — we were the first, so to speak. We discovered the place, the Swedish nudists and I. They all went around in the buff and got themselves tattooed. What shall I get him to do? I asked Benny. Björn and Benny were also there, you see. We'd all recognized them and knew they were world stars, of course, but nobody made a hoo-ha about it because we were all the same on the beach at Pattaya. That's because we were all naked, with free love and all the trimmings, naturally. Benny used to send me an occasional postcard later on, but the phoenix idea was my own. I realized early on it was my symbol — my totem, you know? Life is change, I told Benny, so you have to keep reinventing yourself. You may come a cropper or even get burnt, but you simply have to rise from the ashes. Because, as I told Benny, it's a question of the winner taking it all." Poldi assumed the expression she always wore when immersing herself in sentimental memories. "The winner takes it all," she repeated. "Benny liked that. He knew exactly what a phoenix is."

My aunt also knew a thing or two about phoenixes and rising from the ashes.

Poldi obviously realized that the dead cat outside her door was intended as a warning to drop the Valentino case once and for all. Possibly even to quit Torre Archirafi or Sicily, though she wasn't willing as yet to credit the cat killer with so extreme a demand. His message was unmistakable whichever way one looked at it.

The Via Baronessa was quieter than usual that morning. No moped was blatting, no radio blaring, no one could be seen or heard. It was as if the death of the little creature had expunged all signs of life from the street. Poldi bent down and carefully picked up the animal. A young tortoise-shell tom with a half-chewed ear, very thin and stiff as a washboard, it was only an ownerless stray, but to Poldi that was irrelevant. Someone had snuffed out a life in order to threaten her — had possibly lured the hungry creature with a morsel of fish and then cold-bloodedly slit its throat, just like that. Whoever had done this had no respect for life, no concern for creation, and in Poldi's view he himself deserved no respect or concern for that reason. Whoever it was that had killed the tortoise-shell tom, she hoped he would rot in hell, swore to find him and call him to account.

But first she buried the cat.

Having wrapped the animal in an old pillowcase, she took a spade and drove to a small patch of wasteland that had recently caught her eye not far from the cemetery in Acireale. There, amid gorse bushes and wild fennel, she dug a small hole in the black volcanic soil, carefully laid the bundle in it and weighed it down with a stone to prevent any dogs from digging it up. She improvised a small cross out of two sticks and some florist's wire and stuck it in the cat's grave. She also attached a small note to the cross. It read:

NAMASTE TO THE UNKNOWN CAT

And then, like a big wave after a long ebb tide, everything came back to her. She recalled all that had happened on the night of the wedding — every last thing. She also realized only now that she had recognized the intruder on the roof by one tiny detail.

"*Namaste,* pussycat," Poldi said quietly.

"I'm going to get that swine, I most certainly am."

It was now clear that everything was connected, everything had a deeper meaning. Perhaps the little tomcat had prevented her from getting drunk last night, so that she would find its corpse with a clear head and then recover her memory. This meant that she now owed it to the dead cat to solve the case, not just to Valentino.

Now more than ever.

The first thing Poldi did when she got home was re-examine her corkboard, which she had put back on the wall, and go through her notes. What did she know? Where had she got to? Who could be ruled out?

She made another list.

UNRESOLVED
  red sand
  topographical map
  cash at Valentino's
  knockout drops Femminamorta
  Valérie's phone
  murder motive
  ~~Montana (personal)~~

RESOLVED
  Tannenberger (Mr. X)
  Montana (personal)

A definite misunderstanding. Poldi felt in her handbag and found the paper napkin with the list of names.

RUSSO
PATANÈ
TANNENBERGER
VALÉRIE
~~HÖLDERLIN~~ MIMÌ
TURI

One of them had called Valentino from Valérie's phone. All of them had been at the wedding party. One of them must have slipped the knockout drops into her wine. One of them had broken into her house and possibly killed the unknown cat as well.

One of them had killed Valentino. But why?

Poldi stepped back from her corkboard for a better overall view, but it wasn't enough, so she went up to the roof. To the sea, Etna and the lion. And there she asked herself another question: why had the intruder run such a risk for the sake of a stone lion that might earn him a mere thousand euros? The lion itself clearly disapproved of this question, because it promptly looked a trifle more dyspeptic, but Poldi was undeterred. The only explanation she could find was that the intruder must have been interested in something more than just the lion.

In no time at all Poldi had armed herself with a hammer and chisel and was preparing to take up where the intruder had left off. It was a devil of a job. Valentino must have used the hardest cement in Italy. The sweat was trickling from under Poldi's wig after only a few hammer blows, but she persevered until she had chipped off the cement all round the base of the lion and was able to detach it from the wall completely with a vigorous jerk.

Panting hard, Poldi hefted the lion off the wall and onto the floor of the terrace. *Clunk, clunk, clunk.* Something went rolling across the floor. A small metal capsule that had been lodged in a recess in the base of the stone gatekeeper: an old, egg-shaped tea infuser composed of two halves screwed together. Inside was a closely written inventory with prices listed in date order. In short, the murder motive.

"The winner takes it all," I said when Poldi told me all this.

"As I told you," she said. "At that moment I also recalled what Tannenberger had said in Munich — that Valentino had found something someone would pay him a lot of

money to keep quiet about. I naturally realized that that something could only be this
list."

"And who was Valentino putting the
squeeze on?"

"My, aren't you impatient. One thing at a
time."

Poldi did, of course, have a definite suspicion, but she had to prove it before she
could rub Montana's nose in it. And in
order to do that she first had to stir up a lot
of dust. Red dust.

But one thing at a time. First came some
arithmetic. Poldi added up the individual
sums on the list and arrived at a total of
over two million euros. The most expensive
item was a complete seventeenth-century
fresco for half a million. There couldn't have
been a better motive for murder.

Still taking one thing at a time, Poldi
found that the last item on the list was dated
more than a year earlier. She compared that
date with the newspaper reports of thefts
from old country houses and found a match.
The first report of such a theft was dated
one day later. The subsequent dates also
predated similar newspaper reports by a day
or two. Poldi said "Bingo," kissed her
corkboard and blessed Uncle Martino for
his thorough research work. Uncle Martino

had Swiss ancestors, and that leaves its genetic mark on a person. Swissness combined with oriental generosity and Sicilian crisis management produces psychological mettle of the very finest quality.

Poldi made it her next step to check off all the listed dates on a calendar, and was surprised to find that every one of them had fallen on a Saturday.

"And what does that tell us?" she asked me later.

"No idea."

"Think. Why Saturday, do you reckon?"

"Go on, tell me."

"A little tip: because Sunday is the Lord's day, and one can have a good lie-in."

"What's the connection between that and theft?"

"Why, nothing as a rule. Not unless the thief has a strenuous full-time job and needs to recuperate if he spends the whole night stealing from country houses."

"That's pretty far-fetched," I ventured to object.

"But I'd recognized the intruder, don't forget, so I was bound to put two and two together."

At that point in her investigations, Poldi had a flash of inspiration. She was "in the zone." It was pure intuition. She had simply seen the full picture. She went to the phone and called Valérie.

"Just a quick question, my dear. I need an address from you."

That evening she rang the doorbell of a small house situated on a bend in the Provinciale just before Riposto. Not the best of locations, it must be said, and the house itself was a little old cottage with peeling walls. Behind it, however, Poldi made out an almond orchard, and no one who owns a cottage and an almond orchard is a total pauper.

The windows of the little house were tightly shuttered in the usual Sicilian way, and no sounds were coming from inside. It wasn't until she had rung the bell a second time that Poldi heard a suspicious voice.

"Who is it?"

"Donna Poldina."

Poldi heard shuffling footsteps and coughing. Then the door opened a crack, and a face filled with suspicion and apprehension peered out of the frowsty interior.

"What do you want?"

"Good evening, Turi. I think we need to talk."

The old agricultural labourer peered around mistrustfully.

"I'm on my own, Turi, and that's the way

338

it'll stay if you let me in."

"I can't think what you want from me, Donna Poldina."

Poldi said nothing.

Turi hesitated, then sighed and let her in. The house was gloomy and stuffy. The heat of the day still lingered in its interior, which was redolent of sweat, old age and solitude. Two well-fed cats were romping around on the worn old sofa in the living room, which also contained a shabby carpet and a flat-screen television. The whole house shook as a lorry thundered past outside.

"Let's go into the orchard," said Turi. "It's quieter out there. Would you like some iced tea?"

"Please," said Poldi. The old man was limping, she saw. "How's the leg?"

Turi turned and gave her a sorrowful look. "Oh, Donna Poldina, you almost shot me like a mad dog."

Poldi nodded. "You shouldn't have jumped over the wall like that."

"But you fired at me."

"I didn't. I just shouted 'Bang.' "

"You shouted *what*?"

"Bang."

"You didn't fire?"

"Certainly not."

"But I heard the bullet whizz past me."

"Pure imagination. My old musket can't fire."

Turi shook his head in bewilderment. "I'm getting too old for these things."

"How old are you, Turi?"

"Seventy-two."

"You really ought to retire."

"How can I, Donna Poldina? I can't survive on my pension alone." Having rinsed two glasses, he took an old mineral water bottle full of amber-coloured iced tea from the refrigerator and filled them.

"Would you care for some lemon ice in it?"

"Yes, please."

Taking a spoon, Turi scooped some water ice from a plastic mug, carefully stirred it into the golden liquid, and then led the way out into the orchard. The forty-odd almond trees arrayed there in neat rows were heavy with furry green capsules. Turi had planted a vegetable garden along the wall and installed a plastic table and two chairs nearby. In the background the traffic on the main road roared past like an unpleasant but inextinguishable memory, though the orchard itself made a quiet, peaceful impression. The two cats, which had followed Turi and Poldi outside, were aimlessly roaming around and mewing. Turi coaxed them over by clicking his tongue. They played coy at first, but then the fatter of the two leapt onto his lap and consented to be stroked. The other did the honours with Poldi.

"Nice orchard," said Poldi.

"A lot of work."

Poldi stroked the cat, sipped her iced tea, which tasted both sweet and bitter, and waited.

"How did you recognize me?" asked Turi.

"When you raised your hands on the roof, one finger of your left-hand glove hung limp."

Turi held up his left hand, the one with the little finger missing. "*Madonna*, you mean to say you noticed that in the dark?"

"To be honest, it only occurred to me this morning." Poldi's cat had evidently had enough. It leapt off her lap and retired into the shade of an almond tree, leaving a warm patch of white hairs on her skirt. My aunt stroked the cat hairs into a little ball with her fingers. "Somebody left a dead cat outside my front door this morning. With its throat cut."

"*Madonna*," Turi exclaimed in dismay. "Surely you don't think I —"

"No, not now. Any idea who it could have been?"

He slowly shook his head, which might

341

have meant either that he really didn't know or that he didn't want to say. "May he roast in hell."

"He will."

"I didn't kill Valentino."

"So who did?"

"If I knew that, I'd have gone to the police a long time ago, believe me. Valentino was a good lad."

"And there's no one you suspect?"

Turi shook his head again, this time decisively. He stared at his almond trees in silence.

"Who was Valentino blackmailing?" asked Poldi. "Russo or Patanè?"

"I don't know, Donna Poldina. I had an idea Valentino was in some kind of trouble, but he never spoke to me about it."

"Then why did you call him from Valérie's phone the night before his death?"

"What? I didn't. Why should I use Signorina Belfiore's telephone, anyway? I have a mobile phone of my own. Besides, everyone knows that phone is rubbish."

Poldi thought for a moment. "We're getting nowhere, Turi."

The old man stroked his cat. "Are you going to the police, then?"

A difficult question. Poldi sighed. It was such a nice evening, too. The moon was rising above the almond trees, greeted by countless cicadas.

"You know the joke about God making Sicily out of bits of clay left over from the five continents?" asked Poldi.

"The one where He creates the Sicilians to even things up?"

"That's the one."

Turi nodded. "Great joke. Why?"

Poldi shrugged her shoulders. "I suddenly remembered it, that's all. You're still a thief and a burglar, Turi."

"I'm really sorry I broke in. I shouldn't have got involved, but I'm no thief."

"No? What about all those country houses?"

"But Donna Poldina, those weren't robberies." And he proceeded to explain.

When Poldi got home late that evening with a basket of ripe tomatoes and a big lump of *pasta di mandorle,* she was in high spirits. The first thing she did was strike Turi off her list of suspects, which now read:

RUSSO
PATANÈ
TANNENBERGER
VALÉRIE

HÖLDERLIN MIMÌ
TURI

Only five names left, and one of those she
could really have struck off after listening to
Turi's account, but she was reluctant to be
overhasty. One thing at a time. She didn't
want to call Montana either, for one thing
because of the lido episode but also because
she had given Turi her word. Besides, one
important piece of the puzzle was still missing: the scene of the crime.

But Poldi was a step closer to that as well.

Despite the lateness of the hour, she called
Aunt Teresa.

"Has something happened?" Teresa demanded, instantly on the alert.

"Don't worry, I'm absolutely fine."

"Have you been drinking?"

"No, I'm stone-cold sober. Listen, I need
your help — or rather, Martino's. Could
the two of you drop in here early tomorrow
morning?"

Teresa's suspicions were promptly
aroused, of course.

"What's it about?"

"Why," said Poldi with lamb-like innocence, "the case, of course."

A brief silence.

"I thought you intended to drop it."

"I did, but there's just been an important development. It's like a stalled car. If we give it a little push, it may start. Then the case will be solved."

Teresa reinjected some steel into her voice. "Tell all that to Montana. You're off the case, Poldi."

"You've no idea how utterly depressed I'm feeling."

My Auntie Poldi was adept at subtle hints, disguised threats and delicate allusions.

"Is that a threat, Poldi?"

"No, it's just that I'm so emotionally unstable."

Teresa emitted a grunt of disapproval. "What sort of help?"

"Just local knowledge, that's all. We might go on a little trip."

"A trip?"

"Not far. Please, Teresa."

Poldi heard her sister-in-law say something unintelligible to Martino, the only word she distinguished being *amore.*" Soon afterwards she heard Totti bark and knew it was a done deal.

Martino, Teresa and Totti appeared on the doorstep on the stroke of nine the next morning. Poldi, who was again wearing her khaki linen outfit with the uniform jacket, had everything ready. On the table in the courtyard was a pitcher of ice-cold almond milk made with Turi's *pasta di mandorle,* and beside it the photo of the topographical map, the rolled-up strip of paper from the lion, and a map of Sicily with the thefts of recent months marked on it. Poldi was trembling with excitement. So was Totti, and Martino was only just controlling himself. Aunt Teresa alone remained entirely cool because Poldi's little attempt at blackmail still rankled with her. She calmly sampled the almond milk.

"Excellent. How did you make it?"

"With my informant's *pasta di mandorle.*"

Teresa ignored the keyword. "It's really excellent."

Poldi got the message. "Please forgive me, Teresa. The bit about being depressed just slipped out."

Teresa put her glass down. "So who is this informant?"

When describing this scene to me, my Auntie Poldi broke off to interpolate a little footnote. "The thing is," she said, "all your aunts are Taureans, which means they never bear a grudge. They're the opposite of Scorpios, and I know what I'm talking about. Make one mistake with a Scorpio, drop one little clanger, and you'll be on their blacklist for the rest of your days.

Sooner or later, when you've forgotten all about it long ago — ouch, they sting you."

"Who was the Scorpio in this case?" I asked.

"Oh, that would be going too far."

"I mean, did that play a role in your investigations?"

Poldi looked at me as if I'd just discovered the formula for world peace. Without another word she disappeared into her bedroom, rummaged in the cardboard box containing her investigative notes, and eventually turned up what she was looking for.

"Hallelujah," I heard her cry. "Now I'll believe anything."

"So who was the Scorpio?" I asked when she returned.

Instead of replying, she showed me a slip of paper.

"All three?" I exclaimed in bewilderment.

"You bet. And one of them is Valentino's murderer."

But back to that morning in the courtyard. Poldi kept quiet about the identity of her "informant," as she had promised. With due brevity, she gave an account of recent developments, including the dead cat, the restoration of her memory and the discovery of the antiquities price list.

347

"My informant confessed that he took part in the thefts with Valentino. But they weren't real thefts because they all took place with the tacit approval of the owner of the houses, who naturally took his cut."

"Why on earth should he do such a thing?"

"Because he's broke."

"Then he could simply have sold the houses."

"Yes, but only with the land that goes with them, and that's what the gentleman wanted to hang on to."

"Who?" demanded Teresa.

"Mimì Pastorella di Belfiore, of course. All the looted houses belong to him. That's to say, the ownership of some of the properties is unclear. He may not have wished to go shares with his relations."

"Then it remains theft," said Teresa.

"In principle, yes," Poldi conceded. "Valentino used that to blackmail Patanè, too."

"Are you sure?"

"It's obvious."

"Patanè is Valentino's murderer, you mean?" Uncle Martino chimed in.

"I'm convinced of it. Patanè compelled my informant to break in and steal the lion. That's why it was probably him that slipped the knockout drops into my wine, the same

348

as he did with Valentino. So he's the murderer. I'm sure it was also him that left the dead cat outside my door."

"You must speak to Montana at once, then."

Poldi shook her head. "I must prove it first, and for that we must find the scene of the crime."

"We?"

"Yes. The thing is, Valentino told me before his death that he had something important to do at Femminamorta, so I assumed that Valérie had something to do with it, because of the lion and Russo and so on. But yesterday my informant hinted that this wasn't necessarily so. Because — brace yourselves — there isn't just one Femminamorta in Sicily, there's a whole bunch of them."

Teresa and Martino exchanged a look.

Poldi was momentarily speechless.

"You knew that?"

"Of course," Teresa said with a shrug. "In Italy, Femminamorta is a far from uncommon name for small villages. Just like Donnafugata."

"Or Donnadolce," Martino amplified. "Or Occhiobello, Campodimiele, Buonvicino, Fiumelatte, Bastardo — even Baciaculo. They're all over the place."

Especially in the south, where people think more floridly and express themselves more bluntly. Poldi should really have thought of that, because place names such as Lovely Eye, Honey Field, Good Neighbour, Milk River, Bastard or Kiss Arse have similar counterparts in Bavaria. Many place names are coloured by stories and personal destinies dating from times gone by, and many personal destinies repeat themselves in one way or another. At Valérie's Femminamorta, near Riposto, a consumptive signorina whom everyone loved was said to have died during the eighteenth century. In another Femminamorta the "dead female" might have been murdered by a spurned admirer. At all events, the name was popular and catchy. Uncle Martino estimated that there were at least half a dozen Femminamortas in Sicily alone.

Poldi couldn't take it in. "But for God's sake, why did you never say anything?"

Embarrassed shoulder-shrugging. "You never asked."

That was true, too. Pragmatism was the only answer. My Auntie Poldi had never been one to fret for long over mistakes, faux pas or missed opportunities, because she knew a thing or two about coming unstuck, tripping up, making a fool of yourself and getting a bloody nose, just as she also did about starting afresh, picking yourself up, laughing at yourself and standing for no nonsense. I sometimes think that her only blind spot is not letting go.

She briefly vented her feelings with a characteristic obscenity, then spread out her map of Sicily on the table. "All right, Martino, where are all these Femminamortas?"

Uncle Martino vaguely tapped various places in the east and centre of the island.

"Can't you be more precise?"

He scratched his head uneasily. "It's been a while."

"Amore," Aunt Teresa said sternly. "Concentrate — don't let us down."

Us.

Poldi beamed.

Half a packet of MS later, Uncle Martino had made five red squiggles on the map. They were scattered all over the island and well away from towns.

"Is that the lot?" asked Poldi.

He raised his hands defensively. "They're as many as I can remember, and as I say, they're unofficial place names. Landed estates, small villages, sometimes just an old bridge described as such by the local peasants."

Poldi eyed the map morosely. "They're far

too scattered for us to visit them all." She firmly drew a line through two red squiggles in the north and south of the island. "Too far away."

Teresa and Martino said nothing.

Poldi compared the remaining sites with the photo she had taken in Taormina of the topographical map in Russo's transparent folder. The details did not correspond, but she tried nonetheless, turning the map this way and that. Unable to find a match, she angrily thrust it aside.

"Hell and damnation."

"Beh." Uncle Martino stubbed out his cigarette and looked at his watch. "Nearly midday. I'll just nip over to the fish market in Riposto."

"You're staying here. I won't be a moment."

Uncle Martino and Aunt Teresa looked at each other. Teresa almost imperceptibly shook her head, probably hoping that the situation would resolve itself and that Poldi's addiction to the thrill of the chase would gradually subside.

No such luck.

Poldi fetched her father's magnifying glass from the chest of drawers in the living room and used it to study the three remaining squiggles. She traced roads with her finger, deciphered place names, discovered churches, monasteries, archaeological sites and ruins, estimated distances, sighed, muttered to herself and denied herself a beer. At the edge of a squiggle which Martino had made near Piazza Armerina, near Enna, and almost obliterated by red ink, she eventually made out a cartographic symbol: an inverted miner's kit consisting of two crossed hammers.

"What does that mean?"

"An abandoned mine."

Poldi considered this. An idea took shape in her mind. Only a crumb of an idea, it detached itself from the depths of her subconscious and headed for the surface. Sluggishly borne upwards by the magma of molten memories, it got stuck halfway and made no further progress.

"What sort of mine?"

Uncle Martino glanced at the map. "An old sulphur mine, I should think."

Poldi could almost hear the pop as the little plug of an idea came adrift, shot into her consciousness and crystallized there. Jumping up, she dashed to the corkboard in her bedroom and returned with the photograph she'd taken in Valentino's room of his little collection of minerals. She tapped the yellow crystal at the edge of the print.

"Could something like that be found there?"

Uncle Martino put on his reading glasses. "Certainly. Sicilian sulphur mines contain the finest sulphur crystals in the world."

Poldi triumphantly folded up the map. "Let's go, then."

13

Tells of sulphur, kisses and unresolved trivialities, and of what Poldi found at Femminamorta with the aid of radar-beam technology. What matters is finding something, not looking for it, and who knows that better than Inspector Chance? Totti tries to look good and succeeds brilliantly, but so does Montana. There is coffee and marzipan, good and bad news, and an unexpected visitor.

"The history of sulphur mining in Sicily is a ballad of superabundance and wealth, greed and suffering," Uncle Martino told me once.

Sicilian sulphur formed on the Messinian Plateau when, over five million years ago, the waters of the Mediterranean evaporated and left behind vast deposits of sulphurous gypsum. The Greeks and Romans, who already knew of these immense deposits, extracted the yellow element from numerous mines near Agrigento and in the Enna-Sciacca-Gela triangle. Miners burrowed into the local mountains for many centuries, perforating their interiors like a sponge. The mountainsides are covered with heaps of spoil, and among them are the primitive, mounded furnaces in which sulphur was melted out and cast into rectangular slabs.

In the nineteenth century came the boom. Budding industrialized countries needed sulphuric acid, and Sicily could supply it. The island was then the world's leading supplier of sulphur with a market share of eighty per cent, which gave it a near monopoly in sulphur production.

But working conditions in the mines were murderous. The miners, who worked naked because of the heat underground, seared their lungs with sulphur dust and the poisonous fumes given off by melting and "roasting" sulphur ore. Thousands of children, the so-called *carusi,* had to tote sacks and baskets filled with iron pyrites up the steep shafts that led from the mines to the furnaces — for twelve hours at a time, day after day. Few of them even reached puberty. Tens of thousands of miners perished, either underground or from tending the furnaces or from starvation in their homes.

The poverty must have been unimaginable, for the mine owners, who belonged to the Bourbon nobility and were becoming ever wealthier thanks to their monopoly, paid starvation wages and had absolutely no concern for their miners. Blinded by their monopoly position and inexhaustible deposits, they saw no reason to improve working conditions or invest in new technologies. On the contrary, greed impelled them simply to carry on regardless — the "Sicilian disease," as Uncle Martino always calls it — until the boom abruptly came to an end. Why? Because the Americans soon invented a cheaper process for extracting sulphur, large quantities of which were obtained as a by-product of petroleum processing. By early in the twentieth century, one mine was closing after another, and today there is not a single active sulphur mine left in the whole of Sicily.

I picture Uncle Martino telling Poldi all this on the drive to the sulphur mine near Piazza Armerina. I picture Aunt Teresa sitting in the passenger seat, cheerful and rather excited, behaving as if she had heard it all a hundred times before — which she undoubtedly had. However, I'm sure her face glowed with pride at her husband's encyclopedic knowledge of Sicily, any little gaps in which he liberally and imaginatively papered over. I picture Poldi sitting in the back with Totti's heavy head on her lap, stroking it thoughtfully and filled with dark forebodings.

Beyond Catania, Uncle Martino turned off onto the A19, direction Palermo, a motorway that runs straight through the heart of Sicily past hills mantled with wheat fields and sun-baked relics of antiquity, past ruined bridges leading nowhere and illegal rubbish dumps, across expanses of desert and through magical variations in light.

Midway between Catania and Palermo lies Enna. Visible from a long way off, the city is situated high up on a plateau, and the outlying buildings break off flush with its edge, almost as if they had sprouted from the mountain itself — like an impure mineral, thought Poldi, who of course knew that Enna was still regarded as a stronghold of the Mafia. But they weren't bound for Enna.

Uncle Martino left the motorway and turned off south in the direction of Armerina, which is noted for its late-Roman luxury villa with a wonderful mosaic floor depicting — among other things — ten girls wearing a kind of bikini. But they didn't want to visit the bikini-clad girls; they were bound for Femminamorta.

The abandoned mine lay a good mile outside the town, beyond a small hill and pinewoods. Access was barred by a rusty metal pole with a prohibitive notice attached to it, so they had to leave the car. Totti, who enjoyed long road trips with Uncle Martino as little as I did, leapt out in relief and disappeared into the woods. A rutted sandy track led through the trees. The air smelt of resin and herbs and sulphur.

Beyond the wood, a steep slope strewn with spoil led down to the mining site. Poldi made out the ruins of a pithead frame, dilapidated buildings with drystone walls, the collapsed, round-arched entrances to the mine shafts in the hillside opposite, and the old, grass- and gorse-covered smelting furnaces, which reminded her of prehistoric barrows. Everything was covered with a film of dust, dirt and oxidized sulphur compounds. The sand had a reddish tinge in places, Poldi noticed. She could still smell sulphur. Sharp and evil-smelling, it stung her nose, irritated the mucous membranes, and seemed to shout a warning to her to be gone. This wasn't what Poldi had expected. She could see no sign anywhere of a country mansion, or even of an ordinary house. Valérie's Femminamorta was a miniature paradise, whereas this one was the forecourt to hell. Or had been in the past.

"What an eerie place," Aunt Teresa said uneasily.

"And so utterly remote," said Poldi. "You can't hear a thing. No traffic, not even a bird. Would you two prefer to wait in the car?"

"Are you crazy?"

Uncle Martino lit another cigarette as if this were one of his usual sightseeing trips and led the way down a winding track just wide enough for a single vehicle. Poldi noticed that Totti, who had reappeared, was staying close beside him. The dog seemed to feel that nothing good could come of this excursion. Neither wagging his tail nor barking with excitement and the spirit of adventure, as he usually did, he looked as if he would have preferred to be invisible. He kept sneezing, and Poldi did likewise. It occurred to her that the stench of sulphur was the best protection against uninvited visitors, but there could be no question of turning back.

"So where is Femminamorta?" she called to Martino.

"This is Femminamorta," he called back over his shoulder. "It's the name of the mine."

"Oh, so you've suddenly remembered

that, have you?"

Martino tapped his forehead. "It's all in there, all filed away. It sometimes takes a while, but everything comes back to me sooner or later. I was shown this mine by the branch manager of the local Banco di Sicilia, who had got out of a tricky situation with my help. Must be over twenty years ago. He'd planned to convert it into a sort of sports centre for young people, but the owner squelched the idea."

"Who was the owner?"

"A certain Count Pastorella di Belfiore."

Poldi wasn't even surprised. Having reached the mining site, she looked around. It formed an elongated L flanked by wooded hills and mounds of spoil covered with scrub. Invisible from outside, it was a place without shadows, dazzlingly bright in the afternoon light, a dead, forgotten place that seemed to have been carved out of the world. The air was fraught with heat, dust and the memory of multitudinous suffering. Sweating from every pore, Poldi pictured what life must have been like for the miners and the *carusi*. She half expected the ghosts of the dead children to come shuffling out of the mine shafts at any moment.

"What are we looking for?" asked Teresa, who was clearly feeling ill at ease.

Poldi hadn't the faintest idea.

"I'm not looking, I'm finding," she declared, and strode boldly off through the dust and the smell of sulphur.

"That's what Picasso said," she explained to me. "That's the way he worked: simply take the plunge and see where you end up. You might bear that in mind for that novel of yours. You've got to find, not look. Stay open, be receptive, be ready for anything, know what I mean? Take things as they come, make hay while the sun shines —"

"Thanks, I get the picture," I broke in rather irritably. "Perhaps you'd also explain how it works, this finding business?"

"Of course I will. It's dead easy — even you could master it with a bit of practice."

The prime essential was a roving eye. Like a Bushman in the Kalahari, Poldi swept the site with her gaze, back and forth, to and fro, because concentrating too hard on individual objects blinds one to the rest. Hunters, mushroom pickers, professional photographers and tour guides all know this. Poldi's gaze traversed the site like a radar beam. One step forward — radar beam. One step sideways — radar beam. Teresa and Martino did likewise, step by step — cautiously, like skaters on thin ice.

It was an evil place, that was beyond

doubt. Not even animals wanted to live there, it seemed. Not a bird to be heard, nothing rustling in the gorse bushes that had conquered the whole area despite the contaminated soil. Perhaps, thought Poldi, because yellow plants fare better in sulphur dust.

She strove to concentrate in spite of her mounting uneasiness and an almost over-whelming urge to quit the place as fast as possible. She saw ruins, rusty machine parts and weather-worn refuse on the hillside, together with a covered cistern and, in front of it, some brightly coloured plastic toys. Two cars had evidently driven in and out of here since it last rained, or within the last two months, one with wide tyres with coarse treads and the other with narrower ones. There were footprints everywhere, too, but Poldi couldn't detect how many people had been walking around here. Not that all of this meant anything, because the site appeared to be unguarded. Anyone could come here, but the longer Poldi surveyed the place the more certain she became that no one visited it willingly. No wonder the sports centre had come to nothing, she reflected.

Her thoughts strayed. They yielded to the urge to flee before her legs did, but her legs followed suit, surreptitiously retreating. When she noticed this — when she sternly called herself to order and refocused her radar beam on the ground — she spotted the little fragment of pottery.

It was lying beneath a gorse bush and might have continued to lie there for all eternity: one small, blue, insignificant particle in the infinity of all things. But Inspector Chance had evidently just come on duty, conducted a brief review of the progress of the investigation, cleared his throat, said a few words, and then withdrawn from the proceedings to get himself a coffee.

Poldi did not make the mistake of picking up the potsherd or even touching it. She had instantly recognized its blue glaze, which glinted at her in the afternoon sunlight. She merely took a photograph of it and made a note of the spot.

"Valentino was here," she called to Teresa and Martino.

"Why, have you found something?"

"A piece of glazed pottery. It probably fell out of his pocket."

"So we'll call the police, right?"

Aunt Teresa couldn't wait to leave the place.

"No, we aren't finished yet."

Poldi was quite sure now. Absolutely no urge to flee; on the contrary. She whistled through her fingers for Totti, whose nose she now needed.

"You can whistle through your fingers?" I broke in, when she told me this weeks later.

"Of course. Can't you?"

"Show me."

"My, how suspicious you are," she sighed. Sticking her thumb and forefinger between her teeth, she produced a whistle that nearly punctured my eardrums. "Convinced? May I go on, or are you tired or bored or something?"

"*Forza* Poldi," I told her.

Totti pricked his ears and came scampering up, obviously relieved that they didn't intend to abandon him there. He had something in his mouth which he proudly presented to Poldi: a dog's toy in soft yellow plastic, rather chewed and the worse for wear.

"Ugh, what have you got there?" Poldi exclaimed, trying to relieve Totti of his find. "No, drop it. It's mucky."

Totti reluctantly released his treasure and wagged his tail, preparing to retrieve it at once if the nice lady with the deep voice would please, please consent to throw it for him. But she didn't. She tossed it carelessly aside and held him back by the collar when he tried to dash after it.

"Be a good dog. Look, my pet, I know it's asking a lot of you, but you've got to concentrate, you hear?"

My aunt dragged the unhappy and bewildered Totti to the spot where the potsherd was lying and gently applied his nose to the ground. "There, smell anything? Can you smell Valentino? Go on, sniff."

Totti squinted at his treasure one last time, then gave up and dutifully sniffed the ground around the gorse bush, periodically sneezing. When Poldi was kind enough to release him at last, he stared up at her uncertainly for a moment.

"Well, go on. Seek."

Poldi wasn't very hopeful. Suspecting that Totti had specialized too exclusively in Etna mushrooms, she was doubly gratified when he eventually trotted off and sniffed the ground here and there, giving at least the impression that he was a tracker who knew what he was doing.

In the knowledge that artists and detectives must not be disturbed at their work, Poldi and Uncle Martino followed Totti at an appropriate distance, urging him on with cries of encouragement. Aunt Teresa, by contrast, had sat down in the shade of the pithead frame and was hoping that they would all be able to leave this sinister place before long.

Despite his professional manner, Totti seemed to find it hard to pick up Valentino's scent anywhere. The longer she criss-crossed the site in Totti's wake, the more convinced Poldi became that this had been a thoroughly daft idea. She looked over at Aunt Teresa, who raised a limp hand in her direction, and took out her mobile phone. "That's it; I'm going to call Montana. Not even the best-trained sleuthhound could find anything in this stench."

But Totti, who was steadfastly continuing to sniff away, had begun to scrabble at the base of the old cistern.

"What's he doing?"

Uncle Martino shrugged. "Improving his *bella figura*. He's a Sicilian, after all."

Poldi whistled through her fingers again. "Leave it, Totti. Knocking-off time."

But Totti went on scrabbling at the cistern. He barked, looked over at Poldi and Martino, and barked again — loudly.

Aunt Teresa got to her feet and emerged from the shade. Poldi looked at Martino. "What does that mean?"

"Sounds like mushrooms."

Poldi hurried over. Totti, beside himself

by now, was scrabbling at the cistern like a mad thing and barking excitedly. The circular coping, composed of rough-hewn stone that had once been rendered, came up to Poldi's waist. The mouth of the old reservoir was sealed with a rusty iron plate secured with a padlock. Poldi made out some reddish-brown splashes on the iron plate and the part of the surround Totti was scratching. A lot of splashes. She didn't need a lab report to be sure. She kissed and patted Totti and called Montana.

"Vito, it's me. Can you come to Piazza Armerina? I've got something for you . . . The scene of the crime."

It was evening by the time Montana got there. Streaky red clouds were glowing in the sky like a monstrous projection of Valentino's blood spatter. Possibly a warning from higher authority that his death would not be forgotten or unavenged, thought Poldi. *Namaste,* cirrostratus.

The Polizia di Stato had already cordoned off the area around the cistern. Forensics officers in paper overalls were busying themselves with their brushes and sticky tape, scratching off blood samples, taking photographs while the light lasted, making plaster casts of the tyre tracks, and sticking little flags in the ground.

Poldi and Aunt Teresa were watching in silence from the sidelines when Uncle Martino returned from the town with panini and mineral water. They also ate in silence, depressed by their discovery, the mine, their own impotence and the sight of the policemen's dispassionate professionalism. Only Totti looked cheerful and interested in everything, as if he'd just been dunked in a fountain of youth. "Why don't you go home?" Poldi suggested. "I'm sure Montana will give me a lift."

"Out of the question," said Aunt Teresa.

When Montana arrived — in his crumpled work suit as usual — Poldi rose, straightened her wig and patted the dust from her linen trousers.

"Salve." Montana greeted Teresa and Martino with a handshake, Poldi with two perfunctory kisses on the cheek.

"Hello, Vito."

Montana surveyed his surroundings. "So this is the place."

Poldi said nothing.

"How did you hit on it, Poldi?"

"I put two and two together, that's all."

"Can you be more precise?"

"Valentino mentioned Femminamorta, you remember?"

"And?"

She spread out her arms in the direction of the mine.

"Femminamorta."

"There are *two* of them?"

"At least six," Uncle Martino put in.

Montana groaned. "*Madonna,* what an idiot I am."

"Don't blame yourself. I didn't hit on it by myself either."

"But why this particular one?"

Poldi handed him the photograph of Valentino's collection of bits and pieces and pointed out the sulphur crystal.

"Crystal, sulphur, mine, Femminamorta. That's the name of the mine. It was worth a try." She felt in her bag and handed him the tea infuser containing Valentino's price list. "I found that in the lion yesterday. It proves that Patanè is behind the thefts."

Montana opened the infuser and glanced at the strip of paper, then rolled it up again and put it in an evidence bag together with the infuser.

Poldi was expecting a reprimand for having failed to report the discovery earlier, but Montana merely looked over at the policemen around the murder site. "Anything else I should know?"

Poldi shook her head.

"Okay, I'll be back with you in a minute." Montana sauntered over to the uniformed inspector in charge of the operation.

Poldi saw Montana show his ID, saw him receive a brief rundown from the inspector and accompany him over to the murder site — unhurriedly, with the professional arrogance and composure she found more and more exasperating.

"Let's go," she said to Teresa and Martino. "We aren't needed here any more."

It almost broke Totti's heart to leave the scene of his criminalistic triumph in such an unobtrusive, unacknowledged way. He had to be dragged off.

"Poldi." Montana beckoned her over to the cistern.

Sullenly and reluctantly, Poldi returned to the spot where Valentino had died. "Well?"

"What's that?" asked Montana.

"An old cistern, I guess."

"I meant *that*." Montana pointed to the rusty iron lid.

"A cover to prevent anyone from falling in."

"Have you looked at the padlock?"

The sun had disappeared behind the hill long ago, flooding the mine with shadows and effacing all the light and colour from the dip in which it lay. Poldi had to bend down to see what Montana meant.

"It looks new."

"Brand new, I'd say. A brand-new padlock on an old iron lid."

Poldi stared at him.

Montana turned to the inspector. "I need some bolt cutters right away."

Not long afterwards, when Montana lifted the iron lid, a smell of decay assailed them from the dark interior of the old reservoir. Montana shone a flashlight into it. Poldi could see little at first. An oblong, cement-lined water tank of indeterminate dimensions, the cistern was a good ten feet deep. It no longer contained any water, and the bottom was covered with dust and soil. The beam of the flashlight flitted to and fro until Poldi spotted something that looked like a bundle of clothes. Rotting, colourless articles of clothing, they were also covered in dust. When the beam came to rest on them, Poldi detected something else.

"Oh, my God, is that — ?"

"Looks like it," Montana said harshly.

Wrapped in those dusty articles of clothing on the bottom of the dried-up reservoir was a human skeleton.

Poldi heard nothing from Montana for the next two days. Then she'd had enough.

372

Sleep was out of the question in any case, because the air above Torre Archirafi had been rent every half-hour from early in the morning onwards by monstrous whizzbangs fired from the nearby church square so as to explode — *boom* — just above the roof-tops. Poldi was no stranger to this sort of thing. It was doubtless some local patron saint's name day, which had to be duly celebrated — *boom* — all day long. That evening there would probably be a concluding firework display and a little street festival in the church square. Until then — *boom* — these half-hourly salutes would make the walls shake and make Poldi's ears ring, so a quick exit from town was called for.

Poldi drove to Acireale, parked the Alfa in a no-stopping zone on the Corso Umberto, and strode resolutely towards the gloomy, neo-baroque building that housed police headquarters. Dapper policemen wearing shades and nursing coffees to go were lounging in front of the courtyard entrance as though re-creating a scene outside pre-cinct headquarters in Manhattan South. Confronted by this image of state police and carabinieri united in nonchalant self-importance, Poldi resisted the impulse to take a photo and strode past the uniformed youngsters without a word.

It was pleasantly cool in the prefecture's inner courtyard. Populated by dolphins and nymphs and surrounded by parked patrol cars, a marble fountain sang its sibilant song of hidden beauty, a small orange tree stood to attention in each corner of the courtyard, and the scent of the jasmine on the walls competed with the stench of exhaust fumes. Poldi had seen numerous police stations and headquarters in her time, but never one like this. The prefecture of Acireale was one big apology in itself.

Seated in a glassed-in box at the entrance was a pallid young desk sergeant with sorrowful eyes and an outsize Adam's apple gracing his scrawny neck.

"Commissario Montana," said Poldi.

"Do you have an appointment, signora?"

"No, I don't, but that doesn't matter. The commissario will see me."

A long look from those sorrowful eyes. Poldi saw the Adam's apple slide up and down as if sawing its way out of that far too slender neck.

"Name?"

"Oberreiter, Isolde." She spelt out her surname. "Otranto, Bologna, Empoli, *doppia erre,* Empoli, Imola, Torino, Empoli, Roma. Oh, just tell him Poldi wants a word with him."

The pallid desk sergeant telephoned, covering his mouth and the mouthpiece with his hand.

"The commissario is coming right away."

"Don't bother, just tell me where to find his office."

The Adam's apple danced a tarantella. "Kindly wait here, signora."

Montana appeared a few minutes later. He was looking exhausted, with dark smudges under his eyes, and a trifle nervous. There was a coffee stain on his suit. He nodded to the mournful desk sergeant, took Poldi by the arm and led her to the exit. No kiss.

"Let's go and have a coffee. There's a bar round the corner."

"We could go to your office."

"No, Poldi, we can't."

"Because your pretty young colleague is there, or because there are envelopes full of hush money lying around on your desk?"

"Very funny, Poldi. And she isn't my colleague."

"You're welcome to tell me some more about her."

Pursing his lips, Montana steered my Auntie Poldi gently but firmly past his colleagues and out of the gateway.

"I was going to call you this evening, in

any case."

"Oh yes?"

"Yes." He looked stung.

In the bar round the corner he ordered two coffees and a marzipan mandarin and shepherded Poldi to the far end of the counter.

"I've got good news and bad news. Which do you want first?"

"The good news, of course."

"The good news is, you're still speaking to me."

"Very funny." Poldi tried to look sour but failed abysmally, because just then the hot flush of joy in her breast went surging through every part of her.

Montana grinned. "Patanè has confessed to the thefts."

"Is that all?"

"Of course not. One thing at a time."

"That's what I always say."

"Are you going to keep interrupting me, or do you want to hear how the investigation stands? Make up your mind, I must get back in a minute."

"Calm down, Vito. Well?"

Montana swirled his espresso instead of stirring it with a spoon and gulped it down.

"Patanè has been sitting in an interview room since this morning. He was a bit uncooperative to begin with, but he's been babbling like a brook ever since we confronted him with the evidence."

"What evidence?"

"Traces of a dead body in his car."

"Hallelujah," Poldi cried delightedly.

"The tyre tracks at the mine fit his car," Montana summarized. "So we searched it and found traces of a dead body in the boot, and also traces of Valentino's blood identical to those at the crime scene."

"Has he confessed?"

"Only to the thefts as yet, but he claims they weren't thefts proper. Allegedly, everything had been agreed with the owner of the houses in question."

"Mimì Pastorella di Belfiore. Have you questioned him?"

"What do you think? The noble signore didn't deny it. To be honest, he seems a bit gaga — keeps talking about some German poet . . ."

"Hölderlin."

"Is he well known?"

"A genius from Tübingen who went mad. Did Mimì say anything else about the case?"

"No. Where the thefts are concerned, there'll be a separate investigation to determine whether they constituted a crime at all. In my opinion, Mimì Pastorella is just senile."

"He did well out of the deal, though."

"He can do what he likes with his own property. He's guilty of tax evasion at most. Anyway, Valentino worked for Patanè, but Patanè denies that Valentino ever blackmailed him."

Poldi thought for a moment. "Then why was he so keen on the gate lion?"

"A knee-jerk reaction, he claims, like the knockout drops in your wine. He wants to apologize to you, by the way."

"Smarmy devil. Did he say what he and Russo were arguing about in the car park?"

"Outstanding bills for an extension he'd built. Russo has confirmed this."

"He has, has he? Well, well. Be that as it may, with this level of evidence Patanè may as well give up."

Montana spooned the remains of the sugar out of his espresso cup. "He vehemently denies having murdered Valentino."

"Let him. The weight of the evidence is overwhelming."

Montana evidently needed sugar. He bit off some of his marzipan mandarin. "Delicious, really fresh. Try some."

"The evidence is overwhelming, Vito, isn't it?"

"Pretty well. We'll have to wait for the DNA comparison with the traces from the scene of the crime. The murder weapon is still missing. Patanè also claims that he lent the car to Valentino the day before his death. He found it back outside his house the next morning, so he assumed all was well."

"And he said nothing all this time? I ask you, Vito. Does he have an alibi?"

"No."

"There you are, then. Have you arrested anyone else for the thefts?"

"Should we?"

"I'm only asking."

"Poldi?"

"I'm only asking. Has Patanè at least admitted killing the cat?"

Montana shook his head. "He denies that, too."

"He's a liar. What about the skeleton in the cistern?"

"Hm, that's the next thing. Clearly a young woman, but we haven't managed to identify her yet. Forensics estimate that she could have been lying down there for thirty to fifty years. We're going through all the missing-persons records, but without a DNA comparison it won't be easy."

"A cold case," Poldi exclaimed eagerly.

Montana pulled a face. "It'll be difficult

to nail anyone for murder after such a long time, but we discovered the dried-up remains of some flowers beside the skeleton."

"Flowers?"

"Roses."

"You mean someone knew the woman was lying down there and threw some roses onto her?"

"Yes, within the last few years, too. Some of the roses were relatively well preserved. Romantic, eh?"

"What does Mimì say about it? He owns the mine, after all."

"He was flabbergasted. But he claims he never bothered about the mine — only ever went there once with his father as a child. Somehow, I don't think there's any connection with Valentino's murder."

"What about the new padlock? You think that's a coincidence too, Vito?"

Montana sighed. "We're working on it, okay?"

Poldi bit off some of the marzipan fruit, allowed the sweet almond paste to dissolve on her tongue and cogitated, troubled by a triviality as impalpable as the confectionery in her mouth. Just a triviality like a distant, irritating clicking sound one can't locate or turn off, an unpleasant smell that pursues one throughout the day, or a question mark

380

without a question. It meant she'd over-looked something. Only a triviality, but the vital piece in the puzzle.

Montana glanced at his watch. "I must go."

"So what was the bad news?" asked Poldi.

"Oh yes, the bad news." Montana drew a deep breath. "I believe him. Patanè, I mean."

Poldi tried not to show that this didn't surprise her somehow. "Why?"

He suddenly looked even wearier. "I can't tell you. Call it instinct. There's certainly enough evidence to charge him, even without a confession. Valentino's body was transported in a car, Valentino put the squeeze on him, Patanè is a thief who drugged you and organized a break-in at your house. The chief wants the case closed as quickly as possible."

"But you don't believe Patanè is the mur-derer."

"It's just a feeling, as I say."

"How long have you been doing this job, Vito?"

"Thirty-six years."

"Has your instinct ever let you down?"

"Innumerable times."

He ran a hand nervously over his face and beard as if trying to wipe off an annoying film of something. His bright green eyes looked dull, almost grey. Poldi could tell he hadn't slept much in the previous two days.

"I really have to go now, Poldi."

"And I'd really like to kiss you now."

A little colour came back into the pale green eyes, but his smile remained pained. Poldi construed this as a crystal-clear sign of mixed feelings, and she knew a thing or two about those.

"Let's have a talk when the case is closed, shall we?"

"Oh, Vito."

He wanted to go, couldn't wait to return to his office in the prefecture, the familiar world of investigation and lies. Poldi pictured his lovely colleague waiting for him there, not only impatiently but — with a bit of luck — consumed with jealousy.

But before he went, he drew Poldi to him and kissed her.

"What do you mean by 'kissed'?" I cut in at this point in early October, before she could go on. "Details, please."

"You mean that interests you now? You're usually so bashful about such things."

"And you're usually more precise. All right, how did he kiss you? With tongue or without? Did he take your breath away? Was he greedy, desperate, frantic as a drowning man? Was it an explosion of sensuality, a bit of sophisticated foreplay or more of a cursory peck on the mouth? Were his lips dry or moist? Did his beard tickle? Did the kiss seem to last an eternity, or was it agonizingly brief? Did his breath smell fresh or just stale? I mean, did you click?"

Poldi looked at me intently. She might have been looking at a cute little hamster which has unexpectedly performed a new trick in its cage.

"In the first place," she said, "you obviously don't have a clue about kissing, or you wouldn't ask such daft questions. Secondly, the man is a detective chief inspector and a Sicilian — a sexual force of nature, in other words. Thirdly . . ." Poldi closed her eyes and opened them again. "Thirdly, he tasted of Sicily. Bitter from the coffee, sweet from the marzipan, sour from cigarettes and salty from the sadness and lies he has to put up with every day — from suppressed passion and the pain of falling between two stools again and again. His beard tickled, but in a way that went right through me. It's like walking through a field of corn in summer and feeling you're alive. He smelt sweaty the way a hard-working man smells — of warm skin and a trace of aftershave, of longing and relief that he's back with you and can be himself once more. It was a kiss that tells you, as plain as can be, 'I want you, and I don't give a damn about anyone else.' And, at the same time, it was a farewell kiss that suddenly tears itself away from your lips before they can say 'Come' — one that severs all the ties between you and rips your heart out as well. It was that sort of kiss. Is that good enough for you?"

If anyone knew something about love, Sicily and farewells, it was my Auntie Poldi. On the other hand, she didn't intend to take that farewell kiss lying down — *piacere, grazie e buona giornata* — or file away her heart and give up the commissario just like that. Neither him nor the case. Why not? Because my Auntie Poldi had the feeling she was arriving in Sicily at last.

Back home again she sat bolt upright on the sofa, composed herself for a moment and shut her eyes, trying to forget about the kiss and instead remember the triviality that had so worried her in the café. It wasn't easy because of the whizz-bangs that kept going off in the church square. *Bang.* More and more exasperated, Poldi rooted around in her recollections like someone trying to dislodge a morsel of salami stuck in the gap between two teeth. No use, so she did what she had been taught to do when meditating at the ashram: she took the unresolved triviality by the scruff of the neck, like someone teaching a puppy to sit, and put it back on its blanket.

"And stay there till you tell me the answer yourself."

Boom. The unresolved triviality winced at the next bang, whimpered a little, gazed meekly up at Poldi and tried to slink off its blanket. Poldi drew a deep breath, grabbed it by the scruff of the neck again and gently, patiently, put it back.

"Maybe you can tell me why Vito's bad news didn't surprise me. I mean, Patanè is a thief, a fence, and he damned nearly killed me with knockout drops. He's got a motive and there are masses of clues that seem to incriminate him, so why have I suddenly stopped thinking he murdered Valentino?"

The unresolved triviality looked up at Poldi attentively.

"Good dog," she said. "All right, let's assume it wasn't Patanè. What does that mean? It means I'm wrong about the murder motive, right?"

The unresolved triviality wagged its tail.

"Aha. And it also means that the only candidates left are Valérie and Mimì. Or

385

Russo. Right?"

The unresolved triviality wearily rested its chin on its paws and dozed off. Poldi didn't know what to make of that. She opened her eyes.

The house was hushed and cool. A tap was dripping in the bathroom, and the shutters creaked gently in the midday sunlight. The whizzbangs had temporarily ceased, it seemed. Poldi could hear Signora Anzalone talking to someone outside in the Via Baronessa. She could only hear her neighbour's voice, though, not that of the other person, who was either saying nothing or speaking very softly. She got up from the sofa, intending to peek through the shutters. Just then the doorbell rang. She froze, momentarily overcome by the notion that outside her door were two unshaven, tracksuited thugs with shades and silencers, and, just beyond them, Signora Anzalone lying on the ground in a pool of blood. But then she heard her neighbour say something. "Yes, yes, she's in, I saw her come home a while back." She sounded encouraging and familiar somehow. Not like someone talking to Mafia hitmen. Poldi opened the front door.

It was sad Signora Cocuzza from the bar. Still wearing her white apron over a grey skirt and a pink T-shirt dusted with flour, she looked shorter and more frail than she usually did behind her till — almost transparent but very erect. Poldi had only ever seen her from the waist up before. It now struck her that, despite the sorrow etched into her features, Signora Cocuzza seemed to glow as if there burned deep inside her a light that flickered through all the shadows in her heart. But that might just have been the midday sunlight in the Via Baronessa. Signora Cocuzza was holding out a small package tied up with ribbon. It gave off a delectable smell of fried food.

"I don't mean to intrude, Donna Poldina."

"You aren't intruding in the least."

"I wanted to thank you again for the mushrooms. They were quite delicious. Do you like *arancini*?"

"I'd sell my nephew for a few of your *arancini,* signora."

A hint of a trace of a ghost of a smile. "They're still hot. Two with ragout and two with mozzarella, but they'll keep till tomorrow."

Poldi took the package and stepped aside. "Do come in."

She had expected a shy refusal, but the sad signora needed no second bidding. "I really don't want to intrude, though."

387

"Nonsense. We'll eat the *arancini* together and wash them down with a couple of cold beers, what do you say?"

When Poldi had closed the front door, Signora Cocuzza turned to her. "Are you still looking for Valentino's murderer?"

Slumbering on its blanket somewhere at the back of Poldi's mind, the unresolved triviality sighed in the throes of a restless dream.

"I certainly am."

The sad signora nodded. "Good. Then I may have some information for you." She fixed Poldi with a steady gaze. "I know who the girl in the cistern was."

14

Tells of beauty and death and of what Signora Cocuzza was unable to forget. The Virgin Mary discloses her secret and is celebrated with fireworks and a procession. Poldi draws her conclusions and sets a thoroughly ingenious trap for Valentino's murderer. Things don't go according to plan, unfortunately, and she has to continue her interrogation on the brink of an abyss.

The story Signora Cocuzza told Poldi might be described as a Sicilian ballad about beauty and death. It went as follows: Long, long ago, in the small town of Carruba on the slopes of Etna, overlooking the eastern shores of Sicily, there lived a very beautiful girl named Marisa Puglisi. She was the only child of humble farm labourers who spent their whole existence toiling away for the elderly nobleman who owned the lemon orchard they tended. Despite their poverty, however, Marisa's parents were very happy because Marisa's beauty and her cheerful, outgoing nature constituted the totality of their wealth and happiness. When she laughed the sun rose, buds opened and hearts beat faster. When she cursed the sky grew dark, Etna fell silent and angelic trumpets sounded the Armageddon.

Marisa blossomed early. Endowed with the curves of a grown woman even at the age of twelve, she aroused envy and lust in equal measure. When she was around, her classmates clasped their flat bosoms in despair. As for the men of the town, young and old, they dreamt of the forbidden apples of paradise whenever she walked past. When little Marisa attended Mass on Sundays with her little white dress and her beloved monchhichi bag, every head turned to look at her. It was not long before word spread throughout the district that Carruba was home to a growing girl whose beauty could blind Cyclopes and drive men insane.

And so it turned out. By the time she was sixteen, Marisa's name could be seen all over the place, carved on trees and pews and sprayed on walls. *Marisa ti amo, Marisa ti voglio, Marisa — vita mia.* Her skin was as luminously pale as ricotta with honey and soft as the peaches from Santa Venerina, for Marisa shunned the sun. Her body harboured a multitude of shadowy dimples, secret places and hollows that cried out for tender exploration. Her dark hair fell to her shoulders like ancient streams of lava, and her turquoise eyes were as big and mysterious as the lagoons of Tindari, the gold flecks in them resembling the glitter of morning sunlight on the sea. Her lips, which were always slightly parted as if to utter a major question or a minor reproach, were as full and red and glossy as cherries from Sant'Alfio. Everything, but everything about Marisa was soft and rounded and graceful. Her arms and legs were firm and strong from housework, her hips resembled those of an ancient fertility goddess, Persephone perhaps, and she shook the world's equilibrium with every step she took. And oh, her bosom. A yearning shore, a quiet bay between two wonderful hills visible from afar, a place where a lost fisherman could safely drop anchor and drowse away his sorrows. All in all, it must be said that Marisa had been created by a generous God. Created for love. Marisa thought so, anyway, and she was ready to bestow love, laughter and pleasure with equal generosity. But not on the first poor wretch who came along.

In order to attain true perfection, however, all beauty requires the minor flaws that alone can render perfection discernible and our own mediocrity — our oversized noses, crooked teeth and meagre breasts — tolerable. In Marisa's case they were some insignificant skin blemishes, feet that were on the big side and a predilection for bad language. Above all, though, lack of intelligence. For all her beauty, it must, alas, be said that Marisa Puglisi was rather stupid. She began to be overly proud of her beauty, flirting and boasting of her effect on boys and men. She needed admiration and adoration as gods need nectar and junkies need a fix, yet she gave all her admirers the brush-off. Well, most of them at least, because her heart wasn't made of stone. She was young, and her passionate nature needed an outlet. However, she was firmly resolved not to squander the gift of her beauty but to use it as a ticket to happiness. And to Marisa happiness meant a house with a fitted kitchen and a cleaning woman, a fur coat and a permanent pass to the smartest lido in Catania. In short, Marisa Puglisi was dead set on marrying a rich man. No one less than a *dottore* or an *avvocato* would be considered, and it seems that a suitable candidate soon presented himself.

At this point in her Sicilian ballad, Signora Cocuzza herself appeared on the scene. A shy and sickly young girl in those days, she was occasionally taken into Marisa's confidence. Marisa confessed to her friend that a young man from a good family was not only passionately in love with her — nay, worshipped her — but also wrote her ardent love letters. This appealed to her because none of her other swains had ever thought to do so. She further disclosed that she had to keep the whole affair a strict secret and only meet her admirer on the sly because his father sternly opposed their liaison. They would soon reach the point of no return, however. She would then tell her friend everything and, of course, appoint her a bridesmaid.

Two weeks later Marisa Puglisi disappeared without a trace, somewhere near the Provinciale between Carruba and Acireale. She was never seen again until the day Vito Montana opened the cistern of an old sulphur mine fittingly named Femminamorta.

Poldi listened to the whole ballad in silence, sipping her beer while it was still cool and never once interrupting Signora Cocuzza.

"It broke her parents' hearts, naturally,"

said the sad signora. "Mine, too. I had never forgotten Marisa. Yesterday, when I heard that the police had found a woman's skeleton at Femminamorta, near Piazza Armerina, I realized it could only be hers."

Poldi nodded. "True, but how come *you* already know of the discovery?"

Signora Cocuzza made a weary gesture. "One hears things."

"Didn't the police investigate Marisa's disappearance?"

"Yes, of course. They combed the whole area for weeks, but without success."

"Did they ever discover the identity of Marisa's secret admirer?"

"Hm . . ." The sad signora sighed. "I think the police needed to show some results. The only lead they had was something Marisa told me the day before she disappeared: that she would be meeting her admirer at Femminamorta the following night to clear the air."

"Clear the air?"

"Give him his marching orders."

"I thought she wanted to marry him."

"Well, yes, but he wasn't her only admirer, and she found him rather weird. Too eccentric somehow. His love letters were starting to get on her nerves, if only because she found it hard to decipher his handwriting.

On top of that, she had fallen head over heels in love with someone else, a centre half who played for Calcio Catania. And besides, she was . . . well, pregnant."

"By the footballer?"

The sad signora nodded. "Second month."

"So that night at Femminamorta," Poldi summarized, "Marisa intended to give her mysterious admirer the push."

"Yes, and return all his letters."

"Very romantic of her."

"No, the footballer was insanely jealous, that's all."

"And who was this mysterious admirer?"

"Well . . . Her allusion to Femminamorta pointed to the father of your friend Valérie. He came under suspicion and was questioned for days without success. Nothing could be proved against him, but everyone around here, me included, considered him a murderer — because, of course, we realized eventually that Marisa must be dead. Signor Raisi spent the rest of his life trying to refute the suspicion. He bravely lived among us and never avoided people, but at some stage it all became too much for him."

"What do you mean?"

"He killed himself, didn't you know? Of course, that finally convinced us that he really had murdered Marisa."

Poldi drew a deep breath. "And Marisa's parents?"

"The tragedy destroyed them. They divorced two years later. Marisa's mother died last year. I don't know where her father is living now." Signora Cocuzza was looking even sadder than usual.

"You ought to tell all this to the police again," Poldi told her.

Signora Cocuzza shook her head. "What would be the point after all these years? Besides, the police hardly acquitted themselves with glory back then. I got the impression they weren't all that eager to solve the case."

"Someone was pulling strings, you mean?"

"There's no proof, of course."

"Russo?"

Signora Cocuzza shrugged her shoulders. "Russo was nineteen at the time. He was after Marisa too, of course. In fact they may even have had a fling. But Russo wasn't stupid; he knew he wasn't good enough for Marisa — not at that stage. And he was stunningly good-looking himself; he could take his pick. Besides, he was too bound up in his first business venture."

"Which was?"

"He dug up some big palm trees on wasteland and sold them to the American airbase at Sigonella. It must have been a profitable deal, because he bought his first plot of land and set up Piante Russo soon afterwards."

"You mean his career began just after Marisa disappeared?"

"I mean nothing at all, Donna Poldina. I just can't forget her, that's all, and I thought you might be interested."

Poldi looked at her. "What has all this got to do with Valentino's death?"

Another shrug. "From what I hear, Valentino was killed where they found Marisa's body, so her murderer must have killed him, too. It's only logical."

Poldi hadn't looked at it like that. Signora Cocuzza's reasoning wasn't particularly forensic, but once it had been voiced, its simplicity struck Poldi as being so logical that she could only shake her head in bewilderment.

"My dear Signora Cocuzza, do you know something? You're a genius."

Outside, the whizzbang salutes in honour of the local saint had started up again. The unresolved triviality, too, had perked up. It was standing on its blanket, wagging its tail excitedly and barking at Poldi. All at once, it had something in its mouth: a small, brightly coloured toy.

"And at that moment," my aunt told me later, not without a certain self-satisfaction, "everything became clear to me. I knew who had killed Valentino and why, and I also knew how I might be able to prove it."

"Well, go on."

"Have you guessed already?"

"What's this supposed to be," I asked evasively, "an intermediate examination in inductive logic?"

"Just tell me."

But I wouldn't play. I hate tests and always have. I break out in a sweat even if someone asks me the way in my own home town. Also, I'm no Sherlock Holmes and I don't like spoiling other people's stories.

"It's *your* story," I said firmly. "*You* finish it off."

Poldi's train of thought was as follows: Valentino had blackmailed his killer with his knowledge of Marisa's murder. He had probably discovered the body in the cistern, but he must have had further evidence. There had probably been an exchange of evidence for cash at the cistern, but something had gone wrong. Badly wrong. Since Valentino's killer had tried to deter Poldi from investigating — *vide* the dead cat — this could only mean that the evidence must still exist somewhere. Valentino had probably hidden it like the price list under the lion, but where? In his room at his parents' place? Unlikely. Montana's men had searched it thoroughly. At her house, like the lion? That seemed too risky to be very likely. So where? What sort of evidence was it, anyway? Glancing at the unresolved triviality, Poldi had a sudden idea.

"How did Marisa get those love letters?" she asked Signora Cocuzza. "By post?"

"Of course not; her parents would have found out. The couple had a dead letter box where her admirer left the letters."

Poldi's theory crystallized.

"Do you know where this dead letter box was?"

"Of course. It was I who had to collect the billets-doux for her."

"Why doesn't that surprise me, Signora Cocuzza?"

The sad signora lowered her eyes a trifle coquettishly, Poldi noticed. "Of course I told the police all this at the time, but the letters had gone. Would you like to see it?"

"The dead letter box? You mean it still exists?"

Where, in Bavaria and Sicily alike, do people still deposit spare keys, prayer requests, lottery tickets and secret messages?

With the Virgin Mary, of course. Every respectable household possesses a statuette of the Virgin, and old houses even have a small niche to accommodate one. But statues of the Madonna can also be found outside one's own four walls, for instance at crossroads, in fishing ports, taverns and places in special need of divine protection. A mineral-water spring, for example. The patron saint of Torre Archirafi is the Madonna del Rosario, a blue-robed Madonna with a rosary in her hand. This large figure, which looks so poignant, is stationed beside the altar in the church. A smaller copy can be found in the side wall of the Acqua di Torre mineral-water factory, just beside the public bottling taps in an old shrine of volcanic rock and glazed tiles.

"The Belfiore family donated it in the nineteenth century," Signora Cocuzza informed Poldi on the way there.

My aunt noticed that a small stage had been set up in the church square. Banners were hanging from many windows and the streets were overarched with colourful streamers and festoons. Padre Paolo, who was supervising two youths engaged in setting off another rocket, bade the two women a jovial "good day." Already intent on the shrine, Poldi waved back absently.

She knew the little shrine but had hitherto paid it scant attention. Flush with the wall of the bottling plant, it took the form of a squat tabernacle. Mounted on a small marble base behind a cast-iron grille, the painted plaster Madonna was draped with plastic rosaries and surrounded by votive candles and artificial flowers.

"*Ecco,*" said Signora Cocuzza. "Marisa's admirer had given her a key to the padlock. But you're wondering where the letters were, aren't you?"

Poldi looked closely at the shrine. The lava stone base appeared to be solid, and there was not enough room inside the shrine to secrete a letter, far less a whole bundle.

"Look closer," whispered the sad signora.

Then Poldi saw it. "*Madonna mia.* Well, I'll be damned." She could just make out a fine, rectangular crack in the marble base on which the Madonna stood. The tiny knob of the perfectly fitting stone drawer was concealed by a small vase.

"That's where the Belfiore family used to leave their prayer requests," Signora Cocuzza explained. "They alone possessed a key to the grille."

Poldi examined the padlock, which looked fairly new and displayed no traces of rust. "Who has the key these days?"

"Padre Paolo, and he was kind enough . . ."

Signora Cocuzza produced a small key from the pocket of her apron and held it under Poldi's nose. No grin, not even a smile. The sad signora was utterly poker-faced. My Auntie Poldi was beginning to like her more and more.

While the signora kept watch, Poldi opened the grille, pushed the plastic flowers a little to one side and slid out the small marble drawer beneath the Virgin. Cautiously but without hesitation, she removed its contents. Then she closed the drawer, re-arranged the plastic flowers and locked the grille again.

"What do you plan to do now?" asked the sad signora.

"Go to the police."

But that was only a half-truth, because Poldi's first step was to go home, spread out her haul on the table in the courtyard and examine it carefully. Lying in front of her was everything Valentino had been able to secrete in the small drawer: four small, pale-blue envelopes addressed in ornate handwriting to someone by the name of Diotima, together with a ringlet of dark hair tied up with cheap ribbon. This could only have belonged to Marisa Puglisi, but Poldi was puzzled by the name Diotima on the envelopes. She laid out the four letters side by side. Small sheets of very thin paper, neatly folded and written on in the same ornate, almost illegible handwriting. The letters were dated, but the dates were several weeks apart, so Poldi surmised that Valentino had fished them out at random from a bigger pile before hiding them under the Madonna — as a nest egg, so to speak. From the look of them they consisted of poems with a personal addition at the end. And then, Diotimawise, the penny dropped. Poldi needed no translation. Two clicks, and she found the original on the Internet. The author of the letters had botched up Hölderlin's celebrated "Ode to Diotima" and adapted it to his own libidinous requirements.

Thy heav'nly bosom me arouses,
makes me yearn to play love's game.
Slip thy hand inside my trousers,
and I to thee will do the same.
For Diotima, my goddess of the Temple of
    Pleasure.
Meet me on the mole at eleven tonight.

D.

" 'D'?" I asked, rather at a loss, when

Poldi was revealing the full details of the case.

"Yes, of course. D for Domenico. Domenico Pastorella di Belfiore, aka Mimì, butcher of Hölderlin and double murderer. I mean, I'm no fan of Hölderlin's stuff, but that was a really tasteless piece of horse-shit."

"Aren't you being too hard on him?" I countered. "The man was besotted, after all, and lovers make monkeys of themselves."

"A fat lot you know about it. At all events, that doggerel of Mimì's gave me an insight into his state of mind. I realized that he must have killed Marisa as well as Valentino; Marisa out of jealousy and wounded vanity, Valentino on account of blackmail."

"I see. And what sparked that revelation?"

"Why, the lion. The lion, get it?"

"The lion?"

"The plastic lion, of course. The toy dog I took from Totti at the mine and threw away. It was exactly like the one Mimì's Dobermann is always chewing."

"So what? There must be hundreds of the things."

"Don't be such a smarty-pants. Good God, you've got to admit it couldn't have been a coincidence. That little plastic lion at the mine was quite new — Totti found it near the cistern. Cistern, plastic lion, Hölderlin, Valentino, Mimì, bingo. Follow me? It was clear as daylight."

"Then you ought to have called Montana."

"Jesus Christ Almighty. I wanted to solve the case all by myself, and I still didn't have any solid evidence."

"What about a lock of Marisa's hair and maybe some DNA on the letters?"

"Yes, yes, very clever, professor. Congratulations, *cento punti.* But at that moment I was in the grip of something."

"The hunting instinct?"

"Now we understand each other."

My Auntie Poldi was one of the most fearless people I know. She wanted a confession, obviously, and that required her to set a little trap for Mimì Pastorella.

Summoning up all her courage, she telephoned Mimì and informed him, politely but point-blank, that she had established his guilt and could prove it. She would, however, be prepared to keep her mouth shut and hand over all her evidence if Mimì were willing to pay her an appropriate quid pro quo of fifty thousand euros, which she needed in order to renovate her roof.

Giving the startled man no time to respond or prevaricate, Poldi invited him to settle the matter at the Via Baronessa that same night, or she would take her evidence to the police. Then she hung up. Fifty thousand euros for her leaky roof struck Poldi as an affordable but realistic sum for which it wouldn't be worth committing a third murder. She estimated that, if Mimì consented to the deal, it would be tantamount to a confession. She prepared to document their meeting in a thoroughly professional manner by attaching a tape recorder to the underside of her sofa table with sticky tape. She also loaded the Bavarian infantry musket and propped it against the sofa, well within view, in case Mimì showed up with a sawn-off lupara.

"Just a minute," I broke in at that point. "I thought the old blunderbuss was unusable. Officially deactivated and so on."

Poldi sighed. "Of course not. My father never collected any useless weapons."

I stared uneasily at the muskets and pistols hanging on the opposite wall. "You mean they're all, er . . . potentially lethal?"

"They're all in working order, let's say. All right, I admit there was a certain risk involved because it's a muzzleloader, and they aren't easy to load — you have to take care. But in the first place my old man showed me how, and secondly I didn't load a bullet, just a small powder charge with a wad of paper on top, understand?"

"You simply wanted to make a big bang, right?"

"Dead right, professor. I wanted to be prepared for all eventualities, leave nothing to chance. It was all planned in an ultra-professional way."

But, as is the way with plans that leave nothing to chance, my Auntie Poldi found herself in a tight spot.

Because of course the festival in honour of the Madonna del Rosario, Torre Archirafi's patron saint, was taking place on that of all nights. In addition to whizzbangs all day long, this included a grand firework display in the evening, a church service and an ensuing religious procession through the streets, and a party for the young people of Torre with a band from Riposto — in other words, the usual thing where a town's patron saint was concerned. People splashed out on such occasions, especially when they lived beside the sea and needed protection from tempests and tidal waves. The whole of Torre Archirafi was out and about. Summoned by bells and whizzbangs, everyone was flocking into the church. And that, stupidly enough, meant there were no neighbours within hailing distance.

Mimì turned up on the dot, impeccably dressed as ever in a three-piece suit. And accompanied by Hölderlin. The dog was something else Poldi hadn't considered, and no wonder, alas, because she was slightly tipsy by the time Mimì arrived. In spite of all her good resolutions, she had already downed a stiff one for her nerves' sake. Not exactly the best preparation for such a crucial encounter, but that was my Auntie Poldi. Mimì appeared to be unarmed, though. He certainly hadn't brought a lupara with him.

Poldi initially hesitated to invite the old gentleman and his Dobermann inside. She wondered whether she shouldn't simply slam the front door and call Montana. Although she might have been better advised to, she pulled herself together. Stepping aside, she ushered Hölderlin and his master into the house. Mimì surveyed his surroundings while Hölderlin took off on his own, roaming around and sniffing like a cop with a search warrant. Or a professional killer.

"You have a nice house, Donna Isolde, but you say the roof needs fixing already? That certainly wouldn't have happened in

Germany. You might have done better to stay there."

Poldi ignored this. "A glass of wine, Don Mimì?"

"Very civil of you, Donna Isolde, but no thanks."

"A Coke? Some water?"

"No, please don't bother."

"I trust you won't object if I pour myself a glass?"

"Of course not, Donna Isolde."

Mimì was playing the respectable signore, a man of integrity from his gout-ridden toe to his few remaining wisps of hair, his voice soft and tremulous. He looked somewhat more bent-backed than usual — more pre-occupied, too. And no wonder, thought Poldi, when you've done such things and carried a burden of guilt around with you for decades, and now everything threatens to blow up in your face. On the other hand, she thought he seemed surprisingly calm.

"An heirloom of your father's, I gather," Mimì said softly, pointing to the musket propped against the sofa.

"Er, yes . . . it needed cleaning. Please."

Poldi nervously indicated an armchair.

Without taking his eyes off my aunt, Mimì sank back against the cushions and clicked his fingers. Hölderlin came trotting up and sat down obediently at his side.

Poldi noticed with a touch of uneasiness that the Dobermann, too, was eyeing her fixedly. She sat down on the edge of the sofa, pushed the musket aside and poured herself another Scotch. Her hand was trembling, and she hoped the recording machine beneath the table between her and Mimì was picking up every word.

"I had honestly hoped we could be friends, Donna Isolde."

Poldi refused to be intimidated. "Friends don't leave dead cats outside each other's doors."

Mimì made a dismissive gesture. "What does a cat matter? A dog, on the other hand" — he fondled Hölderlin's head — "a dog is a divine creature, and closer to man than any other, woman included."

"Really? I think you must have got the wrong end of the stick in biology or religious education."

A touch of annoyance furrowed Mimì's brow, but he recovered himself at once. "Well now . . . about these outrageous accusations of yours —"

"Which I can prove, Don Mimì. You killed Valentino Candela and — forty years ago — Marisa Puglisi."

Another feeble, dismissive gesture. "In

410

that case, would you kindly show me this alleged evidence of my alleged guilt?"

"Do you have something for me, too?"

Another sigh. Mimì felt in his breast pocket and brought out a wad of five-hundred-euro notes. He fanned them out on the table. "Want to count them?"

"That won't be necessary."

Poldi took a padded envelope from under a sofa cushion, extracted the four letters and the lock of hair, and put them down beside the money.

Mimì nodded. "Ah, the lock of hair. I knew Valentino still had it. If you hadn't included it, I wouldn't have trusted you."

"These are all the letters I found. I don't think Valentino had any more."

"No, I had to burn the others, alas."

"Before or after you shot him?"

This was precisely the moment at which Poldi meant to begin her rigorous interrogation. Unfortunately, events took a different turn.

For one thing, the Madonna del Rosario procession set off from the church square to a deafening accompaniment of whizzbangs, tolling bells and universal pandemonium; for another, Mimì was startled into dropping his senile romantic's pose. Seemingly jolted out of a pleasant daydream into vile

411

reality, he stared at Poldi as if realizing for the first time whom he was up against. Quick as a flash, more nimbly than Poldi would have believed and before she herself could react, he snatched up the letters and the lock of hair. Then he shouted, "Hölderlin, attack!" In German, mark you.

Hölderlin needed no second bidding. He seemed to have been waiting for that moment, and no wonder, after a life spent worrying cashmere sweaters, terry towels and plastic lions — and occasionally, perhaps, being allowed to inflict an experimental bite on the leg of a Moroccan manservant or the arm of a clumsy child in the Corso. He hadn't even been permitted to touch Valentino, because that would have left telltale marks, so it was only understandable that Hölderlin's innocent Dobermann psyche had developed a certain pent-up pressure, a bloodlust fantasy, a war cry of the wild which he now obeyed with alacrity.

In response to Mimì's command and without any superfluous barking or growling, he flew at my Auntie Poldi. It was nothing personal; Hölderlin was a pro. My aunt, on the other hand, was somewhat short-winded and not as quick on her pins as she used to be. Nor, as already mentioned, was she entirely sober. Situations of this kind are eternally surprising, however, for she reacted with undreamt-of, *Matrix*-like agility, as if time had slowed down for her.

"I saw Hölderlin spring at me in slow motion," she told me later. "It was like my last hour had come and I'd entered another space-time continuum."

Be that as it may, a person's reflexes take over at such moments. Poldi spun round, grabbed the musket and, while Hölderlin was still in mid-air, clouted him on the head. The Dobermann uttered a yelp and landed with a crash on the coffee table. There was another crash as the old musket simultaneously went off. The powder charge erupted from the muzzle with plenty of smoke and flame, blowing a hole in the ceiling and generating a recoil that tore the weapon from Poldi's grasp. Profoundly shocked by both occurrences — the crash and the detonation — Mimì shied like a startled horse, then froze. Although the blow with the musket had not been enough to put Hölderlin completely out of action, it did at least gain Poldi some time. Still moving with unwonted agility, she dived over the back of the sofa and ran up the stairs to the roof — a typically irrational thing to do, because she could easily have reached the front door instead. That, however, would

413

have entailed dodging past Mimì and the dazed Dobermann, which formed a kind of optical-psychological barrier. Meanwhile, Mimì unfroze and Hölderlin scrambled to his feet.

"After her."

Breathing heavily, Poldi reached the roof terrace.

"Help. *Heeeeelp!*"

But no one could hear her. Everyone in town was joining in the procession. Skyrockets, brass band and fervent singing combined to produce a din that reverberated around the streets and rose into the night sky, which was tinged with the glow of torches and candles.

"*Heeeeelp!*"

Not a chance. Poldi briefly considered escaping onto Dottore Branciforti's roof terrace like Turi, but didn't think she was up to it.

So there she stood, all alone on her expanse of roof, feeling rather frightened because Hölderlin, overwrought and still slightly dazed, appeared a moment later. That he bore her an unmistakable grudge was evident from the way he herded her towards the parapet overlooking the street. Mimì, who came toiling up the stairs after him, left Poldi in no doubt as to how the night would end.

"Germany is such a lovely country, Donna Isolde. Why couldn't you have stayed there? Why did you have to poke your nose into things that don't concern you?"

"It's an old failing of mine," Poldi gasped with Hölderlin's slavering muzzle inches from her face. He had both forepaws planted on her chest as though he meant to push her off the roof, and her supposition to that effect was probably correct.

"How did Valentino get hold of the letters and the lock of hair?" she called to Mimì, more to gain time than for information's sake.

"Pure chance. I had an arrangement with Patanè concerning the, er, 'exploitation' of my various properties. That was how Valentino must have come across the letters. I had mentioned Femminamorta to Marisa in the last one I wrote her. Valentino put two and two together and looked around the mine. He saw me throw a rose into the cistern on the anniversary of Marisa's death."

"How romantic."

"I didn't kill Marisa," Mimì snapped. "It was an accident. She meant to leave me for that — that *footballer.* She wouldn't even keep my letters, the silly girl."

"That doesn't surprise me somehow."

"Hold your tongue. I worshipped Marisa. It was an accident. She was so scared by Hölderlin the First, she staggered backwards and hit her head on the side of the cistern."

"You could have explained all that to the police."

"The police were the least of my worries. It was the scandal. You didn't know my father. He would have torn me to pieces and disinherited me."

"A pity he didn't."

"And so, with a bleeding heart, I laid my goddess, my Diotima, to rest in there, hoping to preserve our love and our secret for all time."

"You simply dumped her down there like rubbish."

Mimì was growing calmer. He peered over the parapet. Then, serenity personified, he stepped back.

"Believe me, Donna Isolde, everyone in town will mourn your death. I shall contribute a wreath and recite some poems by the Master at your funeral. It will be extremely moving."

"Oh, don't go to any trouble," gasped Poldi.

Mimì shook his head. "No one will be surprised, Donna Isolde. The drinking, the

416

depression, the foreign country — no wonder you longed for death like a far-off, unattainable lover. That's what people will think." Thus spake the romantic in him. Then he turned prosaically pragmatic. "And now, Donna Isolde, you have a choice: either you jump of your own free will, or Hölderlin will assist you by tearing your face off."

"Can I phone a friend?" Poldi gasped bravely.

Mimì was infuriated. "Go on, jump, Hölderlin."

Hölderlin snapped at Poldi's throat and she shrank back even further over the parapet, unable to go much further. She pictured Death getting out his ballpoint and preparing to strike her name from the list on his funny clipboard. Behind her, the Madonna del Rosario procession was still blaring its way through the town at a snail's pace. She estimated that it would take another twenty minutes to reach the Via Baronessa. Twenty minutes too long, alas.

"And that's why Valentino had to die?"

"He wanted two hundred thousand euros."

"My God, Mimì, why didn't you simply pay him off? All Valentino wanted was to get out of Sicily. You'd never have heard from him again."

"The swine didn't give me all the letters or the lock of hair at our first meeting. He'd have gone on blackmailing me forever."

That was why he'd called Valentino on Valérie's phone and summoned him to Femminamorta for a final payment. At their second meeting he'd wasted no time in setting Hölderlin on him the way he had once set Hölderlin's predecessor on Marisa and was now menacing my Auntie Poldi. Then he had cold-bloodedly fired a load of buckshot at Valentino's face, loaded him into the boot of Patanè's car, driven him back to Torre and laid him out on the beach at Praiola.

"Why didn't you simply dump him in the cistern?"

"Beside Marisa? Never. No one was going to lie beside Marisa."

"Maybe that was your big mistake."

"That's enough. Jump, or Hölderlin will do for you."

Hölderlin came even closer. His breath stank of tartar and rotting meat. Poldi shrank back further still. Behind her, only thirty feet of thin air separated her from the potholed surface of the Via Baronessa. Not far away, the brass band leading the procession was blaring out a slow march. End of the line. Death was impatiently fiddling with his ballpoint.

And then Etna erupted.

Etna is regarded as a good-natured volcano whose lava is low in gas content and relatively inexplosive, and it regularly releases its internal pressure. A stream of lava will flatten a village once in a blue moon, it's true, and half of Catania was destroyed in the seventeenth century. But everything happens nice and slowly, so there's always time to clear out the *salotto,* tie the children's shoelaces, drink a coffee and watch the catastrophe from a safe distance. In any case, the lava tends to run down into the uninhabited Valle del Bove, of which Poldi's terrace affords an excellent view.

Good-natured or not, though, when Etna *does* erupt it transfixes you. The mountain with the picturesque plume of smoke then becomes a gigantic living creature that roars abruptly like a furious old man roused too soon from his siesta. The air quivers with each eruption, galvanizing one's nerves and imagination. Just such a roar, a gigantic *boom* issuing from the bowels of the earth, rent the air behind Mimì, went thundering through the salty night air, rolled down the slopes, surged over tranquil Torre Archirafi and its bitter mineral-water spring, and pierced Poldi to the marrow. Having lived with their volcano since time immemorial, Sicilians treat its eruptions and its irksome showers of ash with equanimity, but when Mongibello makes its presence felt, no one remains unaffected. Everyone turns to look.

Mimì did, too.

Even Hölderlin did.

Poldi saw a huge fountain of lava erupt from the volcano — a wonderful sight, a last farewell. Things happen like that sometimes, so unforeseen, so immediate, so unmistakable. Suddenly everything becomes clear. With this greeting from the volcano and death before her eyes, my Auntie Poldi was transfixed by a frisson of unbridled *joie de vivre*. In that brief instant she realized how good it was to live between the sea and the volcano in company with the aunts, the mushrooms, Valérie, the sad signora, Montana and all, and that she wanted to survive for a while longer, not just for this very last moment.

She didn't really register Etna's second exhalation because everything happened very quickly after that.

Hölderlin released her and spun round in alarm as Montana came storming out onto the roof.

"Get him, Hölderlin," screamed Mimì,

but before the Dobermann could respond to changed circumstances and fly at Montana's throat, the policeman opened fire and Hölderlin collapsed with a death rattle. Shocked by the volcanic eruption and his dog's swift demise, Mimì Pastorella clutched his heart, groaned and collapsed likewise. Heart failure. Fatal. Nothing to be done.

15

Describes my Auntie Poldi in close-up on her terrace, an embrace and a promise. The weather changes and Poldi has to turn up at police headquarters. Various matters need sorting out, not always with agreeable results. It's always the same: just when you think something's over, something else gets in the way yet again.

Stirred and inspired by my Auntie Poldi's account, I devoted the next day — my last day in the Via Baronessa for the time being — to rewriting the first chapter of my novel. Before immigrating to Munich, my great-grandfather Barnaba has to solve a murder. Decades earlier, the aristocratic landowner Calogero Macaluso brutally set his dog on an innocent peasant girl and hounded her to death for refusing him. Since then, legend has had it that the ghost of a monstrous dog haunts the district and commits atrocities.

422

When Macaluso's last surviving grandson is found torn to pieces in my great-grandfather's orange grove, Barnaba has to find the murderer in order to prove his own innocence. He succeeds in doing so thanks to his brilliant inductive logic and the assistance of the lovely Eleonora. Barnaba lays a trap for the dead grandson's rival, a relative of the murdered peasant girl, in the bleak Valle del Bove, shoots his trained Dobermann, and ensures that the murderer gets his just deserts. As the chapter draws to a close, Barnaba and Eleonora make love al fresco while Etna erupts above them in a meaningful manner.

I rewrote the chapter in a sort of frenzy. That evening Poldi asked me to read it aloud to her. She listened attentively without interrupting, never fidgeted once or rolled her eyes. When I had finished and was regarding her nervously, she shook her head.

"It's crap. Dump it."

"Any *constructive* dramatic or stylistic comments?"

She poured herself a Scotch. "No. You can do much better, though. It's all a question of practice."

My Auntie Poldi knew a thing or two about storytelling.

■ ■ ■ ■

But back to Poldi's showdown.

In the background, the erupting volcano and the oom-pah-pah of the procession, which was just turning into the Via Baronessa. In close-up in the foreground, my Auntie Poldi. Pale, wig askew but otherwise all right. She stared in shock at the two corpses on her terrace, Mimì's and Hölderlin's, and at Montana, who felt Mimì's pulse and shook his head. He holstered his gun, rose to his feet and walked slowly over to Poldi, deliberately obstructing her view of the dead bodies.

"Are you all right?"

Poldi couldn't get a word out, just stared at him.

"Poldi."

She whispered something almost inaudible.

"What did you say?"

"Could you —"

"Could I what, Poldi?"

"Could you please put your arms around me?"

No problem. Montana put his arms around my aunt and held her tight. He held her, silent and strong and rather sweaty, until her shock subsided at last and she was able to weep. And he continued to hold her in his arms, as if he never wanted to let go of her, until she gradually stopped trembling.

"Better?"

Poldi nodded and sniffed.

"I have to call my team now, okay?"

Poldi nodded again but continued to hold him tight.

He gently detached himself and looked into her eyes. "Like to sit down?"

She shook her head. "How did you get in?"

Montana held up one of the spare keys. "Assistente Rizzoli got this from one of your sisters-in-law. I'd been meaning to return it for ages."

"I'm glad you took your time."

"I'm glad you can smile again."

The procession was now making its way along the Via Baronessa. The Madonna del Rosario, a meek but majestic figure, swayed past in her canopied palanquin carried by eight young men of Valentino's age. Poldi didn't recognize the march because the brass band's off-key rendition was mingled with the singing of Torre Archirafi's candle-bearing townsfolk, but she didn't care. It sounded wonderful. Heavenly.

"*Namaste,* life," she whispered.

"Did you say something, Poldi?"

"No, nothing."

Having alerted his colleagues, Montana shepherded Poldi down to the living room, sat her down on the sofa, thrust the musket aside and poured her a glass of grappa.

"Drink this, it'll do you good," Poldi said in a low voice.

"What?"

"You've got to say that. They always say that in films. Go on, say it."

"Drink this, it'll do you good."

"But I don't want to."

"Don't be silly, Poldi. And don't budge, I'll deal with everything."

"Don't go, Vito."

"I'm not going."

"Promise me."

"I won't go, I promise. Shall I call your sisters-in-law?"

"Please don't. There's no rush."

Poldi registered little of all the forensic palaver that went on. She nodded absently to Assistente Rizzoli, who was once more involved, answered questions she forgot the next moment, and saw Montana telephoning. She shuddered and started crying again despite herself when the zinc coffin containing Mimì's corpse and Hölderlin's plastic

426

body bag were carried past her. Although she gradually recovered after two double grappas, it took her quite a while to grasp the full extent of what had happened. Montana had to tell her several times.

He had intended to speak to her that night in any case, he said — on a private matter. He'd wanted to clarify something, straighten things out, clear the decks emotionally, shed light on the darkness, put his cards on the table. But that wasn't all. Their conversation that morning in the bar near the prefecture had haunted him all day long like a persistent salesman harassing an irresolute customer. He had been possessed by a strange kind of nervousness and vague irritability that spoilt his concentration and made him feel queasy — meteorologically speaking, all signs of an approaching cyclone. Montana detested indecision, especially in himself. He hated unresolved situations as much as unsolved cases. Falling between two stools and not knowing what to do infuriated him, made him insufferable towards his colleagues, and had become blended with his instinctive feeling that Patanè could not be Valentino's murderer into a vile cocktail of ill humour and heartache.

"Did you say heartache?" Poldi cut in.

"Let me finish, will you?"

"*Forza,* Vito."

He hadn't been entirely honest with her, he went on. Her instinct hadn't, of course, deceived her. Alessia was a colleague, though in the administrative branch. He hated lies, he said. Lies were the worst thing of all, lies were the enemy, the poison he had to swallow every day, the thing that could destroy you if you didn't take care. That was why he had meant to call on Poldi after work and clarify a few things. He had been eating a sandwich in the car when he received this anonymous call. Number withheld, unfamiliar voice, brief message to the effect that the German signora might be in danger and he ought to hurry.

"Who was it?" asked Poldi.

"I told you: anonymous. Obviously, someone who knew what Mimì had in mind."

"A woman's voice?"

"No, a man's."

"How did he get your number?"

"*Madonna,* Poldi, I don't know. Anyway, I slapped the blue light on my roof at once and stepped on the gas."

Needless to say, Poldi was itching to know what he had originally intended to clarify with her — in other words, which way the cookie would crumble as far as she was concerned. But Montana wasn't having any

428

of it. He was tired, hungry and sweaty, he'd shot a dog and failed to prevent a heart attack, saved my aunt's life and solved a murder case.

"I've had enough for one day," he said.

And that's the way it stayed.

The next day Poldi had to go to police headquarters to make a statement. The volcanic eruption seemed to have ushered in a change in the weather. Towering above Etna, which was growling to itself, was a column of smoke and fire thousands of feet high. But the weather wasn't as hot as it had been. Veiled all over in cirrostratus, the sky dispensed a soft, milky light that smoothed the edges and outlines of the world and dispelled the lethargy of the summer. Sky and sea merged, and even Signor Bussacca looked as energetic and supercharged as Livingstone preparing to cross the Kalahari. Signora Cocuzza, who was obviously in the know, went so far as to wink at Poldi when she dropped in for a cappuccino and a *cornetto*. It was a good day. My Auntie Poldi had often been in places she never wanted to leave but was compelled to, but this morning she felt she'd really come home at last.

She told Signora Cocuzza about the

anonymous call to Montana, but her new friend merely frowned and shook her head, and Poldi believed her. She then made a brief call to Teresa from the bar. She had informed her sisters-in-law of events in the Via Baronessa the previous night, although it had been late. She felt she owed them that, and besides, she needed Teresa's help in regard to an official matter.

At nine on the dot, cheerful, sober and smelling of spring flowers, she presented herself at the prefecture in Acireale in a pistachio-coloured pencil skirt and a cream-coloured, very low-cut silk blouse. Sensually dark lipstick, sunglasses and Nefertiti eyeliner for the requisite touch of drama, and, beneath a headscarf with lemon motifs, a sort of tribute to Etna in the shape of her towering black Sunday wig. Everyone turned to look at her. She said good morning to the desk sergeant with the outsize Adam's apple, winked at the young policemen lounging against their patrol cars, and swung her hips like a sixties film star ready to mount the nearest Vespa or jump into the nearest fountain. Assistente Rizzoli found it hard to concentrate on his PC as Poldi dictated her statement.

Attracted by the click of her ballpoint like a cat by the sound of a tin opener, Montana appeared in the doorway as soon as she had signed her deposition. He was wearing a dark suit with a black T-shirt and looked like a cross between a Russian oligarch and a star architect from Milan. In other words, by Poldi's standards: hot. He led her into his office at the end of the passage and shut the door.

"Are you going to have me on the floor?"

"Don't be silly, Poldi."

She got the message. The cookie hadn't crumbled her way.

"Pity. May I sit down?"

"Of course, please do. Like something to drink?"

"Some water."

Montana disappeared, giving Poldi a brief opportunity to inspect his office. It looked the way she'd expected: too small, too chock-a-block, too old, too stuffy, too depressing. A steel desk, a decrepit office chair with butterfly-pattern upholstery, a prehistoric computer, folding chairs for visitors, a filing cabinet, stacks of papers on the floor, a crucifix on the wall, a map of Sicily, and a desk diary with no entries.

It was just the way Poldi had always pictured Inspector Chance's office somewhere at the end of a passage. She was surprised they didn't keep the cleaners' mops and buckets in there as well.

"See what I meant?" Montana asked from the doorway.

She turned to look at him. "It's a shame. A disgrace."

"Only another three years." He sat down beside her on one of the folding chairs and handed her a glass of water. "We found the murder weapon at his house in Acireale. Together with the recording you made, that dispels any doubt: Domenico Pastorella shot Valentino and very probably killed Marisa Puglisi as well. He was almost bankrupt, by the way. Hence the deal with Patanè."

"All I wonder is, who set up the deal?"

"What do you mean?"

"Patanè is a scumbag and an idiot. He'd never have approached Mimì without protection."

"Russo, you mean?"

Poldi made a dismissive gesture. "Pure speculation; forget it. What did Mimì's wife Carmela say?"

"She seemed quite calm. Almost . . ."

"Relieved?"

Montana nodded. "She denies it, of course, but I think she knew the truth all along — not that there's much of a chance we'll be able to prove it. I could spit."

"Oh, Vito."

"What you did was foolish and dangerous, Poldi, not to mention the fact that you obstructed my investigation. You should have informed me far earlier."

"You kept withholding information from *me."*

"I'm a policeman."

"And I'm me. The next time —"

"There won't be a next time, Poldi."

She said nothing.

"Still, the chief did congratulate me earlier."

"That's good. You know the joke about God creating Sicily out of a few offcuts and offsetting such a paradise by creating the Sicilians?"

"Yes, it's a classic. A good one."

"No, Vito, it's balls. Sicily is a paradise, Sicilians and all. You saved my life yesterday. Which reminds me: have I thanked you yet?"

He grinned at her. "Don't mention it."

"If you go on smirking like that, I'll get naughty ideas. Well, now would be a good opportunity to tell me what you really meant to say last night."

Montana squirmed for a moment. Then he pulled himself together and awkwardly, long-windedly, explained that he and his colleague Alessia had been an item for the past three months. Well, more or less an item, because their relationship was rather complicated, too, but he had recently introduced her to his children and it had gone really smoothly. But then the thing with my aunt had hit him like a bolt from the blue — he was only human, after all, and he couldn't help thinking of her all the time, but he was also a man of principle and had had to learn to control his feelings, so he'd carried out emergency open-heart surgery on himself and, well . . . he'd decided in favour of Alessia.

He wound up looking like a marathon runner breasting the tape.

Poldi remained silent. She could have recited the words of his monologue along with him, they sounded so familiar to her.

"Poldi? Say something."

She drew a deep breath. "What utter crap," she said eventually, getting to her feet. "If you think we're history, Vito, you're making a big mistake. It isn't over between us, not by a long chalk. Why not? Because you need me. What's she talking about, you may be thinking, but I know I'm right. I know it because I know a thing or two. One way or another, Vito Montana, you need me."

The day had begun so well, but before she

knew it, Poldi was back outside the prefecture with a knot of sorrow and disappointment in her heart. The sorrow she bravely ignored because she had no wish to spoil such a nice day, which had felt like a twentieth birthday. But the disappointment. The disappointment that no Mafia tie-up had emerged throughout the case, as she had always assumed it would. The disappointment that she'd been unable to prove anything against Russo. Although she had kept the promise she'd made Valentino's lifeless body on the beach at Praiola, the case did not *feel* solved, and that bugged her. That was why she needed Teresa's and Martino's help.

Having arranged to meet her in the Caffè Cipriani, they sat round a table spooning up granitas. Uncle Martino chatted with one of the waiters and lectured him on the absurdity of eating granitas in the evening. He asserted that the same thing applied to them as applied to Bavarian weisswurst — the white sausages traditionally eaten in the morning, preferably for breakfast with a brioche — because the soft sorbet became crystallized and inedible in the bar's freezer compartment.

"You're looking well, Poldi," said Teresa.

"I'm feeling well, too," Poldi lied. She

ordered another *granita mandorla caffè* to fortify herself. "You think they'll open it all up, just like that?"

"Martino knows one of the officials, an old friend he once showed where to find the best mushrooms on Etna, so there shouldn't be any problem. After all, they aren't secret documents and we aren't the NSA."

"True. In that case, let's go."

Only a short walk from the Piazza Duomo, the land registry of the Commune di Acireale was housed in a magnificent baroque palace. It might from its appearance have been a luxury hotel or the headquarters of the Spanish Inquisition, but no, it was the seat of local government. Poldi had been there once before to complete her resident's registration formalities, and she well remembered the chaos that arose when the automatic queue ticket dispenser broke down. She did not have to take a ticket this time, however. She was greeted by a pale, ill-shaven, middle-aged man with protruding eyes who kissed Teresa's hand and hailed Martino warmly like a pupil greeting the mentor who has taught him all he knows.

"This is my sister-in-law, Isolde Oberreiter," Martino told him.

"A pleasure to meet you, signora."

"I hope we're not being a nuisance."

"Certainly not, signora, I'm delighted to be able to do my dear friend Martino a favour. If you'll come with me, I'll show you the records."

Poldi emerged from the baroque palace two hours later with Teresa and Martino and several photocopies in her hand, confident that she would, after all, be able to put the finishing touches to the Valentino case.

"Shall we come with you?" asked Teresa.

"No need, I'll manage."

A little later, on nearing the archway leading to Femminamorta, Poldi saw that the second lion was back in its accustomed place. It was looking sulkier than ever.

"*Namaste,* lion," she said, and tooted twice.

Word of Mimì's guilt and death, which had evidently spread like wildfire, had reached Femminamorta long ago.

"*Mon Dieu,* so it's really true?" Valérie cried in dismay after Poldi had given her a preliminary account of what had happened.

"Beyond doubt," said Poldi. "And I must apologize for suspecting you — I only found out yesterday what your father must have been through. Is that why you left France and took over Femminamorta?"

Valérie pensively stirred her day-old,

reheated coffee. "I don't know. Perhaps. I hardly knew him. You've no need to apologize."

They didn't speak for a while. The palm trees around them rustled as the mice in them tussled for ripe dates, while Oscar and Lady did the same lower down.

Poldi spotted a dark shape wriggling through the tall grass between the avocado trees.

"It's not poisonous," Valérie told her. "On the contrary, they bring good luck."

Poldi nodded. "I could use some."

Valérie looked at her. "I'm not sure why I came to Femminamorta. Perhaps you're right. But I do know why I've stayed. Femminamorta is a good place — a place that protects its occupants. It also protected my father for a very long time, and it's a place that attracts good things and people. You, for instance, Poldi. As long as you come to visit me, I shall feel at home here. Understand?"

My aunt nodded. She knew a thing or two about good places, friendship and things that sustain us.

"Maybe," said Valérie, "you'll introduce me sometime to the German nephew you're always talking about."

"Hello?" I cut in at this point. "You're

always talking about me?"

"No, not *always.* Just occasionally. More in passing."

"What do you tell her about me?"

"The sort of thing one says when conversation starts to drag."

"Like what?"

"Enough of the third degree. I don't owe you an explanation."

I sighed. "So Valérie would like to meet me sometime, would she?"

"You can put that out of your head for a start. You wouldn't hit it off, the two of you."

To change the subject quickly, she told me what she'd had to talk about with Russo, for it was on his account that she had come to Femminamorta. She had no need to go in search of him, however, because he appeared in the garden as if in response to a presentiment, wearing jeans, a T-shirt and shades. Poldi now knew what the sad signora had meant about Russo's good looks.

"I heard from Turi that you were here," he said, unceremoniously joining Valérie and Poldi at the table. "Glad to see you looking well, Donna Poldina."

He didn't remove his sunglasses.

Poldi looked at him. "And I owe it all to you, Signor Russo. Isn't that so?"

"I don't understand."

"You were the anonymous caller who informed Commissario Montana I was in danger last night."

"Mon Dieu!" Valérie exclaimed.

"I'm afraid I've no idea what you're talking about, Donna Poldina."

Poldi gestured impatiently. "You knew all about Marisa Puglisi's murder. Valentino's, too, perhaps."

She paused, never taking her eyes off him.

Russo sat back in his chair. "Thin ice, Donna Poldina. Do go on, though."

"By all means. I won't be able to prove you knew about Valentino, but I know one thing for sure: Valentino wasn't the first person to blackmail Mimì. The first was you."

"Really?"

"Mon Dieu."

Poldi produced the photocopies she had made at the records office in Acireale and spread them out on the table. "Thirty-nine years ago, shortly after Marisa's disappearance, you bought your first plot of land and set up your nursery."

"So what?"

"I wondered how you managed to amass so much money by selling a few wild palm trees, but you didn't need much money because Mimì Pastorella sold you the land

440

for peanuts."

"He needed the money."

"No, he needed your silence." Poldi tapped the photocopies. "These are just a few excerpts from the land register. In the past forty years you've repeatedly bought plots of land from Mimì Pastorella for a song. You blackmailed Mimì. You set up the deal between him and Patanè. You built up your palm tree empire on your knowledge of a murder, Signor Russo. The murder of a girl you were presumably once in love with."

Valérie said nothing. Russo didn't touch the photocopies, just glanced at them from a distance.

"So why did I warn Commissario Montana last night?"

"Because you knew that Mimì was done for. It was only a matter of time before everything came out, and you didn't want him to cause any more chaos — chaos that might affect you, too."

Russo sighed. "I like you, Donna Poldina, I really do, but with all due respect, you're barking up the wrong tree. You can't prove anything, anyway. Look, I'm just a hard-working man who loves his land and his people. I've always worked hard. I come from a very humble background. My parents had nothing, but *I,* with a lot of hard work and a bit of luck, have made something of my life, and now I'm happy to be able to give a lot of people employment. That's all. I've never been involved in blackmail or any other form of sharp practice."

He rose. "And now, if you'll excuse me, I must get back to work."

"One more thing," said Poldi. She opened her bag and produced the photo of the topographical map she had taken in Taormina and had never been able to identify. "Can you tell me what this is?"

Russo examined the photograph, turning it round three times.

"Some land I recently acquired, up at Trecastagni. A vineyard."

"Oh, you're going in for wine-growing?"

Russo handed the photo back. "I hope we see each other again soon, Donna Poldina."

"I'm quite sure we shall, Signor Russo."

An unequivocal statement.

My Auntie Poldi drove home and removed the corkboard from her bedroom wall. She was sitting alone over the grappa bottle that evening when the doorbell rang.

Montana.

He was looking poorly — a nervous wreck, in fact. Poldi could see at once what the matter was, because she knew a thing or two about conditions of that kind.

"Poldi, I —"

"Don't say anything, Vito," she said, putting a finger to his lips and towing him into the house. "Not a word."

When I called my Aunt Luisa a few days later to say I'd be paying another visit soon, she told me how relieved everyone was that our conspiratorial *joie de vivre* project had turned out so well. Poldi seemed far better adjusted, she said. She was showing a surprising interest in mushrooms and the fish market, meeting Valérie almost daily and whispering now and then with the sad signora. She apparently received gentlemen visitors on a regular basis and had recently developed a keen interest in viticulture.

"Hey, what does *namaste* mean?" Luisa asked.

"I think it's an Indian form of greeting."

She giggled. "Know what Poldi's been doing every morning lately? She goes up to the roof terrace stark naked, puts her hands together and sings out '*Namaste*, Sicilia,' followed almost immediately by 'The rest of the world can kiss my ass.'"

That was good news.

With many people, however, *joie de vivre* resembles a volcanic eruption. No matter how fervent and intense, it sooner or later gives way once more to calm and melancholy, so the sisters and I were relieved when my Auntie Poldi encountered her next murder case soon afterwards.

444

ACKNOWLEDGEMENTS

My heartfelt thanks to:
Rosaria, Fini, Nuccia and Piero for everything.
Gaetano for our conversations.
Julia for the light-bulb idea.
Jan for his active encouragement.
Sibylle for her splendid efficiency.
Anja, Johannes, Barbara, Jochen and Daniela for their kindness and exactitude.
Marie-Luce, Paola, Gianni, Ciro and Stef for their hospitality, anecdotes and wine.
And, of course, my Auntie Poldi.

ABOUT THE AUTHOR

Mario Giordano, the son of Italian immigrants, was born in Munich. He is the author of *1,000 Feelings for Which There Are No Names;* he has also written thrillers, books for children, and screenplays. *Auntie Poldi and the Sicilian Lions* is his first novel translated into English. He lives in Cologne.

John Brownjohn lives in Dorset in the UK. His work has won him critical acclaim and numerous awards on both sides of the Atlantic, including the Schlegel-Tieck Prize (three times), the PEN American Center's Goethe House Prize, and the Helen and Kurt Wolff Prize for Marcel Beyer's *The Karnau Tapes* and Thomas Brussig's *Heroes Like Us.*

The employees of Thorndike Press hope you have enjoyed this Large Print book. All our Thorndike, Wheeler, and Kennebec Large Print titles are designed for easy reading, and all our books are made to last. Other Thorndike Press Large Print books are available at your library, through selected bookstores, or directly from us.

For information about titles, please call:
(800) 223-1244

or visit our website at:
gale.com/thorndike

To share your comments, please write:
Publisher
Thorndike Press
10 Water St., Suite 310
Waterville, ME 04901